Blood Orchid

Also by Stuart Woods
in Large Print:

Cold Paradise
Chiefs
Dead Eyes

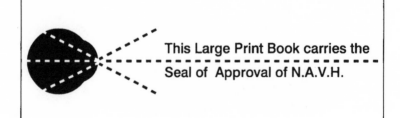

Blood Orchid

Stuart Woods

WHEELER
PUBLISHING

Published in 2003 by arrangement with G. P. Putnam's Sons, a member of Penguin Putnam Inc.

Wheeler Large Print Hardcover Series.

The text of this Large Print edition is unabridged.
Other aspects of the book may vary from the original edition.

Set in 16 pt. Plantin by Christina S. Huff.

Printed in the United States on permanent paper.

Library of Congress Cataloging-in-Publication Data

Woods, Stuart.
    Blood Orchid / Stuart Woods.
      p. cm.
    ISBN 1-58724-395-4 (lg. print : hc : alk. paper)
    1. Barker, Holly (Fictitious character) — Fiction. 2. Police — Florida — Fiction. 3. Police chiefs — Fiction. 4. Policewomen — Fiction. 5. Florida — Fiction. 6. Large type books. I. Title.
PS3573.O642 B58 2003
  813'.54—dc21   2002192405

This book is for Bob and Kay Falise.

1

Sara Tennant arrived at her office building in downtown Miami promptly at seven forty-five A.M., as was her habit. She needed only to park her car and use the private elevator to the penthouse suite of Jimenez Properties; she would be at her desk in the little office next to that of her boss, Manuel Jimenez, when he arrived, promptly at eight o'clock, as was his habit.

As she parked her new Toyota Avalon in the reserved space, next to that of her boss, she was surprised and not a little annoyed to see that his Mercedes was already in its spot. She was going to have to start coming in earlier, she thought; she couldn't have Manny getting there before she did.

There was something odd about the Mercedes, she realized, through the fog of her recent sleep. Until she had her morning coffee, a double espresso, she would not think quickly. She sat in the Toyota with the motor still running while she tried to figure it out.

The lights, she decided. The interior lights of the Mercedes were on, and unless she turned them off, Manny would soon have a dead battery. She gathered her small briefcase, purse, coffee thermos, and the *Miami Herald* and struggled out of her car. She set her things down on the driver's seat and smoothed her skirt before continuing. She was looking forward to reading Carl Hiassen's column in the paper before doing any real work. She loved Hiassen, read all his novels, too, and never missed his column.

She gathered her things once again, closed the car door, and pressed the button on the remote control to lock all the doors and the trunk. Some cars had been broken into in this garage, in spite of the security cameras. She wished Manny had sprung for a garage with a manned entrance, instead of the electronic surveillance; a guard on duty made her feel safer. Embracing her belongings, she walked around Manny's car and saw immediately why the interior lights were on: the driver's door was open. She took another step or two, reaching out for the door, then she peered over the things in her arms and saw what they had concealed until now.

Manny Jimenez was lying on the garage floor in an oddly contorted position.

Heart attack! Sara thought immediately. She had taken a CPR course at her church, and she knew exactly what to do. She put her things on the garage floor, reached out to Manny, and turned him over. Manny had not had a heart attack. A heart attack did not put a hole in his head, and particularly, did not spray his blood and brains across the inside of the Mercedes door. Sara did not pause to take Manny's pulse or put her ear to his chest. He was stiff as a board, and she knew what that meant. She picked up her things and ran for the elevator. As soon as she had opened the door with her key, she was digging in her briefcase for her cellphone.

Steven Steinberg stood on the eighteenth tee of the Doral Country Club's famous course, the Blue Monster, and gazed down the fairway, utterly relaxed and confident. He had played this schmuck from New York like a violin, and now he was going to take his money. Even though Steinberg had an official handicap of six, and even though he should have carried a card that said three, he had allowed his guest to play him neck and neck for seventeen holes. They were now tied at eleven over par, and it was time to crank the handle on the cash register.

Steinberg took his stance, his right foot back a couple of extra inches, and without a practice swing, hit the ball. It started to the right, then turned over and dropped into the middle of the fairway, two hundred and seventy yards down the course.

Fleischman stared after the ball with an expression of disbelief on his face.

"Something wrong?" Steinberg asked.

"Nothing at all," Fleischman replied, teeing up. He swung mightily at the ball and sliced it into a fairway bunker, two hundred and twenty yards down the fairway. He picked up his tee. "So how come, all of a sudden, after seventeen holes, you're outdriving me?"

Steinberg shrugged. "Every now and then I really connect. Don't you, sometimes?"

"Sometimes," Fleischman said. "But not usually on the eighteenth, and not for that kind of length."

They got into Steinberg's customized golf cart. "You know what I'd do if I were you?" he said to his guest.

"No, Steven, what would you do?"

"I'd take a seven wood and go for it."

"Out of a bunker?"

"Why not? It's a shallow bunker; there's enough loft on a seven wood to carry the edge, and you'd find yourself a nice little wedge from the flag. You got a seven wood? You want to borrow mine?" At this stage, he could afford to appear to be generous.

"I've got a seven wood," Fleischman said as the cart drew to a halt next to the bunker. He looked down the fairway toward the flag, checked the depth of the bunker, and pulled his seven wood from his bag.

"Come on," Steinberg said, "you can do it."

Fleischman lined up his shot. "Keep it smooth," he muttered to himself. "Nice easy shot." He swung the club and connected beautifully with the ball. It faded a little but dropped in the fairway, maybe eighty yards from the pin.

"Great shot!" Steinberg said.

"Thanks for the tip," Fleischman replied, getting into the cart.

They stopped next to Steinberg's ball. He didn't even glance down the fairway, just went to his bag and came back with a fairway wood.

"What are you doing with that club?" Fleischman asked. "It's only a hundred and sixty yards to the flag; you'll knock it into the next county."

"This is an eleven wood," Steinberg replied, lining up on the ball. He relaxed, took a breath and let it out, and took a slow-looking, liquid swing at the ball. It rose high into the air, sailed down the fairway, past the guarding bunkers, and dropped onto the green with only a single bounce, stopping four feet from the pin.

"I'm getting one of those," Fleischman muttered.

"You should," Steinberg replied, still holding his finish.

Then Steinberg's head exploded.

For a tiny second before he screamed, Fleischman wondered if cheating at golf could make your head explode.

2

Holly Barker walked into the Ocean Grill in Vero Beach and looked around for her father. Nowhere in sight. She looked at her watch; okay, she was ten minutes early, and Ham was always exactly on time.

"Hi, Holly," the woman at the headwaiter's station said. "How many tonight?"

"Just two," Holly replied. "Ham ought to be here in a few minutes. Tell him I'm in the bar."

"Right. I ought to have a table in twenty minutes or so."

The Ocean Grill didn't take reservations, so Holly always came early. One side of the bar was empty, so she plopped down on a stool there.

"What'll it be?" the bartender asked.

"A three-to-one vodka gimlet, straight up, shaken, very cold."

"Make that two," a man's voice said from behind her, and someone took a seat two stools down. "My favorite," he said to Holly.

Jackson had been dead for nearly a year, but Holly still wasn't ready to be hit on. She half-turned toward the stranger and nodded. She wasn't getting into a conversation. Then she relaxed. He was sixtyish and well preserved, at that. He was beautifully, if casually dressed in a blue blazer, gray trousers, black alligator loafers, and what looked like a silk shirt, pale yellow and open at the collar. A pocket square that matched the shirt peeped from his breast pocket.

"It's a wonderful drink," she said, comfortable talking to someone who was so much older than she, and who, into the bargain, was quite handsome — tall, slim, tanned, and with thick, perfectly white hair, well cut.

"I've never understood the charm of martinis," he said, "except that they look so wonderful. A gimlet gives you the aesthetic reward of the martini, without having to drink it. Three-to-one is just right, too; bartenders never measure, and they always put too much vodka in a gimlet." He glanced at the bartender, who pretended not to be listening. The man picked up a jigger and started measuring.

"Yep," Holly said, "you have to train your bartender to do it right."

The bartender set two frosted martini glasses on the bar, shook the cocktail shaker for half a minute, then strained the pale, green liquid into the two glasses, decorating each with a slice of lime. "Try that," he said.

Holly and the man raised their glasses to each other and sipped.

"You've earned your tip," the man said to the bartender.

"You certainly have," Holly echoed.

The man stuck out his hand. "I'm Ed Shine," he said, "like the shine on your shoes."

Holly took the hand. "Holly Barker."

"From Vero?"

Holly shook her head. "Orchid Beach, up the road."

"Really? Me too, for the past four months."

"I haven't seen you around," Holly said.

"Oh? Do you get around all that much?"

"I sure do," Holly replied. "I work for the city. What do you do, Mr. Shine?"

"Ed, please. I'm retired from the property development business, in New York. Now all I do is grow orchids and play golf."

"What sort of orchids?" Not that she knew much about them.

"Lots of sorts. I develop hybrids. You know anything about them?"

"Not really."

"I was attracted to Orchid Beach first because of the name. Saw it on a map and thought I'd have a look."

"And you liked the town?"

"Orchid Beach is the way Florida should have turned out but didn't," he said. "No high-rises on the beach, beautiful neighborhoods, very manicured."

"I agree," Holly said.

Ham stepped up to the bar. "One of those," he said to the bartender, pointing at Holly's drink. He gave his daughter a kiss on the cheek.

14

"Ed, this is my father, Hamilton Barker, known as Ham. Ham, this is Ed Shine, a recent arrival in Orchid."

The two men shook hands. "Move over here, Ed," Ham said, pointing at the stool next to Holly. "We'll bracket her." He took the stool on the other side of her.

"Ed grows orchids," Holly said.

"Well, I guess Orchid Beach is the place for it. They grow wild everywhere, you know; that's how the place got its name."

They chatted on for a few minutes, then the headwaitress showed up to say their table was ready.

"Join us, Ed, if you're alone."

Shine stood up. "Thanks, I'd like that."

"Can you squeeze in another chair?" Ham asked the headwaitress.

"Sure we can."

They were shown to their table.

"Let me order some wine for us," Shine said, picking up the list. "I assume we're all here for the seafood."

Ham and Holly nodded.

Two hours later, they finished their coffee. Ed Shine had been an excellent companion — intelligent, amusing, and full of stories, and he had chosen a superior wine.

"Why don't the two of you stop by my place for a nightcap on the way home?" Shine asked. "I'll show you some orchids."

15

Ham and Holly consulted each other with a glance. "Sure," Ham said for both of them.

They followed Shine back up A1A, the highway that joins the barrier islands up and down the Florida coast. He took a few turns, and they wound up at a low, nicely designed house on the Indian River, which doubled as the Intercoastal Waterway. Shine led them inside and switched on some lights, revealing a beautifully decorated living room with good pictures on the walls. He poured them each a brandy, then waved them to follow him.

"Come on," he said, "I'll show you my orchids." He led the way through the house, opened a door, and switched on the lights.

They found themselves in a greenhouse some forty feet long, filled with tropical plants and many orchids.

"These are my babies," Shine said, waving a hand. "One in particular." He held up a pot containing a plant with a single, deeply red bloom. "This is my own creation, after a great deal of work: She's called the Blood Orchid."

Then there was the sound of shattering glass, and the pot in Shine's hand exploded. Holly hit the deck, along with Ham, pulling Shine down beside them.

"What was that?" Shine asked. "And why are we on the floor?"

"That," Ham said, "was the sound of a bullet fired into your greenhouse by a small-caliber rifle equipped with a silencer."

"And how the hell would you know that?" Shine asked.

"Believe me," Holly said, "he knows."

"Army," Ham said. "Thirty years of small-weapons use."

Holly crawled over to the door, reached up, and switched off the lights. "He missed you by inches, Ed. I think we should get back into the house," she said.

The three of them crawled out of the greenhouse and closed the door behind them. They sat on the floor and looked at one another.

"You carrying, Holly?" Ham asked.

"I'm afraid not," she replied. "I carry all the time in Orchid, but not when I go to Vero."

"Maybe you ought to carry all the time, period."

"It makes a handbag heavy," Holly said.

Then they heard a car start, and the spinning of tires on gravel.

"He's gone," Ham said.

"Jesus, I hope so," Shine replied. "I guess we'd better call the police."

"I *am* the police," Holly said.

3

Two patrol cars arrived in under two minutes, and Holly was proud. She sent the two cops outside to look for tracks while she sat in the living room and talked to Ed Shine.

"I'm going to take some notes," she said, digging a notebook out of her handbag.

"Sure," Shine said.

"Spell your name for me again?"

"S-h-i-n-e. It's German-Jewish, was originally spelled S-c-h-e-i-n, but the folks at Ellis Island screwed it up. My grandfather thought it was more American, so he kept it that way."

"Born?"

"New York City, seventy years ago."

She was surprised; he looked a lot younger.

"And you've been in Orchid four months, you said?"

"That's right. I sold my development company to my partner earlier this year, and I wanted to get out of New York, for tax reasons."

"Ed, can you think of anyone who would want to harm you?"

"Not a soul," Shine said. "That's why this is

so baffling. Why would anybody want to shoot a retired developer?"

"Are you married?"

"I'm a widower for eight years."

"Have you been seeing anyone in Orchid since your arrival?"

"A woman? Now and then, when I get lucky. Why do you ask?"

"No jealous husbands in the picture?"

Shine laughed. "I'll take that as a compliment, but no."

"You have any kids?"

"None; my wife and I tried, but it didn't work, and we didn't want to adopt."

"Any nephews or nieces?"

"None; I was an only child."

"May I ask, who are your heirs?"

"A number of charities, mostly. I've mentioned a few friends in my will, but they don't know about it."

"What about your business dealings? Have you made any enemies over the years? Somebody who might have felt hard dealt with?"

"Not a soul; I always wanted both sides to like any deal. I'm considered something of a soft touch in the business."

"Any problems with the unions?"

"Always," Shine said, "but I worked hard at being fair with them; they think I'm soft, too. Anyway, it's been a long time since we had *that* sort of problem with the unions. The feds have pretty much cleaned them up."

"How about your neighbors? Any problems with them?"

"No, they're all very nice. I made a point of having them over for a drink after I moved in, and they've since had me over for dinner, the people on both sides of me."

"Once more: can you think of *anybody* who might wish you ill?"

Shine shook his head vehemently. "I've tried to live my life in such a way as not to make enemies. You know what I think? I think this is some kid, some vandal, who just wanted to break some glass, that's all."

The two cops came into the house, careful to wipe their feet. "Chief," one of them said, "we found where the shooter parked his car and stood, right over there about thirty yards away. But the ground is too dry from the drought for there to be any footprints or tire tracks."

"Then how do you know you've found the spot?" Holly asked.

A cop held up a shell casing, hanging on a pencil. "Twenty-two long rifle, magnum load."

Ham spoke for the first time. "With a silencer, that's an assassin's weapon," he said. "Teenaged vandals don't employ silencers. You can't even buy the things, legally; you have to make them."

Holly nodded. "Ed, I think you have to accept that this was an intentional act and behave accordingly. I'm going to leave a squad car here tonight, with one officer, but tomorrow

20

morning I think you ought to consider moving to a hotel, at least for a while. And you really need to think about who might have been behind this. It seems likely that the shooter was hired, and you're the best one to tell us who among the people you know might be capable of that."

"I'll certainly think about it very hard," Shine said, "but I'm not leaving my home. I'm going to buy a gun."

"You can do that in Florida," Holly said, "but I wouldn't advise it. You're more likely to hurt yourself than an intruder, and guns are a favorite target of burglars."

"Thanks for your advice," Shine said, but he seemed determined.

Holly stood up. "Well, I think we can wrap up this stage of our investigation," she said. "Tomorrow morning I'll assign a detective to the case, and he'll want to interview you again."

Shine took a card from his pocket and handed it to her. "I'll be at his disposal."

Holly shook his hand. "Thanks for a wonderful bottle of wine at dinner. Ham and I enjoyed your company."

"I hope to see you both again soon," Shine said. "Do you two play golf?"

"Yes, we do."

"Want to play sometime?"

"Sure, give us a call," Holly said. "You can always reach me at police headquarters."

Holly and Ham walked out into the cool night and stood by their cars. "What do you think?" she asked.

"Mistaken identity?"

"I don't think a pro would make that kind of mistake. Maybe Ed will come up with something when he's had time to think about it." She kissed her father on the cheek. "Good night, Ham; drive safely."

"You too."

Over breakfast the following morning, Holly leafed through the local paper and the *New York Times*, which were delivered to her door. Her Doberman pinscher, Daisy, lay at her feet, having already breakfasted and been for her run in the dunes. Holly and Daisy lived in the beach house that had been left to Holly by her fiancé, Jackson Oxenhandler, who had been killed the year before while a bystander in a bank robbery, an hour before they were supposed to have been married.

There was nothing in the local papers about the previous night's attempt on Ed Shine's life, but the *Times* had something that interested her: The day before, in Miami, two property developers had been shot dead, in different locations, by apparent assassins — one in the garage of an office building, one on a golf course. The investigating detective was quoted in the news article.

It didn't take long to get him on the phone.

"Jim Connor," a man's voice said.

"Detective Connor, my name is Holly Barker. I'm chief of police in Orchid Beach, a hundred and fifty miles north of you."

"What can I do for you, Chief?"

"I read a news report of the two property developers who were homicides yesterday. Are you handling both cases?"

"I am. You got something to tell me about them?"

"No, but last night we had something similar up here. Somebody took a shot at a local man who is a retired developer from New York. The weapon was a twenty-two rifle, magnum cartridge."

"Hollow point?"

"We couldn't tell from the casing, but a silencer was used, so we assume a hired killer. He'd probably use a hollow-point slug."

"That's what killed my golfer yesterday; made a real mess of him. You have any reason to think there's a connection between my killings and your attempt?"

"Only that they're all three property developers," she said. "The intended victim swears he has no enemies, but you never know about a thing like that."

"Both my victims' wives said the same thing. They can't think of anybody who'd want to hurt their husbands. Closest I could come to an enemy was the golfer's playing partner, who

23

thought he was being hustled by the victim. But he's not a suspect."

"I'd be very interested to know what your two developers had in common."

"Same business, is all," the detective replied. "They didn't even know each other, best we can tell."

"Were they direct competitors?"

"We're still working on that. Why don't you send me your shell casing, and I'll compare it to the one we found."

He hadn't mentioned a shell casing before. "After we've had a look at it," she replied. She took note of his mailing address. "Would you let me know if you come up with a connection between the two victims? I'd like to see if it relates to my case."

"Sure, I'll give you a call." He hung up before she could give him her number.

4

Howard Singleton, head of the Miami office of the federal government's General Services Administration, went through the papers on his desk slowly, then he looked up at one of his people, Willard Smith, who was sitting across the desk from him. "Is this all we got?" he asked.

"Three bids," Smith replied.

"I don't get it, Smitty," Singleton said. "This is prime real estate."

"Well, it's not exactly Palm Beach," the man replied. "Orchid Beach is just some backwater. I looked into it; it's pretty, but there's no big-league shopping, only a few decent restaurants, and none of the other stuff you'd expect to find where there's high-end construction going on — very few interior decorators, upscale furniture stores, and all that. Not much in the way of entertainment, either."

"But still, this property has three golf courses, fifty houses already built, a clubhouse."

"There's no beachfront property attached; it's all west of A1A; that holds down the value. Fact is, Orchid Beach isn't the sort of town to support the kind of big-time development that this property would require if someone is going to turn a profit. It's over the top, and by a long way."

"Well, two of these bids are not credible, as far as I'm concerned. Did you read the backup paperwork?"

"Yes, and I agree. There's only one bid that we could properly accept, I think, and it's this BOP, Blood Orchid Properties."

"Weren't we expecting bids from a couple of big Miami developers?"

"Sure, but don't you read the papers?"

"What do you mean?"

"I mean that Manny and Steven Steinberg are both dead. We've had serious interest from both of them, and I was anticipating bids."

"What, they just dropped dead? Both these guys were in their forties, weren't they?"

"They dropped dead from bullets," the man replied. "And on the same day. Less than a week before the bidding closed."

"And what does that tell you?"

"Well, it's suspicious, I'll grant you that, but we're not going to get those bids now. We've advertised this thing, received sealed bids from three parties, and one of them is higher than the reserve, so what can we do but accept it? We're on a deadline here."

Singleton stacked the papers and returned them to his subordinate. "All right, issue the acceptance to this BOP outfit." Singleton watched Willard Smith leave, closing the door behind him, then he called the FBI.

Harry Crisp, the agent in charge of the FBI's Miami office, answered a buzz from his secretary.

"Yes?"

"A Howard Singleton from the GSA is on the phone."

"Is this about my request for additional office space?"

"He didn't say."

Crisp punched the flashing button. "Mr. Singleton, this is Harry Crisp."

"Good morning."

"I hope this is about getting us more office space."

"That request is being processed, Mr. Crisp, but this is about something else."

"What's up?"

"You remember a couple of years back you folks confiscated a piece of property up in Orchid Beach?"

"Yeah, sure; Palmetto Gardens. There was a huge drug-based money-laundering operation being run from there."

"Right. Well, we got authority a few weeks ago to sell the development."

"Yeah, that figures. Did you sell it yet?"

"Yes, but there's something fishy about the bidding."

"Tell me about it."

"We got only three bids, all of them low, only one of them acceptable."

"Listen, Howard, I'm not in the real estate business."

"That's not what I'm calling about. We anticipated bids from two large Miami property developers, and they were both murdered less than a week before bidding closed."

"Murder happens."

"Sure, but why these two guys?"

"Who were they?"

"Manuel Jimenez and Steven Steinberg. According to the papers, they had no connection, except that my office had talked with both of them several times about a bid on Palmetto Gardens. Then they get killed right before it's time to submit sealed bids, way too late for anybody else to get involved who hadn't already prepared a bid. What does that suggest to you?"

"You said you accepted a bid?"

"Yes, from a company called Blood Orchid Properties."

Crisp made a note of that.

"They're a Panamanian company, registered to do business in the U.S."

Crisp kept writing as Singleton gave him what he had on BOP.

Holly's secretary buzzed her. "Harry Crisp on line one."

She picked up the phone. "Harry, how are you?"

"I'm good, Holly, you?"

"Good."

"How's Ham? He all healed up?"

"Sure, a long time ago." Ham had been shot while playing a key role in an FBI investigation.

"We've always been grateful for his help on that thing, you know."

"Then you might tell him so."

"I had the attorney general write him a letter," Crisp said. "What does he want, a hand-written note from the president?"

"Forget it, Harry. What's up?"

"Remember Palmetto Gardens?"

"How could I forget?" She had put the FBI onto what was happening there and had been very important in cracking the case.

"It sold the other day."

"I saw something in the local paper about it. Whoever bought it got a real deal."

"Yeah. Problem is, two Miami developers who were supposed to bid got themselves murdered before they could submit something."

"Oh, yeah. I read about that in the *New York Times*. I even talked to the investigating officer about it."

"Why?"

"We had an attempt on a developer's life up here a couple of weeks back — a retired developer from New York."

"Tell me about it."

"A single rifle shot, missed him by inches, went in one side of the man's greenhouse, came out the other. Assassin's weapon."

"You investigated this?"

"I was standing next to the man when it happened."

"Who is he?"

"Name is Ed Shine." She spelled it for him.

"I'll run it, see if we come up with something."

"Okay."

"Do you know if he bid on the property?"

"I have no idea."

"Can you find out?"

"I can call and ask him. Why? You think that whoever bought the property wanted Shine out of the way, too?"

"Could be. Is he still healthy?"

"Far as I know."

"Let me hear from you. Best to Ham." He hung up.

Holly's secretary buzzed again. "A Mr. Ed Shine, on one."

There was a convenient coincidence. Holly punched the button. "Ed?"

"How are you, Holly?"

"Just fine; you?"

"Couldn't be better. You and Ham up for some golf?"

"Sure, when?"

"How about tomorrow at ten A.M.?"

"Can you get a tee time at that hour this late?"

"Don't worry about it; I just bought the golf course — three of them, in fact."

"Palmetto Gardens?"

"How'd you know that?"

"I'm the chief of police; I know everything."

"Meet me at the front gate at ten sharp tomorrow."

"I'll call Ham; we'll be there." She hung up and called her father.

"Yep?"

"You free for golf at ten A.M. tomorrow?"

"Yep."

"Meet me at Palmetto Gardens."

"I thought the place was closed by the Feds."

"Not anymore; somebody bought it."

"Who?"

"I'll tell you about it tomorrow." Holly hung up. She wouldn't call Harry Crisp back until she knew more. Once Harry got ahold of something, he tended to keep it to himself, and Holly wanted to play out her own string before she turned it over to the FBI.

She got up and walked around to the office of her deputy chief, Hurd Wallace. "Morning. Who did you assign to the Ed Shine thing?"

"I'm doing it myself; it's pretty much a dead end."

"Did you get any prints from the shell casing?"

"Nope. I'm surprised a pro would leave one on the scene."

"A pro in Miami did the same thing," she replied. She handed him the Miami detective's address. "If you're through with it, send the shell casing to this guy, registered mail. Get a receipt."

"Okay."

"You say the Shine thing is a dead end?"

Hurd shrugged. "Somebody took a shot at him and missed, left no trace of himself except the shell casing. There's been no other attempt. I don't know how to make any more out of it."

"Neither do I," Holly said.

5

Holly arrived at Palmetto Gardens to find Ham and Ed Shine waiting for her at the main gate. Two workmen were there, too, hoisting into place a large sign reading BLOOD ORCHID ES-TATES, *A new golf community, home sites from $1,000,000, completed homes from $2,500,000.* There was a phone number at the bottom. Holly rolled down her window.

"Follow me," Ed Shine said, getting into his car.

Holly followed Ed and Ham to the clubhouse, where they got out of their cars. Holly and Ham had played there once before, when the place was a criminal enterprise. "So you bought yourself some property, Ed?"

"Yeah, I did," Ed replied. "I didn't tell you about it the other evening because I hadn't bid yet and I didn't want to jinx it."

"The papers said the price was sixty million dollars, but they didn't mention your name."

"The price was correct, and I consider it a steal," Ed replied. "I like to keep a fairly low profile; I formed a company for the purchase, Blood Orchid Properties."

"Those are pretty hefty prices you're advertising," Ham said.

"Right," Holly added. "I've never heard of prices like that in Orchid Beach."

"A sign like that keeps out the riffraff," Shine replied. "Anyway, when I'm done with this place, people will be lining up to pay those prices," Ed said. "You wait and see. Come on, let's get our clubs."

They retrieved their clubs from their cars and walked out onto the first tee.

"Wow," Holly said, "the course is in beautiful shape."

"The Feds kept on the grounds crew when they confiscated the property," Ed replied. "They knew they'd get more money if the courses were kept in shape, and they maintained the rest of the property, too. Ham, you tee off first, then me, then we'll take Holly down to the ladies' tees."

"Holly drives from the men's tees," Ham said.

"Then Holly, you go first, by all means."

Holly teed up, did some stretching, then drove the ball two hundred and thirty yards down the right side of the fairway.

Ham drove next, outdriving her by ten yards.

Ed drove next. Holly thought he was amazingly flexible for his age; she'd expected a short backswing and a bent left arm, but Ed drove like a pro, even with Holly's drive, but in the center of the fairway.

"I don't drive it as far as I used to," Ed said as

he climbed into a cart with Holly. Ham followed them in a second cart. "I used to be a scratch golfer in my youth. Now I play to an eleven handicap. What's yours?"

"Probably around a fourteen; I used to have a twelve, but I've been too busy to play." She turned and looked at him. "I've got some news for you," she said. "Maybe a reason why somebody took a shot at you."

Ed stopped the cart and looked at her. "Tell me about it."

"This is only a theory," she said, "and I won't know more about it for a few days, but on the day of the evening you were shot at, two Miami property developers were murdered."

"I read about that in the papers," Ed said. "Why does that have anything to do with me?"

"The FBI tells me both those guys were going to bid on Palmetto Gardens."

"Blood Orchid, please," Ed said, holding up a hand.

"Okay, Blood Orchid. Tell me, Ed, who knew you were going to bid on the property?"

"Wait a minute." Ed shook his head. "When you bid on a property the General Services Administration is selling, nobody knows who's bidding or how much they're bidding; that's all very secret. You make your judgment of the value of the property, enter your bid, and hope for the best. Property development is a pretty cut-throat business," he said. "I could tell you some stories. But two murders?"

"Three," Holly said, "but for the grace of God."

Ed laughed and shook his head again. "Nah, couldn't happen. No piece of property is worth that, especially this piece."

"This piece of property looks pretty good to me," Holly said.

"Not from a developer's point of view. Orchid Beach is out of the way, not like Boca or Palm Beach — not even like Vero. This land in Boca or Palm Beach, with three golf courses already constructed and fifty houses built, would cost, what, two hundred million? Maybe more."

"If it's not so hot, why are you so hot on it?"

Ed held up some fingers: "One, because I live here; two, because the price was right; and three, because I had the money from the sale of my business. With me, it's almost a hobby; I don't have any overhead to speak of, though I've opened an office and am hiring a couple of salesmen. Also, since the place already has the important elements in place, it won't take me twenty years to develop it." He smiled. "At my age, twenty years would be too long. Nope, in five years, I'll have this place roaring, and I'll have my own little kingdom to rule. That's how I'll spend the rest of my life."

"Hey!" Ham called from his cart across the course. "Golf, anyone?"

Back at her office, Holly couldn't stand it anymore. She called the Miami detective.

"Hi, this is Chief Holly Barker, in Orchid Beach."

"Afternoon, Chief."

"Did you get my cartridge casing?"

"Yep."

"Was it a match for yours?"

"Yep."

Her theory suddenly held a lot of water. "What's your next step?"

"I don't have one," Connor said.

"What do you mean?"

"I mean, I'm off the case, as of half an hour ago."

"Why?"

"Because the FBI went to the chief of detectives and took it away from me. You want any more, call Harry Crisp, over at their Miami office."

"I'll do that, Jim," Holly said, and hung up. She immediately called Harry.

"Hello, Holly," Harry Crisp said. "I was expecting to hear from you."

"I guess Connor told you about my matching cartridge case, before you snatched the file from him."

"Yes, he did, and I had every right to do that. The case now has federal ramifications, since it was the federal government that was selling Palmetto Gardens."

"Blood Orchid," Holly said.

"What?"

"That's what it's called now. I just played golf

37

out there with the new owner, Ed Shine."

"Oh, yeah. We ran a check on him, came up with no arrests, no convictions. He's clean."

"I'm glad to hear it because he's a nice guy."

"He's a *lucky* guy, is what he is. Clearly, whoever was behind this meant to take him out as well as Jimenez and Steinberg."

"I guess you're checking on the other bidders."

"We are."

"Will you let me know what you find out?"

"Holly, this is a federal investigation now. I can't share information with you."

"Harry, after all we've meant to each other?"

"Holly, I consider you my friend, but I just can't do it."

"Remember where Blood Orchid is located, Harry? It's on my turf. You're going to need me before this is over, so you'd better keep me sweet."

"Holly, Holly," Crisp said, "how could you be any sweeter?" Then he hung up.

"Shit," Holly said.

6

Holly arrived at work the following morning to find all the phones dead.

"They're working on it," Hurd Wallace told her. "We've been down for about half an hour, and they were here in about two minutes; I didn't even have to call them, they were already in the neighborhood."

"That's good service," Holly said. She worked on personnel efficiency reports for a while, deciding how her small budget increase could be distributed in pay raises. It was tough, and she hated doing it. Then she saw a light flash on her phone. She picked it up, got a dial tone, and called Harry Crisp at the FBI office in Miami.

"Good morning, Holly," Harry said cheerfully.

"Morning, Harry. I have a little more for your on Blood Orchid Estates."

"Shoot."

"I confirmed that he paid sixty million for the place."

"Did you find out why?"

"He says it will be a hobby for his old age. He can live there, run it, and maybe even make a buck."

"I guess that makes sense."

"Harry, were there any other bids besides Ed's and the two dead guys' actually received?"

"Two, both inadequate."

"Wouldn't those two companies be a good place to look, since they were obviously trying to buy the property on the cheap?"

"We've already run that down," Harry said.

"And you found out what?"

"They're both South American, one registered in Brazil, one in Bolivia."

"With Colombian ownership, maybe?"

"Maybe, but we haven't been able to nail that down. Their company incorporation procedures are different from ours, and the ownership is harder to track."

"I'll bet you it's some of the same drug money that owned the place before, trying to get it back."

"Could very well be. You ever thought of becoming an FBI agent?"

Holly laughed. "I don't think you could beat my current job, Harry."

"Maybe I could. You go to the academy, and I'll get you assigned to me. Life would be interesting."

"Too interesting. I want to stay home with my dog and my daddy and have fun."

"You having fun, Holly?" Harry asked.

That brought her up short. "Not yet," she said.

"It's been what, a year?"

"You sound like Ham."

"Ham's a smart guy."

"It's not that it's too soon, it's just that I haven't felt like it."

"Felt like what?"

"Having fun, Harry. Now leave me alone."

"Okay, sweetheart. Let me know if you find out anything else that might be helpful."

"I don't suppose there's any point in saying the same to you, Harry."

"I do what I can, Holly. The Bureau frowns on excessive info sharing with local law enforcement."

"Except when there's something in it for the Bureau?"

"Something like that."

"That's what I thought. You ought to talk to them about that, Harry; you might get more local cooperation."

"I get all I need, kiddo."

"Bye, Harry." She hung up. The Bureau annoyed her with its close-to-the-vest way of treating locals like her. She'd talked to some other small-town chiefs who felt the same way.

Hurd Wallace knocked on her door and took a seat.

"What's up?"

"I'm at a dead end on who took a shot at Ed Shine," he said. "There just isn't anything else. I want to put the file into the inactive drawer."

"Okay. If something else comes up, you can

always take it out again. You have any personal theories?"

"Theories unsupported by any actual evidence?"

"Okay."

Hurd shrugged. "What we know is that somebody took a shot at at least two, maybe three property developers, all of whom were bidding or intended to bid on Palmetto Gardens."

"Blood Orchid Estates, now," Holly reminded him.

"Right. That's all we've got. No physical evidence, except for two cartridge cases, nothing else."

"Harry Crisp says that two other companies bid on the property, both of them South American."

Hurd's eyebrows went up. "That kind of rings some bells, doesn't it?"

"Yes, but only for the Feds. We don't have the means or the budget to track down that kind of stuff, and they do."

"I'll bet it's drug money."

"You wouldn't get odds from me," Holly replied.

"I'll bet it's some of the same money that owned it before."

"That's what I just said to Harry, but what can we do? It's Harry's ball game; let him do the pitching and the fielding."

Hurd stood up. "Right, it's in the inactive drawer." He went back to his office.

Holly found herself thinking of Jackson, something she used to do about once a minute and now did more like once a day. She wondered, as she sometimes did, what she would be doing now if Jackson were alive. Probably the same thing she was doing right this minute, she thought.

It wasn't as though they would have pulled up stakes and moved to Paris the minute they were married; after all, Jackson had a law practice in Orchid Beach, and she had a good job. No, they'd probably be doing the same things until they got old.

She thought about the money. Jackson had left her the house, an insurance policy, and some investments. She was worth more than two million dollars now, and she had her salary and her pension from the Army. She could do whatever she wanted, she knew, but apparently what she wanted was just to do her job. It hurt less than anything else.

7

Holly let herself into her house, one arm filled with groceries, and closed the door behind her. She set the grocery bag on the kitchen counter, turned the air-conditioning down a few degrees, and answered Daisy's call for supper.

Then, as Daisy dug into her meal, Holly noticed something odd: There was something different about the kitchen telephone. That morning, hurrying to get out, she had answered the phone and had had to stand very close to the set because the twelve-foot cord to the receiver had been hopelessly tangled. This was true of all the phones Holly used, and she only unwound the cords when she had to. She hadn't done it that morning, but somebody had.

She stood in the kitchen and looked around, then over the counter that separated the kitchen from the living room. Everything looked normal, but too neat. Holly was a neat person, but not obsessively so. But someone was.

On the living room coffee table, a group of magazines, previously tossed onto the table, was now neatly stacked and aligned with the corner of the table. Things on the kitchen counter, too, were neater than she had left them, and she was beginning to get a really creepy feeling. She unsnapped the keep on her holster and lifted the Sig Sauer 9mm that Ham had given her, flipping off the safety.

Daisy looked up at the sound, then went back to her dinner. Holly held the pistol at her side and walked around the counter into the living room, listening. The only sound was the rattle of Daisy's collar against her bowl. The Doberman finished her dinner, drank some water, then looked up at Holly, who was starting up the stairs in her stocking feet, walking on the outside of the treads to avoid squeaking.

She stuck her head into her bedroom momentarily, then with drew it. She heard the click of Daisy's claws on the stairs. Daisy came and nuzzled her hand; she had not had dessert, and she wanted her cookie *now.*

Holly looked around the rest of the house carefully, here and there noting a spot of unaccustomed neatness. Her gun safe was closed and locked, and so was the safe in her dressing room, where she kept what jewelry she had. Finally, she walked back down the stairs, went to the cookie jar, and gave Daisy her dessert. Daisy walked to the back door and waited. After another look around the living room, Holly let her out onto the beach, and Daisy ran into the dunes for her evening ablutions.

Satisfied that no one was in the house, Holly went upstairs, undressed, showered, and slipped into a long T-shirt that she often wore around the house; then she went down to the kitchen to make her own dinner.

There was nothing missing, she mused, but someone had definitely been in the house between the time she'd left that morning and the time she'd returned. But why? Certainly it wasn't a burglar; the TV and stereo were still in their usual places. Had someone come simply to sniff her underwear or shoes, then tidied up before leaving? Her underwear drawer looked the same, and her shoes were as she had left them in her dressing room. It didn't make any sense.

Holly looked at the liquor cabinet and thought of pouring herself a bourbon, but she decided she wanted to remain alert to think about this. She took her salad and pasta on a tray into the living room and turned on the TV, looking for the evening news.

The hell with it, she thought. Why stay sober? She went back to the kitchen, opened a bottle of white wine, grabbed a glass, and returned to her dinner.

"The investigation of the murders of real estate moguls Steven Steinberg and Manuel Jimenez on the same day seems to have come to a complete stop," a reporter was saying. He was standing on a golf course and pointing to the middle of the fairway. "That is the spot where Steinberg was shot as he played golf with a business associate. Miami homicide detectives say they have turned over the investigation to the

FBI, but they won't say what the federal connection to the case is, and neither will the FBI. Both the Steinberg and Jimenez families have demanded answers from the police, but they aren't getting any. Marilyn Steinberg spoke to us earlier today."

The scene changed to the country club deck overlooking the course, where a carefully coiffed and made-up woman in a flowered dress stood facing the reporter, a view of the golf course behind her. "We just don't understand," she said. "Steven had no enemies; he wasn't involved in anything illegal; he never even met a mobster. Who would do this thing, and why won't the Miami police department or the FBI tell us anything? They just say that their investigation is ongoing, and they'll let us know when they have something."

The reporter on the golf course was back. "So, that's where we leave it — in the hands of the Feds, who have been uncommunicative. Back to the studio."

Holly knew just how Marilyn Steinberg felt, she thought. The FBI wasn't telling her anything either. One thing about police work: without evidence, you were nowhere; and she was nowhere. So was Harry Crisp, apparently, and the homicide detective she had talked to had seemed almost somnolent. The phone rang, and she picked up the receiver on the table beside her. "Hello?"

She heard some odd noises, then the line went

dead — no dial tone, nothing. She put the receiver down and picked it up again. This time, she got a dial tone. She put down the receiver and pressed the button that brought up the caller ID log. The word "unavailable" presented itself for the last caller. The one before that was her office, the one before that was Ham. Maybe somebody had called from a cellphone and the call hadn't quite gone through. Maybe he'd call back. She waited, but the phone didn't ring again.

She finished her dinner, switched off the TV, and walked out the back door, across the patio, and onto the beach. She saw Daisy dart in and out of the dunes, amusing herself. The sun was going down, casting shadows across the sand down to the water.

She walked across the beach and let the little waves wash over her feet. It was a beautiful evening, and she wished she had someone to share it with. She and Jackson had liked this time of day on the beach, had taken long walks, returning to the cottage only after dark. Daisy bounded across the beach and joined her, frolicking in the shallow water. Down the beach, toward Orchid, lights were coming on, families were sitting down to dinner, lovers were making love.

Holly was alone, and that hurt, but she still felt she'd rather be alone than with someone other than Jackson. There wouldn't be another Jackson in her life, she knew that, but she hoped there'd be somebody down the line. When he turned up, she hoped she'd want him.

She turned and, with Daisy at her heels, trudged back to the house. It waited for her, warm, inviting, and empty.

8

The following morning Holly phoned the station and asked for Hurd Wallace.

"Deputy Chief Wallace," he said.

"Hurd, Holly. Do you know a really good locksmith?"

"Yeah, sure; Phil Sweat; he does locks, alarms, electronics, the works. I'll give you the number."

Holly wrote it down, then hung up and called the man.

Two hours later, Phil Sweat arrived in a van emblazoned with the name NO SWEAT LOCK-SMITHS, *Your Security Is Our Only Business.* Sweat was short, skinny, and shrewd-looking. He reminded Holly of a ferret.

"Morning, Chief," Sweat said. "What can I do you for?"

"I want new locks on all the exterior doors; excellent locks."

"You had some kind of problem?"

"Somebody came into my house yesterday while I was at work. Nothing was stolen, but I could tell somebody had been here."

"Rearranged things, did he?"

"In tiny ways that only I would notice."

"There are people like that," Sweat said, raising his baseball cap and scratching his head. "They break into people's houses just to experience their lives. Sometimes they steal, sometimes they don't. Sometimes they shit on the floor."

"Nothing like that, but I don't want it to happen again."

"You got an alarm system?"

"Yes, but I haven't been using it."

"Why don't I take a look at it?"

"The box is in the hall coat closet."

Sweat walked into the house, checking the front door lock on the way in. "I could pick that in thirty seconds," he said, "and if I could, so could somebody else." He opened the closet door, pushed the clothing aside, and opened the alarm central box. The key was in the lock. "You made it easy for somebody to get in here and yank some wires."

"That didn't happen; anyway, the alarm wasn't on."

Sweat peered into the box. "It did happen. The front door is no longer wired into the system." He pulled a screwdriver from a vest loaded with tools and worked for a moment. "There, that'll do it, but if I were you, with a problem like this, I'd beef up the system. You're only covering what looks like the exterior doors and the downstairs windows. You got any motion detectors?"

"No."

"Let's take a walk around the house," Sweat said.

Holly followed the man as he checked every door, every window in the house, looked in closets, inspected her safes. Sweat led Holly outside to his van. "You don't have a bad system here, it's just inadequate. What I propose is to replace all the exterior locks with Swedish units that work magnetically." He opened the rear door, rummaged in some boxes on shelves inside, and came up with a hefty lock. "They're very high quality, and hell to get past. Then I'd extend the alarm system to all the windows, and I'd put two motion detectors in — one at the top of the stairs by the kitchen, covering the living room."

"What about Daisy?" Holly said, nodding at the dog.

"I'll align the motion detectors to start reading at three and a half feet; that's over Daisy's head. Something else, I'd rig a video camera at the top of the stairs, attached to a VCR, covering most of the ground floor, and have it triggered by the motion detectors — but only when the alarm system has been activated by you. We're only talking about another five hundred or so, and if somebody gets in, you'll have him on tape."

"I like that," Holly said. "How much?"

Sweat looked at his pad. "A lot of the wiring is already in, so, let's see . . . You're talking about four grand, and I'll give you a police discount of twenty-five percent, so three grand, all in."

"Done," Holly replied. "When can you do the work?"

"It'll be complete by the time you get home tonight. I should meet you here and show you how the system is set up."

"Okay, the place is yours. I'll be home at six, and I'll give you a check then."

Sweat gave her a little salute and went to his van.

Holly went to work.

She had been working on her personnel files for a couple of hours when the phone rang.

"It's Phil Sweat," he said. "I need you to come out here."

"Can we talk about it on the phone?"

"No."

"All right, I'll be there in twenty minutes."

She arrived back at the house to find Sweat running wires up the stairs. "What's up?"

Sweat dug into a vest pocket and came up with a small electronic-looking little thing.

"What's that?"

"I thought I'd have a look at your phone system. I found this in the main box around the side of the house."

"What *is* it, Phil?"

"It's a pretty sophisticated bug. It was attached to the main phone line, so somebody could hear you on any extension, and run to a VHF transmitter under the eaves. VHF is line of sight, so with the transmitter up high like that, it would have a range of, oh, I don't know, maybe six to ten miles."

"Somebody tapped my phone?" Holly said, half to herself.

"Yep. Question is, what do you want to do about it?"

"Rip it out."

"I can do that, but they might just come back and do it again, and better, so that it would be harder to find. On the other hand, if you leave the bug in, you can decide what they hear. I should point out that every phone in your house is a transmitter, whether it's being used or not."

Holly thought for a minute. "Rip it out."

"Okay, but if I were you, I'd watch what I say; you'd never know when it's back in. I mean, I could come over here a couple of times a week and sweep the place."

Holly thought some more. "Okay, leave it in, but can you fix it so it doesn't work very well?"

"I could probably arrange for it to work intermittently, so that a listener would only hear some of what's said. That way, he'd think it was his fault."

"Good idea. If he wanted to come back, would he be able to breach the system?"

"The way I'm rigging it, he would have to be really, really good, and he'd need a lot of time — several hours — to figure out how to get in. But it could be breached — any system can be breached, eventually."

"Right now, the alarm system calls a security company."

"Yeah, I know them. They don't have any cars, they'd just call the police."

"Reset it to call the police station, with a message that the chief's house has been entered."

"Good idea; cut out the middleman. You can stop paying the monthly fee, too; I'll come and check it out periodically."

"Good."

Sweat dug into his trousers pocket and came up with a bunch of keys. "Here are your keys; the locks are already in. All the locks are keyed together, and I've changed the lock on the security box to one of these, too. I'd keep a key in your pocket, one at the office, and I'd hide one somewhere around the house that isn't obvious, because if you're locked out and you can't get ahold of me, you're not going to be able to get in without breaking a window and setting off the alarm."

"Okay."

"By the way, do you want a silent alarm, or one connected to a horn, the way it is now?"

Holly thought about that. "Can you really have it call the station house?"

"Yes, and for a few bucks more, I can have it give a message as to which part of the house has been breached."

"Good, I like that. I mean, Daisy is an excellent watchdog, but it's conceivable that, with the bedroom door closed, she might not hear someone enter downstairs."

"I'll go reconnect the bug," Sweat said.

Holly thought she'd sleep with a gun on the bedside table from now on.

9

Holly went back to her office, wondering what the hell was going on; then she had a thought. She walked around to Hurd Wallace's office and beckoned him out into the hall.

"Did you talk to Phil Sweat?" he asked.

"Yes, he's out there working on a new security system for me right now, and he's discovered a bug on my telephones."

Hurd's eyebrows went up. "No kidding?"

"No kidding. Tell me about how the phones went bad yesterday."

Hurd thought for a moment. "Everything went dead," he said, "and before we could even call the phone company, one of their guys walked in and said they were having some problems in the area and it would be fixed shortly. It was."

"Call the phone company — on your cellphone, and not near one of our phones — and find out if they have any record of anybody working around here yesterday and fixing our problem."

"You think somebody was tapping our phones?"

"I want to find out."

Hurd nodded, took his cellphone off his belt, and walked out the back door. Holly returned to her office and tried to work on her personnel files, but she was having trouble keeping her mind on them.

Hurd came into her office. "The phone company says they did have problems around here yesterday, and they were fixed by a unit already in the neighborhood."

"That's a relief," Holly said, "but I'm still going to get Phil Sweat to come over here when he's done at my place and check out our system. You think he could handle that?"

"Sure. Phil used to work for the state police doing this stuff; he knows his business."

Late in the afternoon, Phil Sweat arrived and spent two hours inspecting their office phone system. Finally, he came back to where Holly and Hurd were waiting for him.

"I think you're okay," he said, "especially since the phone company confirms you had a problem. Think about it: It's one thing to bug your house and have a recorder hooked up that could be checked now and then. It's something else to bug a police station with forty or fifty phones installed and keep track of what's being said on them. I mean, it would be a good-sized job for the National Security Agency, and it's not the sort of thing that some private investigator is going to be able to handle. That's usually who's responsible for bugs like the one on your house — somebody's wife thinks her husband is screwing his secretary, or something like that. Sometimes it might be one business trying to find out about a competitor. The bug at your house was over-the-counter stuff, made of parts you could buy at any electronics supplier. Bugging a police station would require a whole new level of expertise."

"Thank's Phil," Holly said. She wrote him a check for the work at her house. "Send the department a bill for your time here."

"It's on the house," Phil said, pocketing Holly's check. "Now, let's go back to your place so I can show you what I've done and how to run it."

Holly followed him back to her house.

Sweat walked her through the house, reviewed arming and disarming the system with a keypad at each door and one at her bedside. He showed her something that looked like a ceiling light fixture over her stairs. "That's your video camera. I've run it to the TV set in your living room." He picked up a remote control and switched on the TV. "Now, you press the TV/video button until you come to video three, just the way you would if you were going to watch something on the VCR." He handed her another, smaller remote control. "Then you use this to run the VCR in the attic that shows you anything the system has taped while you were out. Remember, it only works if the alarm system is activated. You can rewind and fast forward, as with any VCR, and you press this button to rearm the system. If there's something on a tape you want to keep, you just pull down the stairs to your attic, go up there, and you'll see the unit on a shelf I installed. Take the tape out, replace it with a blank one, and rearm the system. That's all there is to it."

"Thanks, Phil, I feel a lot better now."

"Now that we've been through everything, you want me to get the bug working again?"

"Yes, but intermittently, and then I want it to go out completely."

"Then they'll just come back to see what's wrong."

"That's what I want them to do. You go hook it up, I'll make a couple of calls, and right in the middle of one, you can pull the plug."

"Whatever you say."

"I'll talk outside, on the cordless from the living room, so I can signal you."

"Okay. I'll get back on the ladder."

Holly waited for him to get into position, then she called Ham.

"Hello?"

"Hey, it's me."

"How you doing, baby?"

"I'm okay, I guess. What have you been up to?"

"Did a little fishing today."

"Fishing's a lot of fun, Ham, but doesn't it get old after a while?"

"Not yet."

Holly walked out the door with the cordless phone and looked up at Phil. He gave her a thumbs-up.

"Ham, I'm worried about you out there with nothing but fishing poles."

"Well, don't you worry, kiddo, because fishing poles ain't all I got out here. In fact, right at this moment, there's a lady waiting for me to grill her a steak."

Holly looked up at Phil and nodded. "Ham, you be nice to that lady, you hear? Remember, she's not in the army, and you're not . . ." Phil drew a finger across his throat. ". . . and you're not still a sergeant. Bye-bye."

"See you, kid." Ham hung up, and so did Holly.

Phil climbed down from the ladder. "Got you in mid-sentence," he said. "What I did was loosen one wire so it would look like an accident when the guy comes back to check on it."

"Good work, Phil."

"I gotta go. Call me if you have any problems."

"Will do." She watched him get into his van and drive away, then she called the station and got Hurd.

"Hurd Wallace."

"I'm glad you're still there," she said. "I want you to pull an officer off the night shift and send him out here with another officer in an unmarked car, then I want the car to leave."

"What's' up?"

"I'm going to see if I can't catch me a phone bugger."

"Okay. I'll send Teddy Wright; he's a good kid."

"Fine."

Teddy Wright was the youngest officer on the force and, in many ways, the least experienced, but Holly found him to be bright and willing. "Here's the story," she said, and explained what Phil Sweat had found. "I think they'll send somebody out here to fix it, maybe tonight, and when they do, I want you to apprehend whoever comes." She showed him where the phone box was, and they found a spot where he could watch it while remaining unobserved.

Holly made him a sandwich, gave him a canvas chair to sit in, and handed him a thermos of coffee. "Don't fall asleep, and if the guy shows up, don't shoot him, understand? I want to talk to him."

"Yes, ma'am," Teddy said.

"Just cuff him, and then call me."

"Yes, ma'am."

Holly got him situated and went to have her own dinner. It was getting dark now.

10

Holly woke up at her usual six A.M., showered, dressed, and put some coffee on. She fed Daisy and let her out, then went to ask Teddy Wright to join her for breakfast. He was nowhere to be seen.

Holly was annoyed. She had not told him to leave at dawn, and she expected her officers to follow her instructions. Then she noticed the canvas chair she had put out for Teddy to sit in as he kept watch. It was lying on its side in some long grass. She walked over to it and found Teddy lying facedown in the grass, and there was blood on the back of his head. Alarmed, she turned him over and felt at his neck for a pulse. It was there, but it seemed weak to her.

She pulled Teddy's radio off his belt and spoke into it. "Base, this is the chief."

"Chief, base."

"Get an ambulance out to my house right now, and tell Chief Wallace to get out here, too, and to bring a crime-scene tech."

"Roger, Chief."

Holly dragged over the chair and put Teddy's feet in it; shock was a good possibility. She brushed the hair out of his face, and for a moment she felt something she had rarely felt before — motherly. Teddy's face was cherubic in repose, that of a small boy. A lot of her officers adopted macho attitudes in their work, something she had tried to discourage, but Teddy's face showed none of that now.

She heard an ambulance in the distance, and she walked around the house to meet it. "Back there," she said to the EMTs who spilled out of the vehicle. "You'll need a stretcher."

"What have we got?"

"Unconscious male police officer, apparent blow to the back of the head. Pulse feels weak to me."

She followed them and watched as they went through their routine — placed a collar on the young man's neck, took his blood pressure, started an IV. Minutes later, Teddy was in the back of the ambulance on the way to the hospital.

"I'll follow in a few minutes," Holly said to the driver as he drove past her.

The ambulance had hardly cleared the driveway when Hurd Wallace drove in. He got out of the car. "What's going on?"

"Somebody hit Teddy over the head last night and left him unconscious in the grass. I've no idea how long he was like that before I found him."

Hurd turned to the crime-scene tech. "Check it out — footprints, and anything else you can turn up. Let's go in the house," Hurd said.

"Okay," Holly replied. "I want to go to the hospital and check on Teddy." She led the way into the house. "Coffee's on," she said.

"Thanks." Hurd pulled up a stool to the kitchen counter and accepted the cup. "What do you think is going on here, Holly?"

Holly peeled a banana, which was going to be breakfast. "I don't have a clue, Hurd. What are we working on that might cause somebody to want to bug my phones?"

"It's been pretty quiet," Hurd replied. "I can't think of a thing that would connect to this. Anything in your life that might have brought this on? Anything personal?"

Holly shook her head. "There isn't anything personal in my life, except Ham." It hurt to admit that, especially to her deputy chief. She tossed the banana peel and poured herself a cup of coffee.

"Maybe you ought to get Phil Sweat to sweep Ham's place, too."

"Why?"

Hurd shrugged. "Couldn't hurt."

The tech knocked on the back door, and Holly waved him in. "What have you got?"

"Nothing," the tech replied. "It's a grassy area, and there were no discernible footprints and no other physical evidence, either."

She turned back to Hurd. "Finish your coffee, then please call Phil Sweat and get him back out here. I want to know if the bug is back on the phones, then ask him to go out to Ham's. Call Ham for me, will you? I want to get to the hospital."

Hurd nodded.

"I'll see you back at the station." Holly called Daisy and they hopped into the car and drove away.

The ER was quiet when Holly arrived at the hospital, and she spoke to the young resident who had treated Teddy.

"Blow to the head," the doctor said, "no fracture, but he's concussed, and he required eight stitches. He was showing signs of shock when he arrived."

"Prognosis?"

"He's going to have a hell of a headache, maybe some dizziness. We'll keep him overnight to make sure he's stable, then he ought to take a couple of days off until he feels well again."

"Is he awake?"

"He's been conscious, but he's sleeping now. I don't want him disturbed, unless it's very urgent that you talk to him."

"It's not," she said. "Tell him I was here and to phone me when he feels up to it. I do want to ask him some questions."

A nurse approached. "Officer Wright is awake and asking for the chief," she said.

"Go ahead," the doctor said, "but keep it brief."

Holly nodded and followed the nurse down the hall to a room in which the blinds had been closed. The nurse pressed a button and raised the head of the bed a little.

"How are you feeling, Teddy?" Holly asked, taking his hand.

"I'm sorry, Chief," he said.

"Nothing to be sorry about. You need to just rest until tomorrow, then we'll get you home for a couple of days of R and R."

"It's my fault," Teddy said.

"No it's not; somebody snuck up on you, that's all."

"No, it's my fault."

"Why do you think so?"

"It was my radio; I left it on."

"What happened, do you remember?"

"There was a call on the radio, some traffic thing, and I thought, shit, I forgot to turn it off. Next thing I knew I was on the ground, and then I must have passed out."

"It's okay, Teddy. You're not hurt badly, but you'll be fine in a little while. You just get some rest now, and we'll talk later."

"I'm sorry, Chief," he said again.

"It's all right; don't worry about it." She gave his hand a pat and followed the nurse out of the room.

"Nice kid," the nurse said. "Is he old enough to be a policeman?"

"Only just," Holly replied. "Please see that he gets anything he needs and bill the department.

When he's ready to be released, let me know, and I'll send a car to take him home."

"You bet."

Holly thanked the nurse and drove back to the station. She found Hurd Wallace. "What family does Teddy have?"

"Just a mother; he lives with her." Hurd handed her a slip of paper. "I thought you'd want to call her."

"Thanks, Hurd." Holly made the call.

"Hello?" a woman's voice said.

"Mrs. Wright?"

"Yes."

"This is Chief Holly Barker, at the police station."

"Has something happened to Teddy?" There was real alarm in her voice.

"Teddy's fine, don't worry. He was on a stakeout last night, and he got hit on the head. They want to keep him overnight at the hospital, but he's going to be just fine, and I don't want you to worry."

"Can I see him?"

"Why don't you wait until after lunch? He was up all night, and the doctor wants him to get some sleep."

"Is he really all right?"

"Really, he is. He probably fell off his bike as a kid and got hurt worse."

"He broke his arm, falling off his bike."

"This isn't nearly as bad. Just give him a few hours to rest, then go see him. Is there anything

68

I can do for you? Do you need anything, maybe a ride to the hospital?"

"No, thank you, Chief; I have my car."

"Please call me if there's anything I can do. Teddy will be released tomorrow morning, and he's going to be at home for a couple of days, resting. Don't you let him come back to work until he feels well again."

"Don't you worry, Chief, I'll take care of him. Thank you for calling."

Holly hung up and found Hurd standing in her doorway.

"Ham doesn't want his phones swept," he said.

"I'll deal with Ham," Holly replied. "You just get Phil Sweat out there."

11

Holly drove out to Ham's little island, off the North Bridge, and pulled up to his house. There was a strange car parked out front. Before Holly could make it to the front porch, Ham came out, pulling on a polo shirt.

"Morning, Ham."

"What the hell are you doing here at this hour of the morning?"

"Ham, it's a little past eleven. What happened to your early rising habit?"

"Well, there are times when I just don't want to get out of bed."

Finally, Holly got it. "Oops, my fault; I just wasn't thinking."

"You could say that. And what the hell does Hurd Wallace want to bug my house for?"

"He doesn't want to bug it; he wants it checked for bugs. So do I."

"And why the hell would anybody bug my house?"

"Calm down, Ham. I don't know, and I don't know why they'd want to bug my house, either, but they did."

That stopped Ham in his tracks. "They did?"

"They did. A fellow named Phil Sweat found the bug, and when I disconnected it and put an officer out back to see if anybody would try to reconnect it, he got hit over the head."

Ham absorbed this. "Come on in, I'll make you some coffee."

"I don't think that would be a good idea."

"Oh, what the hell, it's time you met her anyway."

Holly followed him into the house. "Met who?"

"Met me," a woman's voice said.

Holly turned and found a very good-looking redhead standing in the bedroom doorway, buckling the belt on a pair of jeans that fit her slim body perfectly. Her tight, ribbed sweater was a little short, revealing a small expanse of freckled midriff.

"I'm Ginny," she said, offering her hand.

"Virginia Heller," Ham said, "and she is."

Holly shook her hand. "Glad to meet you, Ginny."

"Ham's told me a lot about you."

Holly laughed. "Then you have me at a disadvantage, because he hasn't told me a thing about you."

"Bad Ham," Ginny said, shooting him a glance.

"I just haven't gotten around to it," Ham said, pouring coffee for them all.

"Phil Sweat is going to be here in a few minutes," Holly said, "just as soon as he finishes at my house."

"Tell me about this," Ham said.

Holly led them out onto the back porch, which overlooked the Indian River, and told them about her break-in and the resulting phone tap.

"You sure lead an interesting life," Ginny said.

"This is more annoying than interesting," Holly replied.

"I think it's real interesting," Ham said, "that somebody thinks he needs to hear what you say on the phone. Who's your best guess?"

"I don't have a best guess; it doesn't make any sense at all."

"And who's this Phil Sweat?" Ham asked.

"He runs a locksmith and security service; he seems to be very good at it, too." She turned to Ginny. "You a local, Ginny?"

"For nearly a month," she replied. "I'm a flight instructor out at the airport."

"No kidding?" Holly asked. "I have an interest in getting my private pilot's license."

"That's what I do. Come out real soon, and we'll take an introductory flight."

"How about this weekend?"

"Saturday morning, nine A.M.?"

"I'll do it."

"It's called Orchid Flight Academy."

"I've seen the building. What airplane do you teach in?"

"We'd start you in a Piper Warrior, which is pretty basic but nice, and when you feel like it, move you up to something more complex."

"I'll look forward to that." She heard the

crunch of gravel under tires. "That'll be Phil," she said. She walked to the front door and waved him inside. When the introductions had been made, he asked her to step outside.

"What's up?" she asked.

"I checked the bug, as you asked, and it had not been reconnected."

"I don't know if that's good or bad."

"Turns out, it's bad, and it gets worse."

"How?"

"I thought it was suspicious that they'd go to the trouble to slug a cop, then do nothing, so I had a more extensive look around the house. I ended up in the crawl space underneath, and I found another bug, just like the first one."

"Swell."

"Yeah. What do you want me to do?"

Holly thought about that. She hated the loss of privacy. "Leave it intact," she said. "Let them think I think I'm not being overheard. They can't see into the house, can they?"

Phil shook his head. "Nothing like that. These aren't Peeping Toms; they're looking for information."

Holly nodded. "Go ahead and check out Ham's place."

"Shouldn't take long. If they've bugged it, they'd use the same equipment they're using at your place."

Holly left him to his work and went back inside. "Ham, from now on, when you call me or when you come to the house, be careful what you say. I'm bugged again, and I'm going to leave it that way."

"I wouldn't know what not to say," Ham replied.

"Me either," Holly admitted. They finished their coffee and made small talk.

Half an hour later, Phil Sweat came out to the back porch. "Same deal here," he said quietly. "You want me to leave it in place?"

"Is it just a phone tap?" Ham asked.

"It's more than that; it turns every phone in your house into a microphone."

Ginny Heller spoke up. "Let me get this straight. You mean that somebody could listen to every sound in this house?"

"That's about the size of it," Phil said.

"Oh, shit," she said. "Ham, you're going to have to start coming to my place."

"Ham," Holly said, "I'd like to leave the bug in place; that all right with you? And Ginny?"

Ham and Ginny exchanged a long look. "I guess I'd better start coming to your place," he said to her.

"This is *very* embarrassing," Ginny muttered.

"Yeah, we're probably all over some Internet porn site by now," Ham said, deadpan.

"Ham!" Ginny cried, blushing.

Holly tried not to laugh. "Don't worry, there are no cameras. Are there, Phil?"

"Nope," Phil replied, trying to keep a straight face.

"Thank God for that," Ginny said under her breath.

Ham, looking amused, started to say something, but Holly cut him off. "Well, I guess I'd better get back to work," she said.

Phil spoke up. "I think we'd better go back in the house so I can give a negative report on finding bugs, for the benefit of whoever's listening."

"Good idea," Ham said.

Ginny looked at her watch. "I've got to get going. I've got a student coming at one o'clock, and I've still got to . . ." She left that unsaid.

They went back into the house, Phil gave his report in an audible voice, and he, Holly, and Ginny went to their cars.

"I'll see you Saturday morning at nine," Holly said, waving to Ginny. "Do I need to bring anything?"

"Nope," Ginny called back. "I'll supply everything."

"Good to meet you."

"And you." Ginny drove away.

Holly drove back to her office. When she arrived, there was a note on her desk to call Ed Shine.

12

Holly returned Ed Shine's call, and a secretary answered.

"Mr. Shine's office."

"This is Holly Barker, returning Ed's call."

"Oh, yes; please hold."

"Holly? How are you?"

"Very well, Ed. What have you been up to?"

"Working hard; we've sold two houses already."

"That's great."

"You and Ham free for dinner on Saturday?"

"I am, and Ham probably is, although he has a girlfriend these days."

"Invite them both."

"I'll do that and get back to you."

"I'll be here."

Holly called Ham, made the date, and called Shine back.

"Good. My car will pick you up at seven o'clock. Where do you live?"

Holly gave him directions.

"Then you can direct the driver to Ham's place. Then you'll pick me up."

"Where are we dining?"

"At the Yellow Dog Cafe, just south of Melbourne. It's not a long drive."

"I've heard good things about it. We'll see you later."

Holly hung up and went back to work on her personnel files, completing the job while having a sandwich at her desk. Then her phone rang.

"Holly Barker."

"Hi, it's Harry."

"Hello, Harry. How are you?"

"Good. You free for dinner on Saturday night?"

"No, I've just made plans; Ham and I are dining with friends."

"How about Sunday night?"

"Okay. What brings you up this way?"

"It's not me; his name is Grant Early."

"Harry, are you trying to fix me up?"

"Not exactly. He's one of my people and he's going to be spending some time in your area."

"Doing what?"

"I think we need a presence around there — not exactly an agent in residence, more of a . . ."

"Harry, is he going to be undercover?"

"Well, yes. He'll explain that to you. I'd appreciate it if you'd give him any help you can."

"What could I possibly do for him that the FBI can't?"

Harry paused to think about that. "He might need some on-the-ground assistance," he said finally.

"Well, okay, Harry. Have him call me about Sunday."

"He's right here; I'll put him on."

"Hello?" a man's deep voice said.

"Hello."

"Holly Barker?"

"Yes."

"This is Grant Early."

"Sounds like a bourbon."

"Usually people say scotch. I take it we're on for dinner on Sunday?"

"All right." Holly didn't know why she was agreeing to this.

"Will you book us a table at some place you like a lot? I'll pick you up at seven, if that's all right."

"All right."

"Harry says he'll give me directions to your place."

"Okay."

"How should I dress?"

"We're pretty casual up here; a jacket but no tie should do."

"See you then. Here's Harry."

"Holly, I appreciate this. Don't blame Grant if he can't tell you everything."

"I'll blame you."

Harry laughed.

"Harry, have you been bugging my phones?"

"Huh?" His surprise sounded genuine.

"Somebody has; the FBI is good at that."

"Who do you think it is?"

"My first guess was you."

"Wrong. What's your second guess?"

"I don't have one."

"You working on something exotic?"

"Nope."

"You working on something unexotic that someone might want to know about?"

"Not that I can think of, and believe me, I've thought about it. Whoever it is, is bugging Ham, too, and since he has a new girlfriend, he's not happy about it."

"Why don't you talk to Grant about this on Sunday night? Maybe he'll have some ideas."

"Okay."

"And watch your back; I don't like the sound of this."

"Okay." Holly hung up feeling uneasy. She didn't like the sound of it, either, but she hadn't thought about watching her back.

Her phone rang again.

"Holly Barker."

"Chief, it's Teddy Wright." He sounded sheepish.

"How are you feeling, Teddy?"

"A lot better; I want to come back to work today."

"No dice; you're taking two sick days. I'll see you the day after tomorrow."

"But what am I going to do? I'll go nuts sitting around here."

"Watch soap operas; that shouldn't put any strain on your newly concussed brain."

"I hate soap operas."

"So do I. Try reading."

"I'm not much of a reader."

"Teddy, you're wasting my time. I'll see you the day after tomorrow."

"Okay, Chief." Teddy hung up.

Once again, Holly felt motherly.

13

On Saturday morning Holly drove out to the Orchid Beach airport and found the Orchid Flight Academy. She had been there before, she realized.

The building was broken into a warren of small rooms with desks and computers, and most of them were busy. Ginny Heller was seated in a glassed-in office at the back of the small building.

"Good morning," Holly said, rapping on her open door.

"Good morning," Ginny replied. "What do you think of my place?"

"Used to be a flying club, didn't it? I came out here once for a flight with a friend."

"Right. I bought it from the couple who owned it for thirty years, and I'm expanding the operation. I've installed computers for ground school and hired a couple more instructors."

"I didn't realize you were the boss."

Ginny waved her into a seat. "Yeah, I took my divorce settlement and put it to work here."

"Have you been instructing for long?"

"About eight years. I took up flying because

my marriage was boring me stiff, and then I started instructing. I've got more than three thousand hours now, and a bunch of ratings. It was the only thing I got out of the marriage, except the settlement."

"Good for you."

Ginny handed her a document. "These are our prices for aircraft rental and instructors' fees. The first lesson is free."

Holly read quickly through the price list. "Okay by me."

Ginny picked up a canvas briefcase. "Shall we get started?"

"Sure." Holly followed Ginny out to the ramp to a shiny Piper Warrior, and Ginny began to walk her through a preflight inspection of the airplane.

"We going to fly today?" Holly asked, surprised.

"We always fly on the first lesson; gets the student hooked."

The preflight completed, they got into the airplane, Holly in the left seat.

"You ever flown an airplane before?"

"Yeah. Jackson was a pilot, and he would let me take the controls now and then."

"Okay, let's get started up. Here's your checklist."

Holly worked her way through the list of tasks to complete, and soon the engine was running.

"You steer with your feet; turning the yoke doesn't help at all," Ginny explained. "Tune the bottom radio to the ATIS frequency — that's the automated weather report."

Holly listened and wrote down the data, which was called Information Bravo.

"Now tune the top radio to the ground frequency — it's on your checklist. Call ground control, give them your tail number — it's on the placard over the yoke — and announce that you're ready to taxi from the Orchid Flight Academy and that you have Information Bravo."

Holly did so and was cleared to taxi to runway 18.

"The runways are labeled according to their direction. Runway one-eight is south; runway three-six is north. Keep the nosewheel on the yellow line and follow it, first to the taxiway, then to the runway."

Holly steered with the rudder pedals and found it quite easy to keep the little airplane on track. They stopped at a parking place near the end of the runway and went through the run-up checklist.

"Now we're ready for takeoff," Ginny said. "Call the tower frequency, it's on your checklist, and say you're ready, number one for takeoff."

Holly did so and was cleared for takeoff.

"Now check to see there's no one about to land, then taxi onto the runway and line up the nosewheel with the center line."

Holly followed the instructions.

"Now apply full throttle smoothly, and keep

on the center line. When the airspeed indicator reads sixty knots, rotate — that means pull smoothly back on the yoke."

Holly found the throttle and pushed it in slowly. The airplane began to roll down the runway. At sixty knots she rotated, and they lifted into the air. It was an exhilarating feeling, she found.

"Watch your direction indicator and keep her on a one-eight-zero heading," Ginny said. "At five hundred feet of altitude, turn right to two-seven-zero."

Holly made the right turn.

"Continue to climb to three thousand feet and hold this heading," Ginny said. "You're doing very well."

Holly glanced outside at the flat, central Florida landscape moving beneath her. Her heart was beating fast. "This is wonderful," she said.

"It's like sex," Ginny said. "The more you do it, the better it gets."

Holly laughed. "Losing my virginity wasn't this much fun."

"But it got better, I hope."

"It sure did."

"So will this, the better you get at it. You're coming up on three thousand feet. Push the yoke slightly forward and reduce power to cruise; it's on your checklist. The checklist is your bible. Using it will eliminate half the ways you can get into trouble in an airplane."

"How about the other half?"

"We'll go through those as your training continues."

"Give me an example."

"The most important things are checking the weather before your flight, and making sure you have enough fuel for your planned flight."

"That seems sensible."

"Way too many pilots fail to do one or both. Most of those news stories about small airplanes landing in fields or on the interstate are people who didn't have enough fuel for the flight. And flying into bad weather is the single most common cause of fatal crashes. Now let's make some turns." Ginny guided her through several ninety-degree turns, showing her how to coordinate rudder pressure with turning the yoke. "Just keep the little ball on that instrument centered," she said, pointing.

Holly followed her instructions, learning to make coordinated turns and to fly a compass course.

"Watch your altitude," Ginny said. "It tends to change when you make turns, and keeping your assigned altitude is very important. You're doing extremely well, Holly; you're going to be very good at this."

"Thank you."

"You want to do a little sightseeing?"

"Sure."

"Turn to oh-nine-oh, and we'll fly over to the beach area."

Holly made the turn.

"Now drop down to one thousand feet so we can see things on the ground better."

Holly descended. Ahead of her she saw a long runway on the barrier island. "Look," she said, pointing. "That's Palmetto Gardens — sorry, Blood Orchid. They have their own six-thousand-foot runway."

"I've heard about it. You can get any kind of corporate jet and a lot of airliners onto a six-thousand-foot runway."

"The previous residents flew passengers in and huge sums of money out — the income from drug deals all over the country."

"The place could make a good fly-in community," Ginny said. "There's a place up near Daytona that has a long runway, with houses built around it. You can taxi right into your own hangar, attached to your house. Now make a right turn and fly along the beach; stay about a quarter-mile offshore."

Holly turned the airplane south. She passed a dozen gated communities, then the small Orchid Beach business district, and flew on south, toward Vero Beach. In the distance, she spotted her own house. "That's where I live," she said, pointing.

"Which one?"

"The one with the sea grass around it, white clapboard."

"It's beautiful," Ginny said.

"Jackson took the land in payment for some

legal fees in a case, then he bought an old Florida farmhouse, had it sawed in half and moved it to the property. Then he made some additions and renovated the old house." She stopped talking and looked at the rapidly approaching house. A feeling of déjà vu swept over her. "Something's wrong," she said.

"What is it?"

"There." She pointed. "That van behind the house. That's not supposed to be there."

"I see it," Ginny said.

"How do we contact your office?"

"We use the unicom frequency," Ginny replied, dialing it into the radio.

"Call them, tell them to call the police and tell them to get a partrol car and two officers to the chief's house, pronto."

Ginny made the call.

"Good," Holly said, "now land this thing on the beach. Tide's out, and we've got hard-packed sand to land on."

"We're not supposed to land on a beach," Ginny said.

"I'll square it with the authorities," Holly said. "This is police business."

"I've got the airplane," Ginny said, taking the controls. "We're going in."

14

Ginny made a turn and began losing altitude. "We're going to pretend that the beach is the runway. From the direction of the waves, the wind is from the southeast, so we're going to land to the south." She made another turn and was now at right angles to the beach. "Now we're on base leg, about to turn final for our runway." She made another ninety-degree turn, aligning the airplane with the beach, and continued descending, out of five hundred feet.

Holly was looking for the van, but now it was hidden behind the house.

"Tighten your seat belt," Ginny said. "We're going to make a soft-field landing, which means I keep the nosewheel off the ground for as long as possible before letting it touch down. If the sand is soft that will help keep the nosewheel from digging in and flipping us over on our back."

"Swell," Holly said, staring at her house. They touched gently a hundred yards north of the house, and Ginny eased the nosewheel onto the sand, which was wet and firm. As they swept past the house, Holly thought she saw a dark figure inside. She suddenly realized she was unarmed. Ginny braked to a halt and cut the engine.

"Stay here," Holly said. "Don't let the tide catch the airplane; that nearly happened to Jackson and me once." She unfastened her seat belt, opened the door, and hopped out onto the sand at a dead run. Daisy was in the house, and Holly was praying that she hadn't been hurt.

Holly reached the sliding doors that opened onto the beach, but they were still locked and couldn't be opened from the outside. She saw Daisy lying on the floor, apparently unconscious, but she could not see the intruder. As she ran around to the front door, she wondered why the burglar alarm siren wasn't sounding. She raced up the front steps, and as she did, the door opened and a man wearing dark clothes and a ski mask chose that moment to run out of the house, colliding head-on with her and knocking her off the front porch.

Holly struggled to her feet and started moving toward the man, who was moving toward where his van was parked. She ran after him, grabbed him by the shoulder, spun him around, and kicked hard at his knee. He grunted, and then she saw he had a semiautomatic pistol in his hand.

"Bitch!" he yelled, then slammed the pistol into the side of her head.

Holly fell to her hands and knees, crying out with pain, but she raised her head in time to see the man limp to the van, start it, and tear out of the driveway. Holly felt faint and collapsed onto her belly.

When she woke up, Ginny was pressing a cold cloth to her head, and two of Holly's cops were standing over her.

"Are you all right, Holly?"

"I think so," Holly said, sitting up. "Where's Daisy?"

"She's lying on the living room floor with a dart in her chest, out like a light," one of the cops said. "She appears to be all right, otherwise."

Holly tried to get up, but Ginny held her down. "Easy, there. There's nothing you can do for Daisy until the drug wears off. Do you remember anything?"

Holly tried to concentrate. "A male, six feet, a hundred and eighty pounds, probably under thirty-five. He was wearing dark clothes, a mask, and gloves, so I don't know about race. He drove a late-model van — the family kind, not commercial — medium blue or gray, windows darkened. I didn't register the plate. His gun was a semiautomatic, looked forty-caliber, a little bigger than a nine-millimeter. That's all I can remember."

"An ambulance is on its way," the cop said. "We need to get you checked out." As he spoke, an ambulance turned into the driveway.

"I'm not going without Daisy," Holly said.

"Call her vet and tell him to meet us at the hospital." She gave the name to the cop. "The number is in an address book on my living-room coffee table." The second cop went to get it.

Two EMTs approached with a litter. They looked her over, and one of them put an ice pack against her head and told her to hold it there.

"I can walk," Holly said.

"You shouldn't," the cop replied. "You've had a blow to the head."

Holly relaxed and let them put her onto the litter. "Ginny, you get the airplane off the beach before the tide comes in." Holly dug into a pocket with her free hand and came up with her car keys. She handed them to the cop. "My car's at the Orchid airport; get somebody to drive it to the hospital, will you?"

"I'll come to the hospital after I get the airplane back," Ginny said.

"Don't bother, I won't be there," Holly replied. "I'll call you as soon as I can."

The ambulance took Holly to the Orchid Beach hospital, with Daisy lying on the floor alongside her cot. In the ER a young doctor performed a neurological examination and ordered an X-ray. When a radiologist had checked it, the doctor came to see her and gave her two Tylenols. "There's no fracture, and I don't think you're concussed," he said. "The blow was

91

cushioned by your hair and didn't break the skin. You'll have some bruising, but it will mostly be under your hair."

"Where's my dog?" Holly asked.

"The vet's with her in another room. She's coming around, I think."

Holly hopped off the table and went looking for Daisy. She found the Doberman lying on the table, panting. Daisy lifted her head when Holly came into the room, then lay down again. "How is she?" Holly asked the vet.

"She's all right, just a little groggy." He held up a small dart. "It's a veterinary tool," he said. "The sort of thing they use for small animals at a zoo."

"Can I take her home?" Holly asked.

"Sure. I'll help you carry her out to the car."

A cop was waiting and handed Holly her keys. "You want me to drive you, Chief?"

"No, thanks, I can manage."

"I had a look around your house. As far as I could tell, nothing was disturbed, but your burglar got at the alarm box in a closet and cut some wires. I checked with the station; they never got a call."

"Make a call for me, will you? Phil Sweat at No Sweat Locksmiths. Tell him I've had a break-in and ask him to come out to the house ASAP."

When Holly arrived back at the house, Daisy was awake enough to hop out of the car, although she moved a little unsteadily. Holly opened the door and let her in. "You go get in your bed," she said, and Daisy dutifully walked over to the soft bed next to the fireplace and lay down. In a moment, she was asleep again.

Holly felt surprisingly well for someone who had been hit on the side of the head with a gun. She walked around the house, looking for signs of anything disturbed, but there was nothing. She pulled down the ladder to the attic, walked upstairs, and took the videotape from the VCR that Phil had installed. She put a blank tape in, then went back downstairs. As she arrived in the living room, Ham walked in, followed closely by Phil Sweat.

"You all right?" Ham asked.

"Nothing that a couple of Tylenol couldn't cure." She put a hand to her head. "I'll be a little sore tomorrow, probably."

Phil Sweat was already looking at the alarm control box. "The guy knew what he was doing," he said. "If you find him, tell him I'll give him a job."

"Ginny called me and told me what happened," Ham said.

"I should call her," Holly said, heading for the phone.

"Don't bother; she's flying with another student. Come sit down."

Holly put the videocassette into the living room VCR and sat down next to Ham on the sofa, picking up the remote control. "Let's see what my camera got," she said, pressing the play button. "Phil, come and look at this."

They watched as a snowy image appeared on the screen, then locked into place. It was a good picture, clear and in color. At the bottom of the stairs, the coat closet was open, and they could see a man's back.

"He's disabling the alarm," Phil said.

"Daisy's already down," Ham said, pointing to a black lump halfway offscreen.

"She must have met him at the door, but he was ready for her," Holly said.

"So he knows you've got a dog, and he knows how to disable your alarm," Ham said. "This guy sounds very competent and well prepared."

"He's a regular cat burglar," Phil said, "right out of the movies, or the CIA. You got any jewelry, Holly?"

"Some; it's in the safe upstairs."

"What did he want? You missing anything?"

Holly watched the man turn from the closet and walk up the stairs, passing under the camera. "Not so far. Let's see what else he does."

A minute passed, then the man walked back down the stairs and into the study off the living room. Holly glanced at her watch. When the man left the study, three minutes had passed. He walked around the living room, checking the magazines on the coffee table.

"Look," Holly said, "he's arranging the magazines again; he did that last time."

"Neat freak," Ham said.

The man looked around the room once more, then walked to the front door and opened it.

"That's when I arrived," Holly said. "I collided with him, and I fell off the porch. When I went after him, he hit me with the gun."

"What the fuck is going on here?" Ham asked.

"That's what I'd like to know," Holly replied. "Let's take a look at the study." She led the way into the small room where Jackson had once worked late on case files. About all she used the room for was paying bills. "Neater than I left it," she said.

"He doesn't care if you know he was here," Phil said. "That's weird."

"Weird describes it," Holly replied.

"Holly," Phil said, "if you don't mind, I'd like to work on the alarm system right now."

"Okay."

"What I want to do is to put the original box back together, to look the way it was, then I want to install a second box that really controls the system, and I'll do it where he can't find it so easy."

"Go right ahead, Phil."

"You need to get some rest," Ham said. "I'll cancel dinner with Ed Shine."

"No, don't do that," Holly said. "I've got a touch of cabin fever and I want to get out. I feel all right. I'll take a nap and pick you and Ginny up as planned."

"If you say so," Ham said.

When Ham had gone, Holly left Daisy asleep in her bed and stretched out on the living room sofa, so she'd be nearby when the dog woke up. It took her a few minutes to wind down enough to doze. She dreamed of taking the gun away from the intruder and pistol-whipping him.

15

The car arrived on time, and Holly was impressed. She'd been expecting Ed's Cadillac, but when she walked out of the house she found a Bentley waiting for her, and it looked brand-new. The driver was a nearly silent Hispanic man who greeted her and held the door while she got in.

They cruised up A1A, and, through the darkened windows, Holly watched the expressions of people on the street as they drove through downtown. Nobody had ever seen anything like this in Orchid, she thought.

Ham and Ginny were equally impressed with the car. "Pullman interior," Ham said, referring to the two sets of facing rear seats. "Not as long as those things with hot tubs that people rent so they can get drunk and not have to drive, but long enough."

"How are you feeling, Holly?" Ginny asked. She looked sensational in a red dress that worked with her hair.

"I'm perfectly all right," Holly said, putting a hand to the side of her head. "It's sore under there, but that's all."

"I can't see a bruise," Ginny said. "And nobody who sees you in that dress is going to look at your head."

Holly laughed. "It's Armani; I went down to Palm Beach and bought it . . . before the wedding."

"I didn't mean to bring up a bad memory," Ginny said.

"It's all right; I've learned not to be bothered by things like that."

"Any luck finding your burglar's van?" Ham asked.

"None," Holly replied. "There are dozens, maybe hundreds, like it in the county."

They pulled up at Ed Shine's house, and he came out and got into the car with them.

Ham introduced Ginny. "Terrific car, Ed," Ham said.

"Thank you, Ham; I just got it — ordered it special, six months ago. They custom-made the stretched body." He settled into a seat, then he opened an armrest and pulled out a chilled bottle of champagne and four flutes. "Let's celebrate the car," he said, pouring wine for everybody.

The Yellow Dog Cafe turned out to be a low building squeezed between the highway and the Indian River, just south of Melbourne. The interior surpassed the exterior and they were given a corner table overlooking the river. Holly did not bring up the events of her day, and neither did Ham or Ginny.

When they had ordered drinks, Ed raised his glass again. "This toast is for Blood Orchid," he said. "We've now sold four of the existing houses and one building lot."

"Congratulations, Ed," Holly said, raising her glass.

They ordered dinner, and Ed took the floor again. "Now let me tell you the real reason for asking you here," he said, "apart from the pleasure of your company. Holly, I want to offer you a job."

"A job?" Holly asked, puzzled. "Selling real estate?"

"No, I'd like you to become chief of security at Blood Orchid."

"Barney Noble's old job," Ham said. Noble had been an old army acquaintance of Ham's who had been up to his neck in the illegal operations at the place when it was still called Palmetto Gardens. He now resided at the Florida state penitentiary.

"I never knew him," Ed said. "But Holly, I've got a pretty good idea what you're making in your current job, and I'll increase it by fifty percent, plus a benefits package and a month's vacation every summer. You can hire your own people, invent your own job."

"Well, Ed," Holly replied, "that's very generous of you, but I'm not sure there's going to be a whole lot for a security chief to do, now that the activities on the property are legal and aboveboard."

"As I say, you can invent your own job. Tell you what, you think about it over dinner, and when we're on coffee, you can give me your answer."

"All right."

Their dinner arrived, and they talked animatedly while they enjoyed their food. After dessert, when they were drinking coffee, Ed spoke up.

"What's it going to be, Holly? Will you join me?"

"Ed, I want to thank you for your offer; it's very tempting. May I be frank with you?"

"Of course."

"I think I'd be bored. I love the activity in my present job; something is always happening. I think that no matter what sort of job I invented for myself, it would still be pretty much that of a security guard, gatekeeper, night watchman. The money is certainly attractive, but I'm pretty well fixed as it is. So my answer will have to be no."

"I understand," Ed said, "and I accept your decision." He turned to Ham. "That brings me to my second choice. Ham, how would you like the job?"

"I wouldn't like being second choice," he said dourly, then laughed. "My problem is, I don't want to work. I worked for thirty-odd years, and I'm enjoying not doing it anymore."

Ed nodded, then turned to Ginny. "Young lady, do you have any security qualifications?"

"None at all," Ginny said, laughing.

"Then what am I going to do? Holly, is there anybody you can recommend?"

"I think what you want is a retired police officer, somebody with some experience in running a department, and frankly, I don't know anybody like that. There's a state law enforcement journal. Why don't you run an ad in that and snag yourself somebody who's about to retire?"

"Good thought," Ed said, waving for the check. "I wanted to keep it local, but what the hell."

They drove slowly back to Orchid Beach, this time drinking from a bottle of brandy that Ed had produced from another hidden cupboard. They dropped off Ham and Ginny first.

"Holly," Ed said, "you sure you won't reconsider?" They were on the way to Ed's house now.

"Ed, I really appreciate it, but I'm the wrong person for the job."

"Let me be the judge of that."

"I'm afraid I'll have to be. I need to be really busy at this point in my life, and the Orchid department gives me that. I think you're a great guy, and I know that working for you would be a pleasure, but . . ."

"Okay, okay," Ed said. "How about this: when I find somebody who looks good for the job, will you interview him or her for me? See what you think of their qualifications?"

"I'd be glad to," Holly said.

The car pulled up in front of Ed's house. He pecked her on the cheek and got out of the car. "Jaime, take Ms. Barker back to her home."

"Thank you for a wonderful evening, Ed. I needed it."

"You call me anytime you need *anything*," Ed said.

The car pulled away. Holly sank back in the soft leather and sipped her brandy. Ed's job had sounded pretty cushy; had she made a mistake turning it down? She didn't think so.

16

Holly awoke with the first hangover she'd had for a very long time. Not a bad one, and she was grateful for that, but she was a little fuzzy around the edges, and she was glad she didn't have to work that day.

Daisy seemed hungover, too, and she had just as good a reason as Holly. She had her breakfast and her walk, not run, in the dunes, then repaired to her bed beside the fireplace and went back to sleep.

Holly went into the study and started going through desk drawers, trying to figure out what might have interested the intruder. Her checkbook was kept on the computer on an extension of the desk, and one needed a password, which was DAISY, to get in. Everything else in the desk was mundane — Post-its, paper clips, stationery, files on household repairs, tax stuff, brokerage statements. The guy might have learned something about her income or net worth, but what good would that do him? It wasn't as though she kept large amounts of cash or bearer bonds in the house, and he hadn't opened the upstairs safe. He'd certainly had an opportunity to take the TV or VCR or computer, and she kept her guns locked up, so he didn't seem to be looking for booty, at least not the domestic kind.

She tried to imagine what information or files she might have that somebody might want — for any reason at all — and she came up short. If everything in her personal files was published on the front page of the *Orchid Beach Press-Messenger*, she wouldn't particularly mind everybody reading it. Certainly, she was not harboring some secret that somebody else wanted to know.

The phone rang.

"Hello?"

"Holly, it's Grant Early. How are you?"

"Very well," she replied.

"I just wanted to check in and confirm our dinner date. I'm picking you up at seven?"

"That's good, Grant," she said, then she remembered she hadn't made a dinner reservation.

"Where are we going?" he asked.

"Someplace good; I haven't decided yet."

"You said a jacket and no tie would do?"

"That's right."

"I own a necktie, and I don't mind wearing it."

"You can keep it casual, Grant."

"See you at seven, then."

She said goodbye and hung up. He had a very pleasant voice for an FBI agent, she thought.

Grant Early was on time, and Holly wasn't, which was unlike her, so she had to use the intercom to tell him to come in and sit down. Finally dressed, she came down the steps to find him kneeling and talking to Daisy, who was still in her bed. He stood up to greet her.

"We meet at last," he said, offering a hand. In her cop's habit, she ran his description through her frontal lobe: he was six feet, a hundred and seventy, tanned, with thick, close-cropped, iron-gray hair, a straight nose and a firm jaw, pale blue eyes.

"At last," Holly said. He looked like a runner, she thought — very fit. And he was expensively dressed, in a linen jacket, cream silk trousers, and alligator loafers. For a moment, she forgot this was supposed to be business. "Would you like a drink, or would you rather have one at the restaurant?"

"If you've booked, let's go on," he said.

"We're going to a little French place up the road," she said. "They have a bar."

He led her outside to a silver Mercedes SL600 convertible, which surprised Holly. She fastened her seat belt. "Have FBI agents had a big salary increase?" she asked.

He laughed. "Nope. Until last week, this belonged to a Colombian gentleman who got out of the country just ahead of us. We confiscated everything. I'm undercover, remember?"

"I like your disguise," she said.

"Oh, I still own a gray suit and a white button-down shirt, like all the other agents," he said, smiling and revealing very good teeth.

Holly directed him to the restaurant, and they were seated immediately.

"Drink?" he asked.

"A three-to-one vodka gimlet," Holly said to the waitress. "Straight up and shaken, very cold."

"Make it two," Grant said. "I've never had one, but Harry Crisp told me to trust your judgment in all things."

"That's funny," Holly said, "since Harry almost never does."

Their drinks came, and they sipped.

"Mmmmm," Grant said, "that's perfect."

"It is, isn't it?"

"Harry is a fool not to trust your judgment," he said, "but you have to understand why."

"Why?"

"It's a Bureau thing," Grant said. "The Bureau doesn't like to rely on outside information or advice until it can corroborate everything to its satisfaction. It goes all the way back to Hoover: The thinking is that nobody could possibly know more than the Bureau about anything. That's why we've always been so lousy at things like running snitches."

"I went to a lecture at the FBI academy in Quantico on running snitches, and a DEA agent taught it," Holly said.

"My very point. There probably wasn't an

agent in the Bureau who could have done it as well. Harry's like all other agents, only more so, since he made agent in charge."

"Come to think of it," Holly said, "he was a little more amenable to advice before he got promoted."

They looked at the menus and ordered.

"So, Grant, why are you undercover in Orchid Beach?" she asked.

"If I told you that, then I wouldn't be undercover."

"In that case, you're already not undercover, since I know who you are. Is Grant Early your real name, by the way?"

"It's Grant Early Harrison," he replied. "Early was my mother's maiden name."

"That makes it easy to remember, doesn't it?"

"And anybody who called the Miami office and asked for Grant Early would just get a, '*Who?*'"

"Where are you living?"

"I rented a house on the beach, a few doors north of you, through an agent. I didn't even see it until yesterday."

"So what's your cover? What did you tell the agent?"

"I made a bundle with an Internet company and sold out before the collapse of tech, Net stocks — the company exists, and they'd back me up if anybody checked. I'm thinking of permanently locating around here, and I wanted to rent for a while first to see how I like it."

"How long is your lease?"

"Three months, with an option to renew. It's a very nice house, well furnished. The owners are traveling in Europe for a year."

"Is it as nice as the Mercedes?"

"Yep."

"Good for you. Looks like the way to live well in the Bureau is to go undercover."

"Not necessarily. My last assignment was as mate on a charter fishing boat out of Key West. I had to grow a beard, which itched, and I smelled like fish for eight months."

She laughed. "You got a nice tan, though."

"I get that walking down the street in Miami; it's genetic."

"Did the clothes belong to the Colombian gentleman, too?"

"Nope; they're my own. I'm fortunate in not being entirely dependent on my Bureau salary. I try to hide that from my colleagues by dressing the way they do on the job. They're suspicious enough of me already because I'm a bachelor."

"Me too," Holly said, sipping her gimlet. This really did not feel like business.

Dinner came, and they talked as if they had known each other for a long time. This is a date, Holly thought, any way you slice it. Thank you, Harry Crisp.

17

They lingered over coffee and brandy, and Holly hadn't enjoyed herself so much for a long time. This was different from last night's dinner with Ed Shine: her companion was an eligible male of the proper age and more than proper mien. She found herself thinking improper thoughts.

Grant paid the check with a black American Express card, which, she noted, had his cover name emblazoned upon it. He linked his arm in hers as they walked to the car, and when they were inside and headed south on A1A, he made his move. "Would you like to stop and see my new place, have a nightcap, maybe?"

Yes, she certainly would, Holly thought. "I'm afraid tomorrow is a school day," she said. "Rain check?" She'd had a fair amount to drink, and she didn't trust herself.

"Sure."

She was glad he sounded disappointed. "Anyway, you don't want to take this undercover thing too far, do you?"

"There's Bureau time and my time," he said, "even when undercover." He reached over and squeezed her hand. "This is definitely *my* time, and Harry Crisp doesn't get a report — at least not an honest one."

"Why couldn't you give Harry an honest report?" she asked. "It's not as though we did anything but have dinner."

"Oh, I'll report that — this time — since Harry made the date for us, but I won't tell him what I was thinking all evening."

She laughed. "I'm glad I don't report to Harry," she said.

"Why? What were *you* thinking?"

"There are some thoughts a girl doesn't share on a first date."

"It is a first date, isn't it? Doesn't feel like one, though."

"This is getting terribly close to a line," she said. "Pretty soon you'll be telling me we met in a past life."

"No, we didn't do that; I'd remember. But I've probably had more past existences than anyone you know."

"Tell me about some of your past existences," she said.

"Let's see, I told you about Key West, didn't I?"

"You reeked of fish for eight months."

"Yes. I did nearly a year with a white supremacy group in Arkansas."

"*You?*"

"I had longer hair and another itchy beard. Then I did six weeks in northern California

110

with a motorcycle gang and a couple of weeks as a drug pilot, between Colombia and the Bahamas."

"Only a couple of weeks?"

"They were on to me; I got the hell out by the skin of my teeth."

"What else?"

"I did some bush flying in Alaska, ostensibly fishing trips for rich businessmen, but the business they were in was highly illegal."

"How long you been flying?"

"Since I was in high school; flying was my first great love."

"I took my first lesson yesterday."

"Good for you! You'll love it!"

"I think I already do. And my first day out, I landed on the beach, or at least, my instructor did."

"Lose the engine?"

"No, we were flying past my house, and I spotted a van parked outside that shouldn't have been there. I got there just in time to take a pistol upside the head. Daisy, my dog, got an anesthetic dart for her trouble."

"I've never heard of anybody using a dart on a dog during a domestic break-in," Grant said.

"Neither have I. The guy got past my alarm system fairly easily, and earlier, my phones were tapped."

"You're dealing with a pro," Grant said, "or pros."

"Looks that way." She didn't tell him how

worried she was about this.

"Do you have any idea who's behind this?"

"Not a clue; I'm completely baffled."

He stopped talking and seemed deep in thought.

"You think this might be connected with what you're working on?" she asked.

"I don't think Harry would want me to speculate about that."

"Oh, come on, Grant; you don't have to tell me everything. Maybe you can suggest something about who to take a look at."

Grant shook his head. "I'm afraid not."

Now it was her turn to be silent.

"If I thought you were in any danger . . ."

"How do you know I'm not?" she demanded.

"All right, I'll say this much: it sounds as though someone is doing something around here, and they want to know if the chief of police is on to them. They probably think they'll pick up something in your house or listening to your calls."

"That's a reasonable hypothesis," she said. "Tell me more."

"I can't say any more than that. Suffice it to say that Harry wouldn't have sent me up here if he didn't think there was something to investigate. I mean, the Bureau has pulled hundreds of agents off investigations in order to concentrate on terrorism, since the events at the World Trade Center."

"So it would take something pretty important

for Harry to put an undercover agent on it right now."

"It would take something pretty important to Harry," Grant said.

"As opposed to important to the Bureau as a whole or to the defense of the country?"

"You know," he said, laughing, "the Bureau could use you as an interrogator. You'd have a terrorist spilling the beans in no time at all."

"You may as well fold now, Grant," she said. "I'm going to get it out of you one way or the other."

"I'm looking forward to the other," he said. "I think." He pulled into her driveway and stopped in front of her house. A motion detector switched on the exterior lights.

Grant walked her to the door. "How about dinner this week sometime?"

She fished a card out of her handbag and wrote her home and cell numbers on the back. "Call me," she said.

He leaned forward to kiss her.

She turned her head a little and took the kiss on the corner of her mouth. "It was a nice evening," she said. "I think I'm going to enjoy interrogating you further." She unlocked the door, and Daisy greeted her, nuzzling her fingers.

"You'll find me an impenetrable wall," Grant said.

"Yeah, sure," she said, closing the door behind her.

18

Holly awoke with a feeling she had not had for a year — desire. She stretched her body to its full length, fingers reaching for the headboard, toes reaching for the foot. The resulting feeling was like a tiny orgasm, something she thought she had lost interest in. Clearly a cold shower was in order.

She settled for a cool shower, and she thought about her dinner date of the evening before. A dinner date! Who would have thought it? And who would have thought that she could have Harry Crisp to thank for such an event? Her next job, she mused, was to pry from Grant Early what his assignment was, and, she reflected, she was willing to do just about anything she had to find that out.

Who were these FBI guys that they could send an agent undercover into her jurisdiction, tell her about it, then refuse to tell her why? She'd see about that.

Her phone rang. She grabbed a towel and, still dripping wet, grabbed the phone by the john. "Hello?"

"Good morning, it's Hurd."

"Morning, Hurd. What's up?"

"Somebody phoned in a floater in the Indian River about half an hour ago. Patrol car checked it out, and it was real. The ME is on the way. I thought you'd like to take a look."

"Where?"

"About three hundred yards south of the North Bridge. Sounds like somebody tossed him off the bridge, and the tide took him down. He came to rest against somebody's dock."

"I'll be there in half an hour," she said. "Don't let anybody take the body away before I've seen it."

"Right."

She hung up, dressed, fed Daisy, and let her out while she had a quick bowl of cereal. The floater wasn't going anywhere, so there was no great need to rush. Daisy came back and scratched at the screen door, wanting her cookie for a job well done. Holly gave it to her, then they both got into her car and drove north.

The floater was in a body bag when she got there, stretched out on an ambulance gurney. The medical examiner arrived a minute after she did.

"Let's have a look," she said to the EMT.

The EMT unzipped the entire length of the bag and peeled it back, revealing a white male, thirty to forty years of age, longish black hair, swarthy complexion. She reckoned he was six feet and weighed in at about one-eighty.

The ME walked over and stood beside her. "Look at the mouth," he said.

Holly pulled on a pair of rubber gloves and peeled back the lips, which were tattered. "Missing his front teeth," she said.

"Broken off," the ME replied.

"Let's roll him over." The two of them rolled the body over, facedown. "There's why," Holly said, pointing to the back of the head.

The ME parted the hair on the back of the head to reveal a wound. "One shot to the back of the head, came out the mouth, took some teeth with it."

"Was he kneeling?"

"The angle is right for it."

They rolled the corpse onto its back again, and Holly examined the wrists. "No ligature marks," she said. "He wasn't tied up at the time."

"A gun pointed at the head is enough to get a man on his knees," the ME said. "He didn't need to be tied."

"Anybody go through his pockets?"

"No," the officer replied. "We were waiting for the ME."

"I'll do it at the morgue," the ME said. "Three to one he won't have any ready ID."

"I agree," Holly said. "Do what you can with his clothes."

"We always do," the ME replied. "Okay, fellas, I'll meet you at the morgue."

The EMTs loaded the corpse into their

wagon and drove away, with the ME right behind. Holly looked around. Nice spot, she thought. Nice house, nice dock, nice boat tied up to it. She heard a screen door slam and turned to see a man coming out of the house.

"Good morning," she said. "Sorry to disturb you."

"Thanks for hauling that thing away," the man said.

"All part of the service. Did you hear anything last night? Anything like a gunshot?"

The man shook his head. "Nah. I reckon it happened upriver, probably at the bridge, and the tide brought him down here."

"You should be a cop," Holly said, trying not to sound sarcastic, since it was what she thought, too. "Did you get a good look at him?"

"Yep."

"Ever seen him before?"

"Nope. Looks Cuban to me."

"Maybe."

"He just floated down here and came to rest against one of the piers of my dock. I guess the barnacles snagged some of his clothing. I was going fishing." He pointed at his tackle beside the boat. "You going to be able to identify him?"

"Maybe. The body will be searched for ID, and we'll take his fingerprints and check them with the state and the Feds. We'll check the missing persons reports for somebody resembling him, too."

"How did he die?"

"The medical examiner will have to determine that, officially."

"Unofficially, my guess would be a bullet," the man said.

"Could be. Or he could have been fishing off the bridge last night, fell off and drowned, maybe hit his head on something. We won't jump to conclusions." Even if she had already jumped.

"I guess you know your job," the man said.

"Thanks, yes, I do."

"What are your chances of finding out who he is and what happened to him?"

"Better than fifty-fifty," she said, though she didn't really feel that confident.

"It's organized crime," the man said.

Holly held back a laugh. "We don't have all that much organized crime around here."

"You got a murder on your hands, Chief," the man said.

When a citizen was right, he was right, Holly thought.

"I'd like to know how it comes out."

"Watch the papers," Holly said. She shook his hand, went back to her car, and headed for the morgue. Something had struck her about this corpse, and she wanted her curiosity satisfied.

19

Holly gave the medical examiner a couple of hours' head start, then went to his office. She had seen more than one autopsy, and more than one was enough. When she walked into his lab, the ME was just finishing.

"Hey," he said.

"What's the story?" she asked, nodding at the corpse on the table under the sheet.

The ME consulted his notes on a clipboard. "Well-developed male, closer to thirty than forty, Hispanic, very probably Cuban. Death was from a single gunshot to the back of the head, probably while kneeling, hard-nosed bullet, forty-caliber, went through intact, took out the front teeth."

"Anything I don't already know?"

"Did you know he was Cuban?"

"The man who owned the dock where he was found thought so. Why do you?"

"Amalgam fillings," the ME replied. "They still do them in Cuba, but not here so much. He had a mouth full of socialist-era dentistry."

"Would that indicate that he was somebody special, having access to dental care?"

"Nah. The Cubans pride themselves on their medical system."

"Did you find any other marks on the body?" She didn't want to lead him.

"Bruised knuckles on the right hand; he might have taken a swing at whoever shot him."

"Anything else?"

The ME peered at her. "Sounds like you have something in mind."

"I do, but I'd rather you told me."

"Come on, Chief, tell me."

She walked over to the table and hoisted the cloth covering the body above the knees. "Take a look at that," she said, pointing at the left knee.

The doctor looked at it. "Oh," he said. "All right." He began writing on his clipboard. "Severe bruising of the left knee." He made a note of it.

"How old?" Holly asked.

"Hard to say: a few days, I guess."

Holly parted the hair on her left temple. "Take a look at this."

The ME looked at her head. "You've got severe bruising, too; are you and the deceased related?"

"It's the age of the bruise I'm talking about," she said.

"You think you and the deceased heal at the same rate, and in different parts of the body?"

"Come on, Doctor, could the two bruises have occurred at the same time?"

"You mean, you think the deceased might have bruised his knee while applying it to your temple?"

"No, that's not what I mean. Answer my question, please."

"Well, yes, his bruise and yours could have occurred on the same day. I wouldn't want to put my professional weight behind that in court, if it came to that."

"Thank you," she said. Like pulling teeth. "How long has he been dead?"

"Since the wee hours of this morning," the ME replied. "That's my best guess; his being in the water most of the night screwed up body temperature as a way of determining time of death more precisely. He would have cooled off faster."

"What else can you tell me about him?"

"He's very well built, probably works out on a regular basis. His clothes were expensive — Italian labels — and he had a good manicure. If you blow-dried his hair, he'd probably have a good haircut, too, but river water doesn't improve the look."

"Any jewelry?"

"He's got a whiter band on his left wrist, indicating that he or somebody else removed a wristwatch. And there's this." The doctor walked to a counter, picked up a plastic container, and emptied it into Holly's hand. The contents consisted of a small gold locket on a light, matching chain, and a diamond stud earring of about half a carat.

"Looks like something a girl would wear," she said, examining the stud.

"A lot of men wear earrings these days," the doctor replied. "I can't imagine why."

Holly picked up the locket and opened it. A little Indian River water drained out. Inside was a photograph of a pretty Latino girl, perhaps in her early twenties. Holly dug out the photograph with a fingernail and looked on the back. Nothing. "Looks like a Polaroid, trimmed to fit the locket."

"Well, somebody loved him, then," the doctor sighed.

"Where are his clothes?" she asked.

The doctor pointed to another counter.

Holly walked over to the pile and went through them. Everything was black, the shirt silk and the trousers cotton. He had worn briefs, bikini cut, also black. The socks were cotton, the shoes Italian, Bruno Magli. They were moccasin-like, soft with rubber studs on the soles. "Driving shoes," Holly said aloud. Also good cat-burglar shoes; they wouldn't make much noise against a floor. "No wallet?"

"Nope, though there was some money and some car keys. In the container there." He pointed to the counter.

Holly found a thick wad of bills, a set of keys to a Chrysler product, and some change. "Twelve hundred and eight dollars," she said, counting the damp currency.

"Maybe it was payday," the ME said.

"Maybe it was, at that," Holly agreed. "Or maybe recently. Did you pull his prints and get a dental impression?"

The doctor handed over a fingerprint card. "Here are the prints. I didn't take a dental impression because we're never going to find his dentist, this side of Havana, anyway, and the Cubans are not going to give us his dental records."

"Do you have any other ideas about the body?"

"It was a mob execution, but these days, who knows which mob? Cuban? Colombian? Italian? Mexican? Oh, he could be Mexican; they still do amalgam fillings, too, but this feels Cuban to me."

"Better take the dental impression then, in case he turns out to be Mexican."

"If you say so," the doctor said wearily.

"Tell you what, forget the dental impression, but if we have to exhume him later to get it, you do the digging. Deal?"

"I'll take the impression."

"Thank you, Doctor," Holly said. "I'll get back and run the prints."

"Let me know what you come up with," the ME said. "I always like to match what you find against what I guess."

"What kind of a record do you have, guessing?" she asked.

"Pretty damned good," he said, grinning.

Later, at her desk, Holly shook the locket out of the evidence bag and looked at the photograph inside again. "Well, sweetheart, you won't be seeing him again, and you'll always wonder why." Then she looked at the car keys among the effects. She pressed a button on the phone. "Hurd?"

"Yes, Chief?"

"Got a minute?"

"Sure, be right there." He stood in her doorway a moment later.

She tossed him the car keys. "Track down somebody at Daimler-Chrysler and see if the number on the ignition key will tell us what kind of car it was and give us the VIN number."

"Sure thing," Hurd said.

"And don't forget to log your possession of the keys on the chain-of-evidence form."

"Right. Something I'd like to talk to you about later, if you have the time."

"Talk about it now, if you like."

"This is more important," Hurd said. "Want me to run any prints?"

She handed him the card. "Almost forgot."

Hurd went back to his own office, and Holly wondered what she'd do without him.

20

Holly was about to go to lunch when Ed Shine called. "How are you, young lady?"

"Very well, Ed, and you?"

"I could hardly be better; sold another house, and my ad in the law enforcement journal you recommended has produced a prospect."

"I'd be happy to talk to him for you," she said, remembering her promise.

"That's why I called. He'll be in touch."

"All right, what's his —"

"Gotta run, honey. Let me know what you think, and remember, if for any reason you feel I shouldn't hire him, you just say the word."

"Okay, but . . ."

"Bye." Ed hung up.

Holly stood up and stretched, feeling hungry. She was about to leave when Hurd Wallace appeared again. "That was quick," she said. "You got something?"

"Not yet," Hurd replied. "I'm here for the interview."

"What interview?"

"Didn't Ed Shine call you?"

That let the air out of Holly. "*You're* Ed's candidate?"

"I answered his ad."

"Have a seat, Hurd," she said, trying to collect herself.

Hurd pulled up a chair and sat down. "I saw the ad yesterday, and I faxed Shine my résumé."

"Oh," she replied. She hardly knew what to say next.

"He seemed to think I had a pretty good background," Hurd said drolly.

"Well, of course you do, Hurd. I mean . . . this is something of a shock; I thought you were on board until retirement."

"That's pretty much what I thought," Hurd said, "but next year I'll have twenty-five on the job, and I was thinking of going fishing, anyway."

"You fish?"

"Figuratively speaking. I thought I'd start a little business or do something part-time that would bring me enough income that, combined with my pension, would make life easy. Shine's job looked a lot more attractive than that."

"What'd he offer you?"

"Half again what I'm making, plus a really good benefits package."

"God, I might be able to get you a ten percent raise if I went to the council and made a special request, but I couldn't come close to that."

"I know, Holly, and it's all right. I don't think I'm underpaid here, and I'm certainly not unhappy working for you, but Shine's job looks awful attractive from where I'm sitting."

"Has he told you what your duties would be?"

"Security; that's about it. Between you and me, I believe I'd have to work hard at staying awake. It's certainly not going to be as interesting as working in the department. I mean, we're probably not going to have floaters turning up, like this morning."

"I hope to God not," Holly said. "Palmetto Gardens has made us enough work for a lifetime already."

"Blood Orchid," Hurd said solemnly.

"Oh, yeah, I keep forgetting, and Ed keeps reminding me."

"He especially wanted you to know that he didn't come to me," Hurd said. "I just read the ad like everybody else. I got the impression that he's really interested in my taking the job."

"With my approval, of course," Holly said, chuckling.

"I'm sorry to put you on the spot, but . . ."

"Oh, Hurd, I'll give you the kind of recommendation that would keep him from even thinking about hiring somebody else."

"I appreciate that, Chief."

"How could I do anything else? You've been all I could have asked for in a deputy chief."

"Thank you."

"When would you want to go?"

"As soon as you're comfortable."

"Hurd, I'm *never* going to be as comfortable

with somebody else as I have been with you."

"Thank you, again."

"Tell me, who do you think would be good to replace you?"

Hurd looked at his feet. "Well . . . I thought about that, and — I hope this doesn't sound egotistical — I don't think there's anybody in the department who's ready for the job."

"I'm afraid you're right," Holly said.

"They're all too young and new at it. I admired your wanting to bring in young people, and I understood how that helped with your budgeting, since their salaries start lower, but I guess it's kept us from having an obvious successor."

"You're right about that," Holly said.

"Tell you the truth, it might be best not to hire one. You could parcel out my duties to three or four other people and get along without a deputy. Maybe before long one of them would start to look like somebody who could handle the whole thing."

"That's not a bad idea," Holly said. "At least, it would take the pressure off about searching for somebody to hire. I might get some flak from the city council, though, not having another experienced person around."

"I could make a couple of phone calls that might help with that," Hurd said. "I'd be happy to back you up. My advice would be to hang on to the part of the budget that pays me, though. The council will want to reduce your budget if you don't replace me immediately. You could tell them that you're just taking your time finding the right person."

"You were always a better politician than I, Hurd," Holly said, laughing. "That's a very good idea."

"Well," Hurd said, standing, "I'd better get back to work. We ought to have something later today or early tomorrow on IDing your floater."

"Okay, that's soon enough." She stood up and offered Hurd her hand. "You deserve this."

Hurd shook her hand and went back to his office.

Holly sat down and called Ed Shine.

"Are we speaking?" Ed asked.

"Only just," Holly replied.

"What kind of recommendation can you give Hurd Wallace?"

"Only the very best," she said. "You're very lucky to get him, and you'd better treat him right or I'll arrest you on some spurious charge and put you in jail."

"I didn't go after him, Holly; he came to me."

"I know he did, and I don't blame him a bit. I want to ask a favor, though."

"Shoot."

"I want to hang onto him until I can reassign his duties to others in an orderly way."

"And how long will that be?"

"I don't know; two or three weeks — a month, maybe."

"Take as much time with him as you need, sweetheart."

"You're getting yourself a good man, Ed."

"I'd rather have you."

"You always know how to say the right thing, don't you?"

"I try."

"Bye, Ed."

"Bye-bye."

Holly hung up and sighed. Oh, what the hell, she thought, everything changes. Just make it work.

21

Holly had hardly gotten home when the phone rang.

"I've got some perfect steaks and a couple of bottles of sensational red wine," a male voice said. "You want to join me for dinner?"

"I don't know who this is, but yes," she replied.

Grant laughed.

"I'll do almost anything for a good steak."

"Really?"

"I said *almost.*"

"Oh. Seven o'clock? We'll catch the sunset."

"I don't know how to break this to you, but your house faces east, and in this part of the world the sun sets in the west."

"Whatever you say."

"Those words exhibit a good attitude. Remember them. See you at seven." She hung up, fed Daisy, and took her for a walk, almost as far as Grant's house. It was a good-looking contemporary of wood and stone, not very Florida-like. It suited him, at least from the outside. She walked slowly back to the house, thinking about the evening ahead, while Daisy frolicked in the dunes. By the time they were home, she had made her decision, at least tentatively.

Tentatively meant that, after showering, washing and drying her hair, and dressing fetchingly in short shorts and a low-cut T-shirt that showed a lot of belly, she put her diaphragm in her purse instead of in its final resting place. As an afterthought, she tossed in a condom, too. "Brazen," she said aloud, checking the mirror for signs of wantonness. Then she walked back down the beach to his house.

She could see him through the sliding doors, dressed in Bermuda shorts and a polo shirt, barefoot, fixing something in the kitchen. She tiptoed up the stairs from the beach to the deck and rapped sharply on the glass, making him jump and drop a salad fork. He opened the door.

"An undercover agent must be alert at all times," she said. "I could have snuck in, jerked down your shorts, and tattooed you before you even noticed."

He flung an arm around her and kissed her lightly on the lips. "And what would you have tattooed on me?"

"KICK ME, I'M FBI," she said, "in great big letters."

"Thanks a lot, but you can jerk down my shorts anytime you like."

"In your dreams."

"Let me get you a drink, and I'll start dreaming."

She spied a cocktail shaker on the wet bar next to the kitchen. "I'll get you one." She found a bottle of vodka and some Rose's sweetened lime juice, filled the shaker with ice, added six jiggers of vodka and two of lime juice. She put ice cubes in two martini glasses and swirled them around, then shook the shaker until her hands hurt from the cold. She dumped the ice from the now-frosted glasses and strained the pale, green liquid into them. "Tie that on," she said, handing him one.

He tasted the drink. "Oh, God, can I have another?"

"Easy, kiddo, we don't know yet whether you can handle that one."

He took a gulp, half emptying the glass. "Let's find out."

"What are you fixing?" she asked.

"A Caesar salad," he replied. "I do it the old-fashioned way, in a wooden bowl, with a fork."

"What else do you do the old-fashioned way?"

"Almost everything, especially . . ."

"Not in a wooden bowl with a fork, I trust."

"If that's what rattles your chain."

She pretended to think about that. "No bowl," she said, "but maybe a fork, and I get to hold it."

He handed her a fork, and without another word pulled her to him and kissed her.

She leaned into him, finding what she'd expected, and she was astonished at how quickly her blood rose. She was already wet.

He put his arms tightly around her, pulled her to him, then lifted her a couple of inches off the floor and started walking toward a big sofa in the living room.

Holly went along for the ride, snagging her purse from the bar as they passed it.

Grant dumped her gently onto the sofa and, still kissing her, shucked off his shirt and shorts, while Holly helped him with her clothes. They were both naked in seconds.

"You mind if we skip the foreplay?" he asked, running his tongue over her nipples.

She opened her purse and took out the condom. "Skip it faster," she said, stripping off the wrapper and sliding it onto him, in the process spilling the contents of her purse onto the floor.

He glanced down. "Do you always take a Walther PPK to bed?"

"Only when fucking an FBI man," she said, guiding him into her.

The next ten minutes passed at fast-forward, with no subtleties or anything else except straight sex, enthusiastically conducted. He came seconds before she followed, and they were both noisy about it.

"My God," he said, rolling over on his back next to her. "I wasn't expecting that so soon."

"I was," she said. "Try to keep up, will you?"

"I thought I did keep it up."

"You certainly did, Junior G-Man. Now I'm hungry."

They visited the powder room together, sponging each other clean and dry, then headed for the kitchen, still naked. Grant turned on the built-in restaurant-style grill and turned to the salad. "I need my fork back," he said.

"Dammit," she said, handing it to him, "I forgot to use the fork."

"Don't worry about it, I have enough holes in me already." He separated a couple of egg yolks and dumped them into the wooden bowl.

She fingered a scar on his back. "This must have been one of them."

"Key West," he replied. "I wasn't running fast enough. Fortunately, I had a partner in the bushes with a sniper's rifle."

"He was a little late, wasn't he?"

"Believe me, we had a serious discussion about that later."

"Just like the FBI to be a tad late when it counts."

"You won't get an argument from me about that." Using the fork, he mashed some anchovies, then whipped them into the egg yolks with some Dijon mustard and some chopped garlic. Then he added olive oil slowly, until he had a smooth dressing. He added torn Romaine leaves, tossed them well, and Holly sat down to a table already set with a bottle of the Far Niente Cabernet waiting, breathing. Grant tossed the steaks onto the grill before sitting down.

"When was the last time you had dinner

naked?" he asked, shoveling salad into his mouth.

She rolled her eyes in thought. "Well, let's see; that would have been . . . never."

"No kidding? Well, you certainly do it well, for a first-timer."

"Funny, that's what my first lover said."

"What else did he say?"

"Modesty prevents me from telling you."

"That's what I like, a modest girl," he said, reaching across the table and tweaking a nipple.

"Careful, buddy, or we'll never get to the steak. You better marshal your resources for a while."

"I'm marshaling, I'm marshaling," he said, serving the steaks.

When they had finished their steaks and a bottle and a half of wine, she took a deep breath and sighed. "That was wonderful," she said. "Is there a bed in this house?"

"You betcha."

"Don't tell me, show me."

And he did.

22

They lay on their backs in the moonlight, bathed in sweat, panting, on a bed that had been stripped of everything but the bottom sheet.

"It's been a long time for you, hasn't it?" he gasped.

"Over a year, but I'm always this way."

"Always?"

"Can we do it again, now, please?"

"Oh, God, I'm going to die."

"Not until I'm finished with you." She rolled over, put her head on his shoulder and began fondling him.

He stopped her. "It has to rest."

"How long?"

"I'm not sure. Weeks, maybe."

"You should speak to your doctor about getting that pill that makes it possible for the impotent to get an erection."

"Impotent? How can you say that?"

"Any guy who can't do it three times in an hour and a half is in big trouble."

He dissolved in what seemed to be a combination of laughter and weeping.

"Don't worry, I'm not an impatient person. Take another ten minutes."

"I'm going to die in this bed," he said, "drained of all life by some new kind of vampire."

"One that sucks semen from its victims?"

"Not just that; the whole life force."

"I'll bet you ten bucks I can bring you back to life in sixty seconds."

"You're on."

A minute later, he said, "My money's on the dresser over there; take whatever you want."

She threw a leg over him and slid him inside her, moving slowly up and down. "Nice view of the ocean from here," she said.

"From where?"

"From on top."

"Yeah, I can't see a thing from down here except you, and I like the view from this angle."

"You're sweet, for a G-Man," she said, leaning down and biting a nipple.

"And you have marvelous breasts, for a cop," he replied, holding them in his hands and massaging.

"I have marvelous breasts for a female human being," she said, slapping him lightly across the chops. "Another compliment like that and I'll stop."

She woke first, showered, dressed, and went down to the kitchen. She was turning two omelets when he staggered in. "You're walking funny," she said.

"I'm lucky I can walk at all," he replied, sinking into a chair at the table.

"You FBI guys aren't in very good shape, are you? Maybe you should undertake a program of fitness training."

"I'm of the view that exercise should be activity-specific."

"What?"

"If you want to get in shape for sex, you should have more sex. Maybe you could be my personal trainer."

"I'm sure we could whip you into shape in no time at all," she said, sliding the omelets onto plates and sitting down. She sipped her orange juice. "So, I guess all you think about is sex, huh?"

"Well, I mean . . ."

"I had hoped we could have an actual conversation before this date ends."

"Sure, I . . ."

"But the moment I walk into the house, it's nothing but sex, sex, sex. Is that all you ever think about?"

"Sometimes I think about work."

"So, how's work?"

"So-so. How about yours?"

"You remember the guy who broke into my house?"

"Yep."

"He turned up in the Indian River yesterday, with a bullet through his head."

"Did you do it? I mean, I know you were

139

pretty pissed off about the intruder, but . . ."

"I might have, if I'd had the chance."

"How do you know it was the guy? Wasn't he masked?"

"Yeah, but I fetched him a pretty good kick in the knee, and the floater had a badly bruised knee. He fit the general description, too."

"You run his prints?"

"The FBI computer was running very slowly yesterday; we should know something this morning, if your people can get their act together."

"Did you get anything else from the corpse? I mean, our people usually do."

"Oh, we struggle along, in our own small-town way. He's Cuban — we know that from his dental work — and he had a girlfriend. I found a locket with a picture of a girl."

"That's sweet."

"I thought so."

"You want me to delve into this?"

"I think I can handle it, thanks. Don't you have better things to do?"

"Sometimes it is the duty of an undercover agent to simply sit and wait. I'm looking at some property, though."

"Where, and what for?"

"At a new development called Blood Orchid, and because it's the kind of thing the character I'm playing would do."

"That's Ed Shine's place."

"Who?"

"Didn't Harry Crisp tell you about Ed?"

"Nope."

"You remember the case of the two property developers in Miami who were recently shot dead on the same day?"

"I saw something in the papers."

"Apparently, they were both bidding on the Palmetto Gardens property."

"Where's that?"

"It's now called Blood Orchid. Ed Shine, who ended up buying it, had a shot taken at him around the same time. I happened to be there when it happened."

"So you solved the case instantly?"

"Not exactly. By the time I had finished crawling around on my belly through broken glass, the shooter had dematerialized."

"They'll do that."

"I'd be interested in your impressions of Blood Orchid," she said.

"What's Shine like?"

"Nice guy; you'll like him." She finished her omelet and stood up. "I gotta go to work."

Without rising, he pulled her to him and kissed her navel, running his tongue around it.

"Or I could stay for a couple of days," she said.

He spun her around and pushed her toward the beach door. "Go, while I still have the strength to send you," he said plaintively.

She gave him a quick kiss, then ran out onto the deck and down to the beach. She ran all the way home, happy.

23

Holly arrived at her office whistling, turning heads as she walked by, Daisy at her side. She had hardly sat down when Hurd turned up at her door.

"Good morning. You seem to be in a good mood."

"I'm always in a good mood," she said.

"If you say so. We've got an ID on your floater." He handed her a file folder.

She handed it back. "Tell me about him."

Hurd sat down and opened the folder. "Name: Carlos Alvarez, born Havana, thirty-two years ago. Arrived Miami twelve years ago on a small fishing boat with nineteen others. He was printed by Immigration at the time. He's a partner in a locksmith's shop in Fort Lauderdale; unmarried; has no arrest record — he wouldn't have gotten a locksmith's license if he had. He drives a two-year-old Chrysler Concorde."

"Is that it?"

"His partner's name is here, if you want it." Hurd handed her the folder.

"Thanks, Hurd."

"I'm organizing my workload now, preparing

memos to the people who're going to take over my duties. You want a list of my recommendations?"

She was thinking about the locksmith. "Whoever you want is fine with me, Hurd." This was the sort of detail for which she relied on him.

"I'll let you know if we find anything else," he said. "We're still dealing with Daimler-Chrysler about the car key."

"Notify all the patrol cars to look for an abandoned Concorde," she said. "You got a color?"

"Registration just says green."

"Okay. If we can find the car, then we can dust it for prints, and we might get lucky and come up with the shooter."

"I'm on it." He went back to his office.

Holly read the file folder, then turned to Daisy. "You up for a trip to Lauderdale?"

Daisy was on her feet, wagging everything.

Holly closed her office door and changed into civilian clothes. "You can reach me on my cell if you need me," she said to her secretary on her way out. "Try not to need me."

She drove south on 95, enjoying the seventy-mile-per-hour speed limit at eighty-five. Her car had no markings, but there was the big antenna on the back. Once, a state trooper pulled up next to her and gave her a look; she held up her shield for him to see, and he dropped back. There were some perks connected to being in law enforcement.

Using a map of the city, she found C&P Lock-smiths fairly easily. It was in a small strip mall in a good part of town. She parked the car and, putting Daisy on a leash for appearances' sake, entered the shop. A Latino in his mid-thirties was making a key on a duplicating machine. He looked up and smiled, turning off the machine. "Hello, can I help you?" he asked, in slightly accented English.

Holly looked at the file folder. "Are you Pedro Alvarez?" she asked.

"That's right."

She showed him her badge. "My name is Holly Barker. I'd like to talk to you for a minute."

"That's not a Lauderdale badge," he said.

"No, I'm from Orchid Beach, up the coast."

"What can I do for you?" He had become a little wary, she noticed, but some people did at the sight of a badge, even when they had nothing to hide.

"Do you have some place we can sit down?" she asked.

He went to the door, locked it, and hung up a sign saying he'd be back in ten minutes. "Back here," he said, leading the way to the rear of the shop. It was a room just large enough to hold two desks and a couple of filing cabinets. He indicated where she should sit, then sat behind his desk.

"You're Carlos Alvarez's partner, is that right?"

"Yes."

"Brothers?"

144

"First cousins. We grew up together in Havana and came to the U.S. at the same time."

"Same fishing boat?"

He nodded.

"Do you know where Carlos is now?"

"He's taking some time off," Pedro said. "A few days."

"Do you know why?"

"He said he had some personal business to take care of."

"Do you know where he's taking care of it?"

"He didn't say."

Holly didn't believe that. She took the locket photo, blown up, from the folder and handed it to him. "I expect you know this girl."

Pedro looked at the photo but said nothing.

"What's her name?"

"What is this about, exactly?"

Holly took a deep breath. She hated saying this to people because she never knew what their reaction would be, and it tended to vary widely. "I'm afraid I have some bad news," she said.

Pedro sat up. "Has Carlos been arrested?"

"Was he doing something that he might be arrested for?"

"I don't know. Tell me what's going on, please."

"Carlos is dead."

Pedro's face became expressionless. "How?"

"Someone shot him in the head and threw his body into the Indian River, in my jurisdiction."

To Holly's astonishment, Pedro began to cry. She said nothing, just waited for him to get control of himself.

Finally, he did. "Who did this?" Pedro asked, wiping his face with a handkerchief.

"I was hoping you might be able to help me find out. What was Carlos into?"

"I don't know what you mean," Pedro replied.

"Did Carlos have knowledge of burglar-alarm systems?"

"It's a good part of what we do here," Pedro said. "Carlos was a lot better at it than I am. I tend to stay in the shop."

Holly nodded. "I have reason to believe that Carlos broke into a house in my jurisdiction. Repeatedly."

"Carlos was no burglar."

"Then what was he, Pedro? You must have known him as well as anybody. What was he into?"

Pedro stared at her. "I don't know what you're talking about," he said, then stood up. "I don't want to talk about this anymore. I'd appreciate it if you'd go, now. I have to open the shop."

"Your cousin and partner is dead, and you're going to reopen the shop?"

"I have to make a living," he said. "How do I claim Carlos's body?"

Holly gave him her card and wrote the ME's number on the back. "Have your funeral parlor call this number. I'll see that the body is released tomorrow."

"Thank you," he said, leading the way to the front door. He opened it for her and stood aside to let her leave.

Holly held up the photograph again. "I'm going to have to tell her about Carlos," she said.

"I'll take care of that," Pedro replied.

"I'm going to have to talk to her," Holly said firmly.

Pedro was just as firm. "I'll give her your number," he said. "She can call you in a few days, when we're past this a little."

"Something else, Pedro," she said. "Where were you the night before last?"

"I closed the shop at six o'clock, then I picked up my wife and kids and we went to a wedding. There were more than a hundred people there."

Holly nodded. "Pedro, there's going to come a moment when you realize that if you want to find out who murdered Carlos, you'll need to talk to me. When that happens, call me."

He said nothing, just closed the door behind her.

Holly left, but she wasn't through with Pedro Alvarez.

24

Holly got back onto the interstate and headed north. At seventy miles per hour she put the car on cruise control and called Harry Crisp.

"Hey there, Holly, how are you?"

"I'm real good, Harry, and I could use your help."

"Shoot."

"You'll remember that my house was broken into and my phone tapped?"

"Yes."

"Well, we found the guy who did it."

"Good for you."

"Not so good: We found him in the Indian River with a bullet through the head."

"Oh?"

"Yeah. We ID'ed him as Carlos Alvarez, a locksmith from Fort Lauderdale."

"Doesn't ring a bell."

"No reason why it should; he has a clean sheet."

"That's interesting."

"Why?"

"Well, you'd normally expect somebody with the proficiency to do your burglary and wiretapping to have some sort of record, at least an arrest or two."

"I thought proficient people were the least likely to get caught."

"Yeah, but they don't start out proficient, and they usually screw up early in their careers."

"If you say so. Anyway, I went down to his shop today and talked with his partner and cousin, Pedro Alvarez, broke the news to him. He was shocked, said he didn't know what Carlos was into, but I don't believe him."

"So what do you want from me?"

"Wiretapping's a federal crime, so I thought maybe you might be able to investigate this for me. I don't have the resources to send people all over the state to conduct interviews, and I don't want to go through the red tape with the state."

"I don't know, Holly. What with our push on terrorism, I don't have a lot of agents to put on stuff with a low priority. I mean, some tech gets himself wasted, that's not really our problem."

"You've got enough people to send a guy to my jurisdiction, haven't you?"

"That's different."

"How?"

"You know I can't tell you that."

"Suppose this is connected to what your man is working on?"

"How would you know that? You don't know what he's working on."

"No, I don't, but you do, and if there's a con- nection to be made, you can make it."

Harry was silent.

"I hope you're thinking."

"I'm thinking." He went silent again.

"Just tell me when you're finished, Harry."

"All right, I'll send somebody over to talk to Pedro."

"Carlos also had a girlfriend, but Pedro wouldn't give me her name."

"We'll talk to her, too. We can probably find a way to worm the name out of Pedro. Is he a U.S. citizen?"

"I don't know. Both cousins were born in Ha- vana and came over on the same fishing boat twelve years ago."

"I'll check him out; he'll be easier to handle if all he has is a green card. Easier still if he's an il- legal."

"Thanks, Harry, I appreciate it."

"Glad to help. How are you and what's-his- name getting on?"

"Who?"

"You know who I'm talking about."

"Oh, him. Well, I saw him like you sug- gested."

"And . . ."

"You trying to be a matchmaker, Harry?"

"Me?"

"Talk to you later, Harry." She punched off.

Daisy took a couple of turns around her seat and resettled with her head in Holly's lap.

Back at the station Hurd had news for her.

"We ran down the Chrysler key," he said. "It's not to Carlos Alvarez's car; it's to a year-old van. We ran the VIN number and it turns up rented from a Miami company two weeks ago and not returned on schedule."

"Who was it rented to?"

"For cash to a fictitious name and a false driver's license. It's a small rental agency in a Cuban neighborhood that apparently doesn't do all the checking that Hertz and Avis do."

"Okay, cancel the bulletin on Carlos's car and put out one on the van."

"It was kind of smart to steal the van that way, instead of just grabbing one off the street," Hurd said. "This way, the guy gets a couple of weeks of use without the thing being reported stolen."

"Yeah, that is smart," Holly said, "except that there was a face attached to the fake driver's license, and an employee of the agency would have seen it. Call them and get a description of the renter."

"Okay."

"Also, do a criminal background check on Pedro Alvarez — he's Carlos's cousin and business partner. Check out his immigration or citizenship status, too." No need to rely entirely on Harry Crisp, she thought.

"Okay."

"Let the coroner know that it's all right to release Carlos Alvarez's body, too, and tell him to call me with the name and address of the funeral home."

"Will do." Hurd returned to his office.

Holly sat and thought about Carlos Alvarez. He didn't do this on his own, she knew. Why would a Fort Lauderdale locksmith be interested in her telephone conversations? No, he was hired, and by somebody smart enough to find a man with no criminal background, and to steal a van from a rental agency, instead of off the street.

She tried to figure out how this might all connect to the murder of the two Miami property developers and the attempt on Ed Shine's life, but that didn't work. Whoever was behind those crimes obviously wanted to win the auction of the Palmetto Gardens property, and once Ed Shine had won, there was no further motive for killing him, nor would there be any further motive for coming to Orchid Beach and rummaging around in her life. So her burglar couldn't be connected to the Fed's auction of the property.

Dead end. Unless Harry Crisp could come up with something. She decided to relax and let the FBI do the work.

Then her thoughts returned to the night before. She hadn't heard from Grant today. She called a florist and sent a dozen yellow roses to his house, with a card reading, "Hope you get well soon."

25

The following day, in the early afternoon, Pedro Alvarez called.

"Hello?" Holly said. She hoped he was ready to talk to her.

"The FBI was here in my shop this morning," Pedro said, his voice trembling. "Why are you persecuting me?"

"Mr. Alvarez," Holly said soothingly, "I run a small police department in Indian River County; I don't run the FBI."

"Then how did they know about me?"

"When a person involved in criminal activity is murdered, that information passes to different law enforcement agencies."

"Carlos wasn't into criminal activity!"

"I told you that he committed burglary and wiretapping in my jurisdiction."

"How do you know this?"

"It came out in my investigation of his death. Tell me, did you ever see Carlos driving a rented Chrysler van?"

Pedro was silent for a moment. "It was rented?"

"Did you think he had bought the van?"

"I thought he had borrowed it."

"From whom?"

More silence.

"Pedro, what you don't seem to understand is that the more you hold back, the more this is going to be investigated. You're bringing all this attention on yourself, and there's going to be more."

"I don't know anything; what is it you think I know?"

"Who was Carlos dealing with that might have gotten him into trouble?"

"Why would I know this?"

"You were his business partner, his cousin, and his friend. Who else would know more?"

"I don't know."

"Then perhaps the girl will know. Have the FBI talked to her yet?"

"I have to go," Pedro said, then hung up.

Holly called Harry Crisp. "Thanks for moving so fast on Pedro Alvarez. What did you find out?"

"How did you know we'd talked to him, Holly?"

"He just called me, all upset. Somehow, he thought it was all my fault."

Harry laughed. "Then he's smarter than we thought."

"Did your people get anything out of him?"

"Not really."

"Harry, you're being evasive."

"Holly, you know I can't talk to you about our investigation."

"I put you on this guy, Harry, and now you're holding out on me?"

"My hands are tied, Holly."

"So, I guess I'll have to hold out on you, too."

"You can't do that, Holly; that's impeding a federal investigation. There could be an obstruction charge. Now tell me what you know."

"I did that yesterday, Harry, and I haven't learned anything new since then."

"You'll keep me posted, though?"

"Don't hold your breath, Harry." She hung up, incensed.

Her secretary handed her a message: the name and phone number of the funeral directors who had collected Carlos Alvarez's body. Holly dialed the number.

"Good afternoon, Serene Rest," an oleaginous male voice said.

"Good afternoon," Holly said smoothly. "Can you tell me when the Carlos Alvarez services will be held?"

"Are you a family member?"

"No, just an acquaintance; I'd like to pay my respects."

"Viewing will be tomorrow morning between ten and noon. Services are at two o'clock at the Santa Maria church, with burial to follow in the churchyard." He gave her the address.

"Thank you so much," Holly said. "I'd like to send flowers, too. Can you tell me the name of his fiancée?"

"The next of kin is Mr. Pedro Alvarez," the man said guardedly.

"Yes, but he also had a fiancée, Miss . . ." She hoped he would fill in the blank, but he didn't.

"You may send any floral arrangements here," he said.

"Thank you. Goodbye."

Holly didn't like funerals, but she wasn't going to miss this one.

When Holly got home that evening there was a note on her door. *I'm all better,* it read. *How about I bring over a pizza this evening around seven?*

She looked at her watch; it was a quarter to seven. She fed Daisy and let her out alone, then ran for the shower. She had just dried her hair and was putting on a sexy cotton shift when the doorbell rang. She ran down the stairs, happy to greet him.

A pizza deliveryman stood on her doorstep. "Delivery, prepaid," he said, handing her the box with an envelope taped to the top.

"Then I assume you're pre-tipped, too," Holly said, snatching the box from him and closing the door. She set down the pizza on the coffee table and opened the envelope.

Sorry, but duty calls, it read. *I hope to be through not too late. I'll call you when I'm free.*

"Oh, you will, will you?" Holly said aloud. "You son of a bitch!" She let Daisy in, then got a beer and sat down at the coffee table, switching on the evening news. From the local station menu on the satellite service, she chose a Fort Lauderdale station. The pizza smelled fantastic. She began to eat greedily.

She watched ten minutes of traffic and weather and was about to switch channels when a picture of Carlos Alvarez appeared on-screen.

"Fort Lauderdale businessman Carlos Alvarez was found murdered in Indian River County yesterday. An FBI source said he had been shot to death in a gangland-style killing and his body dumped into the Indian River. His cousin and business partner, Pedro Alvarez, said his family and friends were shocked by the killing."

Pedro appeared, standing in front of his shop. "We don't know who could have wanted Carlos dead," he said. "He was a law-abiding citizen, a small businessman for many years in this city. Who could have done this?" He covered his face and looked away.

"Funeral services will be held tomorrow at Santa Maria church."

Holly switched off the TV and was astonished to find that she had eaten half the pizza.

26

Holly was wakened from a deep sleep by a noise. She sat up and looked around, disoriented; she had been asleep on the sofa. The noise came again: Someone was knocking on the front door. She got up and opened it.

Grant Early stood on the doorstep with a bundle of flowers, the kind that were sold at traffic lights during rush hour. "Hi there," he said. "Any pizza left?"

Holly walked back into the living room, leaving the door open. "Yours is on the coffee table," she said. "Daisy, get the FBI guy a beer."

As Grant watched, Daisy got up from her bed, trotted to the kitchen, opened the refrigerator door with a rope hanging from the handle, took out a bottle of beer, and brought it to Grant, whose mouth was open by this time.

"I don't suppose you've got an opener on you," he said to the dog.

Daisy sat down and looked at him.

"She says it's a twist-top," Holly said.

"You're kind of grumpy this evening, aren't you?" Grant asked, lifting the top of the pizza box and making a face.

"I was asleep," she said.

"Mind if I nuke this?"

"Suit yourself."

Grant carried the box to the kitchen, found a plate, arranged the slices, and shoved them into the microwave.

"So, how was your day?" he asked, sitting down on the sofa and drinking his beer.

"Pretty well screwed up by the FBI," she replied.

"Oh? How so?"

"Well, I drove down to Lauderdale to interview a guy, and —"

"What case was this?"

"Carlos Alvarez, my burglar."

"Okay."

"Carlos's cousin, Pedro, was not forthcoming, so I called Harry, thinking a visit by a couple of agents might get the cousin off the dime."

"And?"

"They talked to him, but Harry won't tell me what Pedro said."

Grant chuckled. "And you're surprised?"

"No, just pissed off. And then I hear the FBI quoted on TV about the case, just like it's their long-standing case, and they know what it's all about."

"Maybe they do."

"I doubt it. All Harry had for leverage was the possibility of an immigration violation to squeeze Pedro with, and I ran my own check, and he's a citizen. Did you talk to Harry today?"

"I don't contact him unless I've got something to report," Grant said. "And I haven't had anything of substance to report since I arrived in Orchid Beach."

"Not even what a great lay I was?"

"You were certainly a great lay, but that appraisal will not find its way into my report."

"Gee, thanks for your discretion."

"Listen, do I have to take it up the nose for everything the FBI and Harry Crisp do?"

Holly was about to fire back a smart answer when the phone rang. She picked it up. "Hello?"

"Hi, it's Hurd."

"Hi, what's up?"

"We found the van."

"Where?"

"Well, this is kind of embarrassing. You know that little park area in the approaches to the North Bridge?"

"Yes."

"It was there all along. I guess I should have sent somebody up there first thing."

"Don't worry about it; finding it a few hours later won't hurt anything. Where is it now?"

"We've towed it into the city garage. I've got a tech on it. We'll have everything by first thing in the morning."

"I'll see you then. Thanks for calling." She hung up.

Grant came back from the kitchen with his pizza. "Developments?"

Holly started to speak and stopped. "First,

160

you and I have to have an understanding," she said.

"What sort of understanding?"

"Whatever I tell you about my cases stops here, it doesn't go to Harry."

"Okay, unless the information is relevant to my work here."

"Nope, relevant or not, you tell Harry nothing."

"Holly, the FBI pays my salary, and Harry Crisp is my boss. I can't withhold information about my case from them, surely you understand that."

Holly made a disgusted noise.

"I could lie and tell you everything is just between you and me, but I want to be straight with you."

Holly said nothing, just looked out the window.

"Look, maybe I can help, offer some suggestions. If it doesn't touch on my case, I'll say nothing to Harry about it."

"But if it does, you'll blab, right?"

"If that's how you want to put it, yes."

"Will you stop me telling you, if you think it's going to relate to your case?"

"If I did that, then you might figure out what my case is."

"You don't give a girl much wiggle room, do you?"

"I don't have all that much myself. I'd love to help, if I can, but I can't hold out on Harry."

Holly thought about it again. "We found Carlos's van," she said. "We're going over it for prints now, hoping that the killer might have left some on it."

"That's a good development, maybe a short-cut to solving the murder."

"You know something?" Holly said. "I know I'm not supposed to say this, but I don't really care all that much about the murder. Carlos played in the wrong pigpen, and he got bit. What I care about is finding out why he was in my house, and if solving the murder will help with that, then okay, I'm interested in the murder."

"You're taking this personally, aren't you?"

"It *is* personal when somebody breaks into your house and taps your phones."

"No it's not, it's work. That's why they tapped your phones, don't you see that? I doubt if there's anything in your personal life that's all that interesting."

"Oh, thanks a lot!"

"I mean for criminal purposes. Obviously, they want to know about something you're working on. What else could it be?"

"I know, but it still pisses me off."

"What could it be? What are you working on?"

"Now? The murder of Carlos Alvarez and who he was working for. But I wasn't working on that when he pulled the job in my house."

"What were you working on then?"

162

"*Nothing!* I mean, what, a stolen car? A stickup at a convenience store? Somebody selling dime bags on the west side of town? That's what we do around here, you know; it's a small town, and we investigate small crimes."

"Then it doesn't add up."

"No, it doesn't."

"Keep digging until you get a break."

"I intend to."

He reached out and put a palm on her cheek. "Truce?"

She looked at him doubtfully.

"Please, I don't want to take the heat for the Bureau." He leaned over and kissed her lightly on the lips.

"Okay," she said, and kissed him back.

27

Holly sat in her car half a block from the church and waited. Daisy was asleep, her head in Holly's lap, her legs moving, giving out muffled barks. "Well, your day is more exciting than mine, so far," she said to the dog.

She still carried a rosy feeling from that morning, when she had wakened with Grant's head on her breast. They had managed to spend the whole night in bed together, naked, without making love. She had made him breakfast and sent him back to whatever an undercover agent did with his time.

It had been wrong of her to blame him for her problems with the FBI. "Speaking of the FBI," she said aloud to herself.

Daisy raised her head, looked at Holly, then went back to sleep with a long sigh.

Holly was looking across the little square at a green SUV that had been sitting there for as long as she had. She raised the pocket binoculars to her eyes, zoomed in, and tried to make out who was inside. Its windows were darkened, as were hers, but there was a sunlit building behind them that allowed her to see the silhouettes of a man and a woman. She smiled. One of them — the woman in the passenger seat — was using binoculars, too.

"Oh, Harry, Harry," she said, "how can you be wasting manpower on an unimportant murder when there are terrorists to be caught?" She wished he were there to answer.

The front doors of the church opened and organ music wafted down the street as a priest in full regalia, followed by eight men carrying a mahogany coffin, came down the front steps and headed for the churchyard, followed by the congregation. A deep hole and a pile of dirt covered by artificial turf awaited them. The group gathered around the open grave, and half a dozen of them took their places in folding chairs that had been set out to receive them.

Holly saw Pedro Alvarez among them, but the crowd kept her from seeing who occupied the other chairs. The ceremony proceeded, then one by one the people in the chairs got up, tossed a handful of dirt into the grave, then stood by. Last was a tall, quite beautiful young woman who added a single rose to the small tributes. "That's my girl," Holly said, consulting the photograph from the locket. "Now, we wait some more."

The ceremony concluded, the crowd took a few minutes to disperse, after offering their condolences. At last, only the family were left. They talked among themselves for a moment, then broke into two distinct groups and departed.

The group with Pedro went to one car, while the group with the young woman walked to another. Holly gave the car, a white Lexus, a head start before following. She noted that the FBI, faced with the choice, chose Pedro's group. Okay with her.

The Lexus drove at a leisurely pace to a pretty neighborhood a few blocks away, nicely painted houses surrounded by neatly kept lawns. Holly stopped as the car turned in to a driveway, where there was already a blue Ford Focus parked. Six people got out and went into the house. More waiting to be done.

Holly sat, fighting the urge to doze like Daisy, and then she got a little break. A mailman was working his way down the street toward her. When he was even with the car, Holly rolled down the window. "Excuse me, sir," she said.

The mailman looked at her. "Yeah?"

"See the house down the street there, with the Lexus parked in the driveway?"

"Yeah."

"Can you tell me who lives there?"

"Who are you, and why do you want to know?"

Holly showed him her badge. "A car answering that description has been reported stolen; I'm just checking it out."

The mailman rummaged in his bag and found a small bundle of envelopes, secured with a rubber band. He walked over to the car and held them up so that Holly could read the name and address on a phone bill. "That do it for you?"

Marina Santos, the name read. "Yes, thank you."

"Lives there with her mother, name of Maria. And they're not the sort of folks to steal cars."

"I believe a visitor is driving the car. Thanks very much."

The mailman nodded and continued on his rounds, eventually crossing the street and working that side.

The sun fell low in the sky, and the shadows lengthened, and still the visitors remained inside. Finally, as Holly saw a light go on in a window, the front door opened and the guests said their goodbyes, getting into the Lexus and driving away. Holly started her car and drove down the block, parking in front of the Santos house. "Stay," she said to Daisy. She got out, went to the front door, and rang the bell.

A woman in her fifties came to the door. "*Sí?*" she asked.

"May I speak with Marina, please?"

The woman turned and spoke some words of Spanish, then Marina came to the door. "You wish to speak with me?" she asked, sounding baffled. Her English was unaccented.

"Yes. My name is Holly Barker. I'm a police officer, and I'm investigating the death of Carlos Alvarez. I'm sorry to intrude on such a day, but it's very important."

Marina stared at her warily; probably Pedro had warned her to expect the visit.

"Marina, I'm trying very hard to learn who murdered Carlos. Unless you are willing to help me, we may never know who did it."

Marina finally made her decision. "Come in," she said.

Holly stepped into a small entrance hall, then followed Marina into a nicely furnished living room.

"Please be seated," Marina said, then she turned to her mother and spoke some words of Spanish. "Would you like some tea?" she said to Holly.

"Yes, thank you."

"Lemon or milk?"

"Lemon, please."

Marina spoke to her mother, who left the room. She turned back to Holly. "You spoke to Pedro?"

"Yes," Holly said. "He wasn't much help."

Marina nodded. "Carlos and Pedro grew up in Cuba; they are, naturally, very suspicious of the police. I was born here. How can I help you?"

Holly took a deep breath; she had rehearsed this. "In the days, perhaps weeks or months, before his death, Carlos began working at a job other than the locksmith's shop. Were you aware of this?" Then she saw the diamond ring on Marina's left hand, around three carats, she estimated.

"Yes," Marina said. "He would not talk about it, but he began to have more money than usual. I see you noticed my engagement ring; that's how he bought it, I think. He said we could get married soon."

"And he never told you who he was working for?"

"No."

"Or what he was doing to earn the money?"

"No. He was very secretive about it."

"Did you ever see him talking to a stranger, someone not usually in his life?"

A little light came on in Marina's eyes. "Yes. Once we went to Miami to have dinner at a restaurant on South Beach. On the way, we stopped at another restaurant, and Carlos went inside for a few minutes. When he came out, a man was with him. They stood in the doorway and talked for a couple of minutes."

"Could you hear what they were saying?"

"No, but from the way they talked — their body language, and the fact that they were both nodding a lot — I had the impression that they had agreed on something. I asked Carlos about it, and he said it was about installing a burglar alarm in the restaurant."

"Can you describe the man?"

"He was a little taller than Carlos, older and slimmer; he was nicely dressed in a suit and tie. He was Italian, I think."

"How do you know that?"

"He was Mediterranean-looking, with an olive complexion that's different from Cubans', and he had a long, curved nose. His suit was Italian, too — you know how the lapels are cut?

Also, the restaurant was called Pellegrino's, like the Italian mineral water. Perhaps he was the headwaiter or the owner."

Good, Holly thought. Good, observant girl. "Do you remember the address?"

"No, but it wasn't on the beach. We had another fifteen minutes to drive before we were there."

"Was it after this that Carlos had more money?"

"Yes."

"How long ago did this meeting take place?"

"About six weeks. I remember because we were celebrating my birthday. It was a couple of weeks after that when Carlos seemed to have more cash. He bought the ring not long after that and asked me to marry him."

"Did you ever see him with this man again?"

"No, but I think I was with him when he talked to the man on the telephone."

"What did he say that made you think so?"

"At one point in the conversation he called the person on the other end of the phone something like *'pisan,'* which, I believe, is Italian for 'friend.'"

"Do you know about any other contact he may have had with this man?"

"He would get calls on his cellphone when we were together. I noticed that he would answer the cellphone every time it rang, when, before, he would sometimes shut it off. He never failed to answer his cellphone after that."

"Did Carlos ever tell you how much money he was getting?"

"No, but I think it must have been a great deal, because when I had the ring appraised for my insurance, it was valued at thirty-five thousand dollars."

"Can you think of anything else that might help me in my investigation?" Holly asked.

Marina thought for a moment, then shook her head.

Holly had a thought. "Was Carlos interested in guns?"

"Yes, he owned a couple of pistols; he kept them at the shop, in case of thieves, he said. He went once a week to a shooting range in North Miami, called Miami Bullseye." She looked down. "Tomorrow night would have been his night for that."

Holly stood up. "Thank you, I won't keep you further." She handed Marina her card. "Will you call me if you think of anything else?"

"Yes, I will."

"And I think it might be best if you didn't mention our talk to Pedro."

"I think you're right."

Marina's mother came back into the living room with the tea.

"Won't you please stay for tea?" Marina asked.

"Thank you, but I have to go."

Marina followed her out onto the front porch.

"Marina, I want to express my sympathy for your loss."

"Thank you."

"I lost my fiancé a little over a year ago, so I understand how you feel."

Marina began to tear up, and Holly embraced her. The two women stood on the front porch, holding each other, for another minute before Holly left, tears in her own eyes.

28

Holly walked Daisy and fed her some of the dry food and water she kept in her car, thinking the whole time. So Carlos had come into money? He wouldn't have been paid so much to bug her phones and jimmy her alarm system, but Carlos had other talents. For the wiretapping and for three murders, he'd be very well paid indeed. Of course, he'd missed Ed Shine, but he'd been very successful with the other two.

But why would the people who'd hired him murder him? Because they were finished with him, of course, and maybe because he'd failed with Ed Shine, and the property went to another buyer.

She wasn't driving back to Orchid Beach tonight; she had two other stops to make in the area, and she began thinking about where to spend the night. There were a lot of motels in the area, but would they take dogs? Then she remembered something. The year before, when she had been working with the FBI on a case, they had put her up at the Delano, a jazzy and elegant hotel in South Beach. What the hell, she was a woman of means, Jackson had seen to that in his will, and she deserved a good night's rest. She called the Delano and made a reservation, getting an okay on Daisy, then she started driving.

She spent half an hour at a mall buying some extra clothes, then headed south. Fifteen minutes from her destination she saw a sign with a familiar name, and she braked hard, nearly throwing Daisy off the seat. She whipped into a parking spot. "You stay here, baby," she said to Daisy. "It's time for your mama to have dinner." Daisy was used to waiting in the car.

She walked into Pellegrino's and looked around; she saw the man almost immediately, talking to customers at a nearby table. He left them and approached her.

"Good evening," he said. "May I help you?"

He was as Marina had described him, sleek and well dressed, about fifty, she reckoned.

"I haven't made a reservation," she said. "Do you have room for one for dinner?"

"I'm very sorry," he said with a regretful smile, "we're fully booked, but you can have dinner at the bar, if you wish. The menu is the same."

"Thank you, I'll sit at the bar." She offered him a smile of her own.

He led her to the bar, which was half full, and pulled out a seat at the less populated end. He snapped his fingers for the bartender, who came quickly. "Perhaps you'd be my guest for a drink while you're looking at the menu," he said.

"Thank you, I'd love one. A bourbon on the rocks?"

"Any special brand?"

"Do you have Knob Creek?"

"Of course." He nodded at the bartender, who went to pour the drink, then he handed Holly a menu. "Would you like me to recommend something?"

"Why don't you order for me?" Holly said, handing back the menu.

The man beamed. "Of course. How hungry are you?"

"Very."

"In that case I will start you with our famous antipasti and continue with our specialty, the osso buco."

"Sounds wonderful."

"May I introduce myself? I'm Pio Pellegrino."

"I'm Helen Benson," she said. "You're the owner, then?"

"It's a family business," he replied. "My father, over there, is still the owner, but we run it together." He nodded at an elderly man sitting near the kitchen door, eating pasta. "He likes to sit there because it's near the waiters' station, and he wants to be sure they don't steal the cutlery."

Holly laughed. "A smart businessman."

"You don't know the half of it. Excuse me, I'll order your dinner."

Holly sipped her bourbon and looked around

the place. It was handsomely designed, fairly large, and filling up fast — obviously a popular place.

Her antipasti arrived, and she had a bit of everything. Delicious. Then came the osso buco, and Pio, with half a bottle of red.

"I hope you'll drink some wine," he said. "With my personal compliments."

"Thank you, yes."

He poured the wine, a very good Chianti Classico, and she made appreciative noises. He left to seat other customers.

Holly loved the osso buco, and when Pio returned, she had finished it. "Thank you so much for ordering for me, and for the wine," she said. "Can I buy you a drink?"

"Not in my own restaurant," he said, "but I'd be delighted to have one with you." He spoke to the bartender in Italian, and two glasses of a golden liquid appeared.

"What is it?"

He settled on a stool next to her. "Strega, an Italian aperitif."

She liked it and told him so.

"So, are you from Miami?"

"No, from out of town."

"How did you choose my restaurant?"

"Pure luck; I was driving past and saw the sign, and I was in the mood for Italian."

His smile turned into a leer, but he didn't rise to the line. "Where are you staying?"

"Over on South Beach." She looked at her watch. "In fact, I'd better be going. I'm meeting my boyfriend at our hotel, and I'm late."

His face fell. "I hope you'll come back again," he said. "And alone. I enjoy your company."

"That's very kind of you; I'll keep it in mind. I'm here for a few more days. May I have a check?"

"There is no check," he said grandly.

"My goodness," Holly said, batting her eyes. "You're even kinder than I thought." She shook his hand, and he held on for a little too long, then she left and went back to the car, feeling that she had only just escaped his further intentions.

At the Delano, Holly checked in, with only a shopping bag for luggage, settled into her room, then called her office and told them where she was. "Don't give out that information, though," she said. "Just take a message."

Then she called Ham. "Hey."

"Hey."

"I'm in Miami for a couple of nights on business," she said. "I didn't want you to worry."

"Me, worry? You don't need my permission for a dirty weekend."

"It's not a weekend, and it's not dirty," she replied. "It's just a couple of days' work on a case."

"Whatever you say."

"Oh, shut up, Ham. I'll see you later in the week." She hung up.

Daisy hopped onto the bed and put her head in Holly's lap.

"Your grandfather has a dirty mind," she said. She thought about Grant and wished it was a dirty weekend.

29

Holly slept late and had a good breakfast. She dressed in her new clothes, the first she had bought since Jackson's death, and took Daisy for a walk, then got into her car. She had nothing to do until evening, so she decided to have another go at Pedro Alvarez.

When she got to his shop, he was with a customer, and she waited, looking carefully at the displays of locks and burglar alarms. She was not surprised that two of the examples on display were identical to the equipment in her house.

Pedro said goodbye to the customer, then approached Holly. "What do you want now?" he asked, his tone unfriendly.

"I want to see Carlos's guns," she said.

"Do you have a warrant?" he asked.

"Oh, I can get a warrant, and very quickly," she replied. "But let me tell you what happens if I get a warrant. I'll bring a team in here, and we will dismantle this shop and take anything we like away with us, including all the guns we find. Then, if any of them has been used in a crime, or if we find any other violation of the law, I'll have your locksmith's license yanked. Now, how do you want to do this?"

"I'll show you the gun," he said.

"There's more than one, Pedro."

"Carlos had two, a nine-millimeter and a forty-caliber. One of them is missing." He led her to a large safe in the back room and began opening it.

So Carlos had been carrying, and he might well have been shot with his own gun.

"Here is Carlos's nine-millimeter," he said, handing her a Beretta.

It was loaded. She popped out the magazine and ejected one from the breech. "Do you have a paper bag?" she asked.

"I didn't say you could take it with you."

"So you want me to get the warrant? I can phone it in, and we can wait together for the team to arrive."

"All right, all right," he said. He handed her a sheepskin-lined leather pouch, and she zipped the gun inside it, putting the cartridges in a pocket inside. She wrote a receipt on the back of her card and handed it to him.

"When will you return it?" he asked.

"When I've finished processing it. If it turns out to have been used in a crime, you won't get it back."

Pedro nodded.

"You must have been aware that Carlos was into something he shouldn't have been."

Pedro shook his head.

"Come on, Pedro. If you want us to find out who killed your cousin, you're going to have to help us. Now we know that Carlos suddenly came into money. Where was he getting it?"

Pedro shook his head again. "I don't know. When I asked Carlos about it, he told me that it was none of my affair, that, in fact, it would help our business."

"Help your business how?"

"He said he was developing new contacts for alarm-system installations."

"Business or residential?"

"There were going to be a number of new houses, he said."

"In what town?"

"I don't know. Not in our immediate area, though; he was talking about opening another shop."

"Where?"

"He said he couldn't tell me yet."

"Did he indicate to you that his new work might be dangerous?"

"Just the reverse; he said it was a piece of cake."

"Did Carlos mention any names to you?"
"No."

"A nickname, maybe?"

"No, nothing."

"What else did he tell you, Pedro?"

"I swear, that's all he told me."

"Did you tell this to the FBI agents who came to see you?"

"No, I didn't tell them anything."

"Did Carlos own a rifle?"

"No, but . . ." Pedro was staring into the middle distance, as if he remembered something. "Once I saw a leather rifle case in the van he borrowed."

"What was his explanation?"

"I didn't ask him about it; he had already told me that his outside work was none of my business."

"How big a case? How long?"

"Just a standard zipper case, like one that would hold a hunting rifle or a shotgun."

"How long ago?"

"I'm not sure; two or three weeks, maybe. I thought maybe he was taking it to the range, since it was his regular day to go."

"Miami Bullseye?"

He looked at her in surprise. "Yes. He fired there every week."

Holly nodded. "I'll see you again, Pedro." She left the shop and stowed the weapon in the lockable bin that held the spare tire in her SUV. Then she went back to the mall and went shopping again. It was lovely to be doing something so normal again, she thought as she shopped for shoes.

At her third stop in the mall, she became aware of a woman she had seen the morning before. She was thirtyish, dressed in a business suit, with fairly short brown hair. Holly felt she was beginning to see too much of her. As she continued through the mall, she kept seeing the woman, and when she came out of the Ralph Lauren store, her tail was sitting on a bench in the middle of the mall, pretending to read a magazine.

Holly went and sat down next to her. "Good morning," she said.

The woman glanced at her, nodded, and went back to her magazine.

"How's Harry Crisp these days?"

The woman looked at her. "I beg your pardon?"

"How's old Harry? Your boss?"

"I'm afraid you have me confused with someone else," the woman said.

"I'm afraid you have me confused with someone who can't spot a tail," Holly replied.

"I'm sorry?"

"I wouldn't go as far as that, but you're not very good. You were outside the church at the Alvarez funeral, weren't you? You followed Pedro home after the burial."

The woman was becoming flustered now. "I would appreciate it if you would leave me alone," she said.

"Sure, I will," Holly replied, "and I'll give you a choice. You can vanish, then call Harry and tell him you lost me, or I'll call him myself and tell him what a lousy job you're doing."

"Goodbye," the woman said, getting up. She walked quickly away, toward an exit to the parking lot.

Holly resumed her shopping, but she kept an eye out for the woman's partner, if she had one.

30

Holly, unable to think of anything else to do, took in a movie at the mall, then after getting the address from the telephone information operator, drove to North Miami and Miami Bullseye. She figured Carlos's shooting group would arrive early evening, after work and supper, so she had a burger at a fast-food joint across the street. When she felt the time was right, she retrieved Carlos's Beretta from her car, shouldered her handbag, and walked into the shooting range.

It was pretty much what she had expected — a long, low building made of concrete blocks, divided into narrow alleys and shooting booths. She stopped at a window and told the woman behind the glass that she'd like to fire for an hour. The woman took her money and signed her in. "Can I buy some cartridges?" she asked.

"What do you need?"

"A box each of nine-millimeter and seven sixty-fives."

The woman went to a steel cabinet behind her, unlocked it, took out two boxes, relocked the cabinet, and returned to the window. Holly paid her, and she took down the serial numbers of both weapons.

"Take position ten," the woman said, pointing.

There were twenty positions, putting Holly right in the middle. She set down her bag, unzipped the pistol pouch, and removed the Beretta. Then she had a thought and returned to the window. "Do you have a tank?" she asked. "I'd like to get a sample."

"Just a minute." The woman picked up a telephone, dialed a three-digit extension, and spoke into the phone. A moment later a man entered the booth and motioned Holly toward a door next to it. He met her and let her in.

"Hi, I'm Jimmy," he said. "This is my place."

"Hi, I'm Helen." They shook hands.

"You want to fire it yourself, or you want me to do it?"

"I'll fire."

Jimmy led her across what appeared to be a storeroom and pointed at the tank, a container a few feet long filled with water.

Holly shoved the magazine into the Beretta, worked the action, flipped off the safety, and fired two rounds into the tank.

"Just a minute," Jimmy said. He went to the other end, opened a flap and, using a flashlight and a pair of tongs, retrieved the two slugs. "Here you go," he said, handing them to her.

"Thanks," she said, dropping them into her purse.

He nodded and let her out of the room.

She went back to her station and flipped a switch that moved her target back to fifty feet. She put on ear protectors, took up a combat stance — knees bent, pistol held out before her with two hands — and emptied the magazine into the target. Then she removed her Walther from her handbag and emptied another magazine into the target. She flipped the switch and brought the target back to her.

"Nice grouping," a voice said from behind her.

She turned to find Jimmy standing there. "Thanks."

"That's a really good grouping with the Walther."

She examined the target. The 9mm shots formed a tight group at the bull's-eye, while the .765 shots were a little more dispersed. "I haven't shot for a while," she said. "At that range, I ought to be able to fire just as tight with the Walther as with the Beretta."

He put another target up for her, and she moved it to 100 feet and fired both pistols. When the target came back, the groupings were looser, but still good.

"Where'd you learn to shoot?" Jimmy asked.

"My father taught me when I was a kid — he's a lot better shot than I am — then I was in the military. I did the twenty."

"Me too," he said.

"Nice little business you've got here."

"Thanks." He put another target up for her, and she moved it to 150 feet. The groupings were wider, but the man-shaped target had taken all the slugs in the chest.

"I'm impressed," Jimmy said.

"Think I'll take a break, then see if I can improve my groupings," she said. "Can I buy you a beer?"

"We don't sell it here, but I'll buy you a cup of coffee." He indicated for her to follow him. A moment later, she was seated in his office and he was pouring her a cup of coffee.

"Thanks," she said, accepting the cup.

"You live around here?"

"No, up the coast."

"What brings you to my place?"

Holly decided to play it straight with him; she figured she had a chance of learning more. "I'm chief of police in a little town called Orchid Beach," she said, laying her ID on his desk.

He picked it up and examined it. "Holly, not Helen."

"Sorry, I was being too careful."

He tossed back her wallet. "So, like I said, what brings you to my place?"

"A customer of yours took one in the back of the head up in my jurisdiction."

"That would be Carlos Alvarez, unless I've lost another customer I don't know about."

"That would be Carlos. I'm working the murder."

"There's a guy named Barker up there. Know him?"

"Ham? That would be my old man."

Jimmy smiled. "I was at Bragg with him a few years back. I didn't know him, really, but I saw him shoot a couple of times. It was really boring, looking at those targets; he'd blow out the middle every time."

"He still does."

"I'd say tell him hello, but he wouldn't know the name. Tell him a fan said hello."

"I'll do that; it'll please him."

"So, Holly, how can I help you?"

"Carlos shot in here once a week."

"Yeah, he did. He was a good shot, too; not as good as your old man, but good."

"Who did he shoot with?"

"Bunch of Cuban guys."

"You think they'd talk to me?"

Jimmy laughed. "An Anglo female cop? Yeah, sure. That would violate four or five different kinds of macho."

"That's what I figured, but maybe you can tell me what I need to know."

"If I can."

"What did Carlos fire when he came?"

"He usually brought a forty millimeter and a Beretta."

"I'm firing the Beretta tonight."

"Oh?"

"Yeah. The forty is missing; I think it might have been used to kill him."

189

"A shame about that. He had a really pretty girlfriend he brought in here once."

"Yeah. Did Carlos ever fire a rifle here?"

"Sometimes he'd swap pieces with somebody. Once, he brought a twenty-two Winchester with a scope in here."

"How long ago?"

"I don't know, three, four weeks, I guess."

"How'd he shoot with it?"

"Sweet, just like with everything else."

"Jimmy, let me ask you something entirely off the record."

Jimmy's expression didn't change, and he said nothing.

"If Carlos wanted a silencer made for the rifle, who would he go to?"

Jimmy didn't move, didn't say a word.

31

Holly waited him out. Jimmy stared at her for the longest moment, before he spoke.

"Why do you want to know?"

"Because there are a lot of pieces to this puzzle, and if I'm going to put them all together, I've got to know everything. The silencer is an important piece."

"I might be able to arrange a brief meeting," he said. "But no names, and when it's over, it never happened."

"That's good with me."

"Pour yourself another cup of coffee," Jimmy said, getting up from his desk. "I'll be back." He left the office and closed the door behind him.

Holly got up and walked around the room. There was a display of army stuff on the walls — Jimmy's shooting qualification certificates, awards for winning competitions.

The door opened and a man followed Jimmy into the room. Small, rat-like, nervous, he took a chair, as did Jimmy.

"Go ahead," Jimmy said.

Holly looked at the man. "Did you ever make a silencer for Carlos Alvarez?"

The man looked at Jimmy, then at the floor.

"This is completely off the record," Jimmy said. "A meeting that never happened."

"I'll never be asked to testify?"

Holly shook her head. "Carlos is dead; you can't hurt him."

The man looked at her again. "I made something for a Winchester twenty-two rifle," he said.

"He does good work," Jimmy chimed in.

"My work is as good for accuracy as for noise," the little man said. "I do rifling; they're perfectly machined."

"He's right," Jimmy said. "I've seen his work."

"How long ago?"

"A month, maybe; I didn't count."

"Thanks," Holly said. "I appreciate your help."

"That it?" he asked Jimmy, and Jimmy nodded. The man got up and opened the door, then closed it again.

"Something else?" Jimmy asked.

"I made something for a forty-millimeter Heckler and Koch, too."

"Same time?" Holly asked.

"Same time. Next time I saw Carlos, he said he was real happy with my work."

"Thanks again," Holly said, and the man left the room and closed the door behind him.

"That what you wanted?" Jimmy asked.

"That was it," Holly said. "One more thing."

"Shoot."

"I noticed that when I checked in, your lady

took the serial numbers of my weapons."

"We always do. Keeps people from bringing illegal pieces in here, and we throw out anybody who brings in something with the number filed off."

"Then you'll have the serial numbers of Carlos's rifle and two pistols?"

Jimmy went to a card file, flipped through it, and extracted three cards. He lined them up on a copying machine and pressed the button. "There you are," he said, handing her the copy. "In Carlos's own handwriting, with his signature."

"That's great, Jimmy. I can't thank you enough." She didn't get up.

"Something else?"

"I think Carlos made a connection here. Does the name Pellegrino mean anything to you?"

"There's a restaurant in Miami by that name; my wife and I have had dinner there a couple of times, on special occasions."

"You remember the headwaiter, Pio, the guy who seats everybody? He's tall, slim, very slick-looking."

"Sure. He owns the place, doesn't he?"

"With his father, apparently. Has he ever been in here, maybe talked to Carlos?"

"No, I'd remember; he's never been in here."

"Then there's a connection between Carlos and Pellegrino, and it may be somebody who comes in here, who's seen Carlos shoot and who recommended him to somebody outside, maybe Pellegrino, or maybe a third party who sent him to Pellegrino."

"Hard to know who that could be," Jimmy said.

"You have any customer you suspect might be connected?"

"You mean mob-connected?"

"Right."

Jimmy thought about it. "I can't even think of anybody with an Italian name, offhand."

"Doesn't have to be Italian. When you visited Pellegrino's restaurant, did you see anybody you knew among the customers?"

Jimmy's eyebrows went up. "Yeah, now you mention it. There's a guy named Trini Rodriguez, he's a regular here. In fact, he's part of the group that Carlos shoots with."

"This is Carlos's regular night; is Rodriguez here?"

"Hang on." Jimmy left the room and came back a moment later. "Trini is shooting in position fourteen," he said.

"I want to get a good look at him," Holly said. "Can you put me next to him?"

"Yeah, thirteen is open. Come on."

Holly followed Jimmy back into the range, and he showed her to position thirteen. Holly put her weapons on the shelf in front of her, then stepped back so she could see around the partition between the positions. His back was to her and he was shooting a 9mm.

She fiddled with the Beretta a little, waiting for him to recall his target.

"Nice group," she said.

He turned and regarded her for a long moment. About Carlos's size, well built, well dressed, slick haircut. "Thanks," he said, then went back to his shooting.

Holly fired both pistols again, then went to a cleaning station, field-stripped both pistols, and cleaned them carefully, taking as much time as she could.

Eventually, Rodriguez walked over and began cleaning his weapon.

"You shoot here regularly?" Holly asked.

Rodriguez looked up at her coolly and nodded.

"Seems like a nice place."

"It is," he said. "Jimmy's okay."

She nodded, then packed away her two weapons and walked away. On the way out, she gave Jimmy a wink, and he winked back.

Connection, she thought — Carlos, Trini, Pellegrino. But who did Pellegrino connect with?

32

Holly was having dinner on the Delano's terrace when she looked up and found Harry Crisp standing a few feet away, staring at her.

"Why, Harry, what brings you to South Beach? I thought the FBI worked in grubbier surroundings."

"Evening, Holly. Mind if I sit down?"

"Please do. Would you like some dinner?"

"Thanks, I've already eaten."

"Drink?"

"Well, why not? I'm off duty." He flagged down a waiter and ordered a mai tai. "And don't put a little umbrella in it," he said to the waiter.

"I guess you tracked me down through Ham," Holly said.

"Yep."

"What's so urgent?"

"I want to know what you're doing down here, Holly."

"Sorry, Harry. I'm tired of the FBI's one-way information highway."

"What do you want?"

"Full disclosure."

"About what?"

"About every aspect of this case."

"Which case?"

"Harry, this isn't getting us anywhere. You know exactly what I'm talking about."

"Yeah, okay."

"Okay, full disclosure?"

The waiter came back with Harry's mai tai; there was a little umbrella in it. "No tip for him," Harry said as the waiter walked away. He tossed the umbrella onto the table. "So, tell me what you're doing down here."

"Harry, I don't believe I received a confirmation of our new arrangement, the one about full disclosure."

"All right, all right, full disclosure."

"That means an answer to any question I ask?"

"Any relevant question."

"Harry, if I ask a question, it's relevant. Now, if you're ready to deal on equal terms, two-way information highway, say so; if not, please go away and leave me to enjoy this very good dinner."

"All right, two-way information highway."

"I'm going to hold you to that, Harry."

"Now tell me what you're doing here."

"I'm solving the murder of Carlos Alvarez."

"Who?"

"Come on, Harry, Grant must have told you about this."

"Not much."

That was good, Holly thought. Grant was being close-mouthed.

"He's the guy who broke into my house repeatedly and tapped my phones. He turned up dead in the Indian River."

"And you've solved it?"

"Not yet, but I'm on the way. Oh, by the way, Carlos also killed your two Miami property developers and tried to kill Ed Shine."

"*What?*"

"No kidding."

"Why do you think so?"

"Carlos was spotted at a Miami shooting range by somebody who was *connected* connected. He was a crack shot. He bought or was supplied with a Winchester twenty-two rifle, went to the range to sight it in, and had a silencer made for the rifle and his own forty-caliber Heckler and Koch semiautomatic. Isn't that what your Cuban developer was shot with?"

"Yes. We recovered a slug from the inside of the guy's car door. The nice Mercedes upholstery kept it from being deformed too much, so we can probably get a match, if we ever find the gun."

"My people are going to start searching the Indian River around the North Bridge for the gun tomorrow morning. I think Carlos was shot there with his own gun, and my guess is the shooter tossed it, along with Carlos."

"Send it to me when you get it, and I'll run the ballistics."

"You send me the bullet and *I'll* run the ballistics."

"I have a better lab than the state."

"Maybe, but this is a murder that occurred in my jurisdiction. If I send you the gun, I want a receipt stating that it will be returned when the ballistics have been run."

"Okay."

"Something else. After Carlos was spotted at the range, I think he was hired by a guy named Pio Pellegrino, who runs a restaurant."

"Pellegrino's? I've eaten there. Good place, if you can get a table."

"I'd like you to run a check on Pio's background, his father's, too, see if they're connected, and if so, to whom."

Harry was taking notes now. "What's his father's name?"

"I don't know. Try the phone book."

"I'll see that it's run down."

"Harry, if Pellegrino isn't running this thing, then he's connected to whoever is, so don't start walking all over this with your big FBI feet, okay? Don't bring him in for questioning, and if you have him watched, for God's sake don't park an FBI van outside his door. Be subtle, Harry."

"We're always subtle," Harry replied.

"Like the green SUV with the two agents inside that was parked at the Santa Maria church? Like the female agent you had following me when I was shopping for shoes? Please."

"I'll take special steps," Harry said through clenched teeth.

"What's Grant Early working on, Harry?"

"That's not relevant."

"So what happened to the two-way information highway, Harry?"

"It's not relevant."

"I should have known you'd do this. I spill everything I've got, saving you many man-hours of legwork, and you stonewall me."

"Holly, I mean it, Grant's case is not relevant to your investigation; it's a whole separate thing."

Holly sighed. "Harry, if I find out it isn't, I'm going to come over to your house and shoot you in your sleep."

"It's a federal crime to threaten an FBI agent, Holly."

"So, arrest me."

Harry smirked at her. "Not yet."

"Not while I'm doing your work for you, huh?"

"You're not doing my work for me; this stuff is just frosting on the cake."

"I want to hear about the Pellegrinos by lunchtime tomorrow," Holly said, sliding her card across the table. "My cellphone number is on the card."

Harry pocketed the card. "I'll be in touch," he said, getting up and tossing a five-dollar bill onto the table.

"The drink's on me, Harry," Holly said.

"Gee, thanks," Harry replied, picking up the note. "Talk to you tomorrow." He walked away.

Holly went back to her dinner, now cold. "You'd bloody well better talk to me tomorrow," she said aloud to herself.

33

Holly got an early start for home the following morning. Once she was on I-95, she called Hurd Wallace.

"Good morning."

"Morning, Holly."

"Hurd, I'd like you to get ahold of our divers and do a search of the waters under and around the North Bridge."

"What are we looking for?"

"A Heckler and Koch forty-caliber pistol with a silencer."

"The weapon used on Carlos?"

"I think so. He owned such a gun, and it's missing."

"Okay."

"Which side of the road was the van parked on?"

"The south side."

"Then search the south side of the bridge first, to a distance that you could throw a semi-automatic pistol. Start at the center of the river and work outward."

"I'm on it. When will you be back?"

"I'm on the way now; see you later this morning."

"Right." Hurd hung up.

Holly continued up I-95. An hour later, her phone rang.

"Hello?"

"Hi, it's Harry."

"Good morning."

"We've run a check on Pio and his old man, whose name is Ignacio."

"Isn't Ignacio a Spanish name?"

"Who knows? Anyway, they've both got a clean sheet, federal and state."

"That doesn't add up," Holly said. "How far back did you go?"

"When they've got a clean sheet, it's from childhood."

"Harry, do a background check on both of them; this needs more than just a records check. Find out how long they've been in business, how long they've lived where they live, all that stuff."

"This is looking like a dead end to me, Holly."

"I don't think it is, Harry. I mean, I think the trail is meant to end with Pellegrino, if somebody investigates, but I don't think that's where the trail ends."

"All right, I'll put a couple of men on it."

"Thanks. My people are on the search for the forty-caliber. I'll call you if they find something."

"See you later."

Holly had lunch at her desk and worked on administrative matters for most of the afternoon. A little after four, Hurd Wallace walked into her office, bearing two plastic-wrapped packages. He held them up for her to see.

"You found the forty-caliber."

"With the silencer attached. You pegged where it would be. And there's this," Hurd said, setting the larger of the two packages on her desk.

"What is it?"

"Open it."

Holly put on latex gloves, then unwrapped the plastic cover. Inside was a leather rifle case. Handling it carefully, she unzipped the sodden case, revealing a Winchester .22 rifle with a scope attached. In another zippered pocket was an eight-inch-long silencer. "Bingo," she said. "Dust them, then collect a specimen bullet and a shell casing from both of them. When you're finished with them, send a patrolman down to the Miami FBI office with them; deliver to Harry Crisp personally. Also, run ownership checks on both weapons. I know the pistol belonged to Carlos Alvarez; it'll be interesting to see if we can trace an owner for the rifle."

"Will do," Hurd said. He took the weapons away.

Holly called Harry Crisp.

"Hello?"

"Harry, I've had a fruitful day. What about you?"

"Did you find the pistol?"

"You first."

"Okay, neither of the Pellegrinos existed six

years ago. I'm going to have them picked up and printed."

"Harry, don't do that. Have them photographed and see if you can get a match from your records. You have an optical matching system in Washington, don't you?"

"Yeah, I guess that's a better idea. Now what have you got?"

"A forty-caliber Heckler and Koch and silencer and a twenty-two Winchester rifle with a scope and a silencer."

"Great."

"They'll be messengered down to you tonight."

"Don't do that, just overnight them directly to Washington." He gave her the address and a case number. "I'll send the bullet and shell casings we have, and they'll have everything tomorrow morning. We should have the report by the close of business tomorrow."

"That's good."

"Question: who was the connection between Carlos Alvarez and Pio Pellegrino?"

"Oh, I forgot to give you that. I think it was a guy named Trini Rodriguez; you should run a check on him, too. He was seen in the restaurant on one occasion, and he was one of a group of guys, including Carlos, who met weekly at the firing range."

"You think the range is dirty?"

"No, the owner is ex-army, and he was very helpful. He's straight."

"Okay, if you say so. My check on Carlos turned up a clean sheet, too," Holly said.

"Yeah, he was straight, until he got involved in this."

"What turned him, money?"

"Yeah, and a lot of it. He bought his girl an expensive diamond ring, for one thing. I think he thought he'd do these jobs, then get out clean. Otherwise, he wouldn't have used his own pistol in one of the murders. He thought nobody could ever connect him to any of his victims, and he was probably right, except he didn't count on getting blown away by the people who hired him."

"They never do, do they?" Harry said.

"Get back to me, Harry." She hung up as Hurd walked into her office.

"The rifle had no prints on it," he said. "I guess they were washed away by being under-water for a few days. But we picked up a pretty good thumbprint on the magazine of the pistol, and it isn't Carlos's print. I think the only reason we got it was because the magazine had some oil on it. We're running it now."

"That's great, Hurd. When you're done with the weapons, send them to the FBI lab in Washington; here's the address." She handed him the paper. "I think we might be getting some-where."

"I'm glad," Hurd said. "Holly, I think this is going to be my last day on the job."

"So soon?" Holly asked. "I'd hoped you'd stay

on for at least a couple more weeks, for a smooth transition."

"It's done; I've broken up my duties and re-assigned them. Here's a list." He put a file on her desk. "Everybody's briefed; I'm now super-fluous."

Holly stood up. "Thank you, Hurd, for always doing a superb job. I'm going to miss you." She shook his hand.

"I'll miss you, too, Holly," he said.

For a moment, Holly thought she saw a flash of emotion on Hurd's usually impassive face.

A few hours later, the phone rang.

"Hello?" Holly answered.

"It's your turn to cook for me," Grant said.

She looked at her watch. "I'll pick up some-thing on the way home. My place at seven-thirty?"

"You're on."

Holly hung up, glowing with anticipation.

34

Holly stopped at the grocery store and picked up the makings for a pasta dish she was particularly good at and a couple of bottles of a Dolcetto, a very nice Italian wine. She got home, fed Daisy and let her out, then started cooking. By the time Grant arrived, the house smelled wonderful.

She threw her arms around him and gave him a big kiss.

"Hey, you're in a good mood!"

"You bet I am. I'm making real good progress on the floater case, and I've even got Harry Crisp onboard."

"Tell me about it."

She told him everything, about Marina and the shooting range, about Pio Pellegrino and his father, who didn't exist a few years back. She told him about recovering both weapons and shipping them to Washington.

"You've had a good couple of days, then," Grant said. "Especially getting Harry onboard. How'd you do that?"

"By coming up with more evidence than his own people were able to find. He's not happy about being onboard, believe me, but I think he's finally learning that he gets further when he trusts me, instead of shouldering me out of the investigation."

"I hope he's that smart," Grant said. "Harry can revert to type at the drop of a hat. He's a good guy to work for in a lot of ways, but — remember that someone once said that there's no limit to how far you can go, if you don't care who gets the credit? Harry has never figured that out. Every time our office makes a big bust, the report has got Harry's palm prints all over it, and the guys who really did the work are mentioned somewhere down at the bottom of the page."

"Well, I'm not competing with him for the credit; I just want to know what the hell is going on in my town."

"Next time I talk to him, I'll see if I can point that out to him, subtly."

"If you're subtle, Harry won't get it."

"You have a point." He sniffed the air. "God, that smells good!"

"Of course it does. You ready to eat?"

"Try me."

They ate.

An hour later, as Holly was dozing off on Grant's shoulder, the phone rang.

"Chief?"

"Yes."

"It's Sally Worth, down at the station. We got a

match on the thumbprint that Hurd asked for."

"Tell me."

"It belongs to a Trini Rodriguez. He has a record of arrests, more than a dozen of them, for arson, robbery, car theft, and attempted murder."

"A jack-of-all-trades, huh? Any convictions?"

"None."

"Thanks, Sally." She hung up and turned back to Grant. "We got a match on the thumbprint; one Trini Rodriguez, whom I recently met."

"You ought to call Harry."

"Tomorrow morning will be good enough," she said, kissing him.

"He'd like it if you called him at home; I've got the number."

Holly rolled over and called Harry. "Harry? Sorry to disturb you at home, but I thought you ought to know that we pulled a print off the magazine of Carlos's forty-caliber, and it belongs to Trini Rodriguez, the guy I told you about earlier today."

"Good news," Harry said. "I'm glad you called. I'll have him picked up."

"Not yet, Harry, please," Holly said. "The people he works for might go to ground, and anyway, the evidence isn't all that good."

"You think we can't get him for Carlos's murder with that evidence?"

"No, I don't think so. He can claim that he put the print on the gun when Carlos showed it to him at the shooting range. Also, the guy has a long arrest record but no convictions, which means he knows how to keep his mouth shut and lawyer up. Rodriguez is very cool, and I don't think you'll be able to get anything out of him that would help us at this stage. Let's find out more about the Pellegrinos before we grab Trini."

"Okay, that makes sense."

"When are we going to have something from Washington about Pio and his daddy?"

"We got photographs of them arriving at the restaurant earlier this evening, and they've been transmitted to D.C. Depends on their case load; if it's light, we'll hear something soon."

"Thank you, Harry."

"Say hello to Grant," Harry said.

"I beg your pardon?"

"Where else would you get my home number? It's unlisted."

"Good night, Harry." She hung up. "Harry says hello."

"Why does he think I'm here?"

"He has an unlisted number."

"Oops."

"Yeah."

"Well, he fixed us up, didn't he? Maybe Harry has a romantic soul after all."

"Maybe," Holly said, cuddling up to Grant again.

35

Holly had been at her desk for only a few minutes the following morning when her telephone rang.

"Miss Barker."

"Miss Barker?" A woman's voice.

"Yes."

"This is Marina Santos. Do you remember me?"

"Of course, Marina. I hope you're well."

"I'm all right. You said I should telephone you if I knew anything else."

"Yes. Is there something you forgot to tell me?"

"Yes, but somebody else didn't forget."

"What is it, Marina?"

"Carlos left something here that he didn't want anyone to see."

"What is it?"

"A notebook."

"What kind of notebook?"

"Leather, with a ring binder."

"What's in it?"

"I've read it but I don't understand it. It's just a lot of numbers and letters."

"You said somebody else didn't forget?"

"Pedro, Carlos's cousin. He was here last night asking about the notebook. He couldn't find it at Carlos's place."

"Did you give it to him?"

"No."

"Do you still have it?"

"I've hidden it."

"In your house?"

"Yes."

"Marina, I'm going to drive down there and pick it up." She looked at her watch. "I'll be there in a couple of hours."

"Thank you. I want to get rid of it."

"If anybody else asks about it, you don't know anything, understand?"

"I understand."

"My cellphone number is on the card, if you need to get in touch with me before I get there."

"Thank you."

Holly hung up. "Come on, Daisy." She stopped at the front desk and told them where she was going.

This time Holly didn't bother staying anywhere near the speed limit. She turned on the flashing lights behind the grille on the unmarked car, and as soon as she was on I-95, she put her foot down, moderating her speed only when she hit 120 miles per hour. Names, she wanted names, and she didn't want Harry Crisp to have them, unless he got them from her. She made the trip in record time, slowing down only when she entered Marina's street.

She drove slowly down the street, passing a car parked in front of the house, a Hispanic male at the wheel reading something. She parked on the other side of the street, three or four houses down, put Daisy on a leash, and walked back up the street toward the parked car, allowing Daisy to water the grass on the way, just a woman walking her dog. The man in the car seemed engrossed in his reading.

At Marina's house she turned up the walk, and as she did, she heard a commotion inside. The front door was wide open, the screen door closed. She put her hand inside her purse, opened the screen with her leash hand, and walked into the house.

The room was in disarray, and there was a man present, wearing a sport shirt, loose at the waist, revealing a bulge, his back to her, his hand drawn back. Holly let the screen door slam.

The man spun around to face her. Holly didn't know him, but Marina Santos was standing behind him, in tears. He said something in Spanish.

"How's that again?" Holly asked.

"Who the fuck are you?" he demanded, taking a step toward her.

"Daisy," Holly said quietly, and Daisy bared her teeth and began growling. The man stopped. "Daisy, guard," Holly said. Then to the man, she said, "I'm a police officer. If you move a muscle, the dog will kill you." The man didn't move.

"Marina," Holly said, "go into the kitchen and call nine-one-one; tell them there's an intruder in your home."

The man said something sinister-sounding in Spanish, and Marina didn't move.

"Don't worry, Marina," Holly said, "he won't hurt you. If he tries, I'll put the dog on him."

Marina backed away from the man, then turned and went into the kitchen.

"You," Holly said, "on your knees, hands behind your head."

"Fuck that," the man said, and his hand went behind him.

Holly shot him through the purse, the bullet striking him in the center of the chest, and he fell backward, a pistol flying from his hand. "Guard, Daisy," she said, letting go of the leash. Daisy trotted over and stood perhaps five feet from the fallen man, still growling. Holly kicked the gun away from the man, then went and stood beside the door, waiting with her gun drawn for the man's companion to enter. Instead, she heard the car start and drive away, burning rubber.

She checked to be sure, then turned back to the shot man. "Quiet, Daisy. Stay." She knelt beside him, her gun under his chin. "Lie very still," she said. "Marina," she called out, "ask for an ambulance as well as for the police."

Holly held the fingers of her free hand to his neck, feeling for a pulse. It was weak and thready.

The man lay on his back, his breathing shallow and labored, his eyes open but unfocused, looking at the ceiling, his lips moving soundlessly. "Nothing I can do for you," she said. She stood up and walked to the kitchen door. Marina was hanging up the phone.

"They're on their way," she said. "I asked for an ambulance."

Holly heard a siren coming down the block. She put her gun back into her handbag and walked out the front door, stopping on the porch, holding her badge in sight.

Two officers, one a sergeant, spilled out of the police car, weapons drawn. "Police officer," Holly said, waving the badge. "You won't need weapons."

The two officers stopped running and walked up the front steps. "I've got a perpetrator down in the living room," she said, "one gunshot to the chest. He doesn't look good, and there's an ambulance on its way."

The sergeant looked closely at her ID. "Orchid Beach? Where the hell is that?"

"Out of town," Holly said.

He looked at her handbag. "Is there a weapon in there?"

"Yes," she replied. "I'll give it to you." She reached into the bag, ran a finger through the trigger guard, and held out the weapon to him.

He took it from her the same way she was holding it and dropped it into an evidence bag. "Is that your only weapon?"

"Yes. There's another on the living room floor that belonged to the perp. He was about to shoot me when I shot him."

The sergeant started for the screen door. "Not yet," Holly said. "Daisy," she called out. "Sit, stay. It's all right."

The sergeant looked at her.

"Who's Daisy?"

"The only witness," Holly said. "You can go inside now."

36

The sergeant opened the screen door and walked in. "Jesus!" he said. "Nice doggy."

"Her name is Daisy. Say 'Hello, Daisy.' "

"Hello, Daisy," the sergeant said. "Can I touch the guy without him eating me?"

"It's a she, and you're friends now."

The sergeant gingerly patted Daisy on the head. "Nice Daisy."

"Yes, she is."

He went and felt the wounded man's throat. "He's dead," he said.

"Let's wait for the EMTs to determine that," Holly said, as they heard a siren coming down the street. "Daisy, come here." The dog padded over, and Holly picked up the leash again. "Good girl, good dog." Daisy nuzzled her leg.

"Now," the sergeant said, "you want to tell me what went down here?"

"Why don't we wait for homicide, so I won't have to do it twice?"

The sergeant produced a portable radio and asked that homicide detectives be sent to the address.

Holly led Marina out to the front porch to

wait. When the sergeant went to look around the house, Holly said, "Where is the notebook?"

"In the freezer," Marina replied.

"Let's leave it there."

The homicide detectives secured the scene and called for a crime-scene tech, then they came back outside. "Can I see your ID?" one of them asked Holly. He examined it carefully. "And where is Orchid Beach?"

"Up the coast a couple of hours."

"And what brings you to our jurisdiction, Chief?"

"I came to see Ms. Santos. When I arrived, the perp was threatening her."

"So you shot him?"

"Not right away, not until he went to his back for a gun."

"And how did you know he had a gun?"

"I saw the bulge under his shirt when his back was to me," she said. "I already had my hand on my weapon. I had told him to kneel and put his hands behind his head."

"Did you identify yourself as a police officer and show him your badge?"

"I identified myself as a police officer, but I had my dog in one hand and my weapon in the other, so I couldn't show him a badge right at that moment."

"I see. And you believed it was necessary to use deadly force?"

"His weapon is lying next to him," Holly said. "I haven't touched it."

"Why was the perp threatening Ms. Santos?"

"It appeared to be a robbery," Holly said. "When I arrived, the living room was in disarray, and his hand was drawn back as if to strike her."

"Was he looking for something specific, Ms. Santos?"

"I don't know," she replied innocently. "He was tearing up the living room when I walked in from the kitchen, and then Chief Barker arrived."

"Did you know him?"

"No, I've never seen him before."

"Was there anyone with the man?"

"When I arrived, there was a car parked out front with a Latino male at the wheel, reading something. After I fired, I heard the car start and leave in a hurry."

"Any further description?"

"Dark hair, a mustache, that's about all I could see. The car was a late-model Lincoln Town Car, black."

"Great," the detective said. "Not many of those around Lauderdale. Are you here on official business, Chief?" the detective asked.

"Yes. Ms. Santos was the fiancée of a man named Carlos Alvarez, who was murdered in my jurisdiction. I was here to discuss that with her."

"And what, exactly, did you discuss?"

"We didn't have time to discuss anything," Holly said.

"And what did you want to ask her?"

"I don't think that's relevant to your investigation of the homicide," Holly said.

"Well, I guess your internal affairs people are going to want to discuss this with you."

"We don't have an internal affairs division," Holly said.

"Lucky you."

"I'd like my weapon back as soon as you're done with it," Holly said, giving the detective her card.

"Sure. Now why don't you come inside and walk me through what happened?"

"Glad to, Detective."

The crime-scene tech handed the detective an open wallet. "Florida driver's license," he said.

"Ernesto Rodriguez," the detective read from the license. "Name sound familiar to either of you?" he asked Holly and Marina. Both shook their heads.

Two hours had passed before the corpse was taken away and the investigation completed. Holly went into the kitchen with Marina. "Now, the notebook, please," she said.

Marina went to the fridge, took an open bag of Tater Tots from the freezer, fished out the notebook, and handed it to Holly.

"Thank you," Holly said, putting it into her

damaged handbag. "What did the man say to you when he came inside?"

"He said he was a friend of Carlos, and he wanted his notebook. I told him I didn't know about a notebook, and he became angry and started to tear the place apart. Fortunately, you arrived about that time."

"Did he hit you?"

"No, he only pushed me against the wall, but he was about to hit me."

"Did you know him, Marina?"

"I've seen him in Pedro's shop," she said, "but I don't know his name."

"Often?"

"Just once. He was talking to Pedro in the office when I dropped in to see Carlos."

"Where is your mother?"

"She's working at the church today."

"We'd better get the living room cleaned up before she comes back. We don't want her to be frightened."

Marina nodded, and the two women went to work, restoring the room to its former appearance, except for the bloodstain on the carpet.

Marina got some spray carpet cleaner from the kitchen and was about to begin using it when Holly stopped her. "Do you have any disinfectant?"

"Yes, some Lysol."

"Better spray the stain well before you clean it. You never know about blood these days."

When the house was in order, Holly made to

leave. "Something else, Marina," she said.

"Yes?"

"You shouldn't speak to Pedro again. If he calls you, tell him you don't want to talk to him, and if he tries to see you, call the police."

"Why?"

"I believe he sent the man here today for the notebook, and since he doesn't have it, he'll still want it. I think Pedro was involved with whatever Carlos was doing. I'll speak to him and tell him to stay away from you."

"Thank you," Marina said.

"In the meantime, I think it's best if you and your mother leave the house for a few days. Rodriguez had a friend with him, and we don't want you to be here when he comes back. Is there somewhere you can go? A friend or relative that Pedro doesn't know?"

Marina thought about it. "My mother has a sister in Sarasota; we can go there."

"Does Pedro know about her?"

"No."

"Good. You'd better pack a bag for your mother and yourself and go pick her up at the church."

Holly waited until Marina was on her way, then got back in her car and drove away, heading for the locksmith's shop.

37

Holly found a parking spot a few doors from the locksmith's shop, then she took the notebook out of her bag. The dead body on the living room floor of Marina's house kept intruding into her thoughts, but she would think about that later. Right now, she wanted to see the notebook before she spoke to Pedro.

She took it from her handbag and opened it, turning the pages slowly. It was in the crudest kind of code; Carlos hadn't been all that smart. There were a series of three-digit numbers, followed by letters. Clearly, the numbers were dates, and the letters were initials. Apparently, Carlos had kept a record of the dates and people he dealt with from the time he got involved in his second job. Three of the dates corresponded to the shootings of the two Miami property dealers and the attempt on Ed Shine's life. TR was surely Trini Rodriguez, and PP Pio Pellegrino; PA was Pedro Alvarez, and he had been involved from the beginning. This was still not enough for arrests, not just yet. She changed her mind about speaking to Pedro and started her car. She was about to back out of her parking place when a car pulled into a spot in front of the locksmith's shop, and Trini Rodriguez got out and went inside. He looked angry. Holly switched off her engine.

Trini was in the shop no more than three minutes, and when he came out, he was in a hurry. Holly started her car again and followed him, keeping well back. She hoped he wouldn't notice the aerial on her car. As she followed Trini, driving west, the surroundings became less prosperous. Once past I-95, they became downright seedy. There was less traffic now, and she dropped back farther. Finally, Trini pulled off the road and stopped in front of a bar called Tricky's.

Holly drove straight past. A quarter of a mile down the road, she made a U-turn and stopped, still able to see the bar and Trini's car. She got out her cellphone and called Harry Crisp.

"What is it, Holly? I'm pretty busy."

"I'm pretty busy myself, Harry. I shot Trini Rodriguez's brother, or maybe cousin, earlier this afternoon, and now I'm tailing Trini. He's at a bar called Tricky's." She gave him the address.

"Did you say you shot somebody?"

"Shot him dead. I've already dealt with Lauderdale homicide. Carlos Alvarez left a notebook containing some incriminating information with his girlfriend, and Trini's brother went to try and beat it out of her. I got there in time."

"What do you mean 'incriminating information'?"

"He used a childish code, but it's apparently a record of his meetings with Trini, Pio Pellegrino, and Pedro Alvarez, plus the dates of the two murders and one attempt."

"That's plenty to bring them all in for questioning," Harry said.

"Not yet, Harry. This has got to lead somewhere, and I want to know where, don't you?"

"I can tell you where it's going to lead, Holly. It's going to lead to Central or South America, where the corporations are located that were bidding on the Palmetto Gardens property. Whoever is running this is out of the country, and we're never going to lay hands on them, so we'd better settle for who we can grab and convict."

"We don't have enough yet to convict anybody but Carlos Alvarez, and he's dead. What have you heard on the background check on Pio Pellegrino and his father? Any news on identifying their photographs?"

"Not yet; the lab is pretty busy."

"What I'd like you to do, Harry, is to get a team out to Tricky's and pick up the tail on Trini. I'm in a vehicle that is an obvious unmarked police car, and if I continue to follow him, he's going to make me, eventually."

"It's going to take me at least an hour, maybe two, to round up enough people and vehicles."

"He may be gone by then."

"Will you stay on him until we can relieve you?"

"I'll try, Harry, but it would help if you could get even one car out here, so we can swap positions from time to time."

"I'll do my best. You on your cellphone?"

"Yes."

"I'll get back to you." He hung up.

Holly sat, staring down the road at Tricky's, wondering whether Trini had business there or if he had just stopped in for a beer. It had to be business, she reckoned. Nobody would come out here for just a drink. She watched Trini's red Ford Explorer until, suddenly, it moved. She hadn't seen him come out of the bar. The car headed back in the direction they had come, and Holly followed, trying to keep a car or two between them.

Her phone rang. "Holly Barker."

"It's Harry. I've got two cars on the way up I-95. You still at Tricky's?"

"Nope, Trini is on the move. We're just coming up on I-95 now." She gave him the exit number. "Tell your guys to get off and follow me east. I'm in a tan Jeep Grand Cherokee with a big antenna on the back. I'll watch for them."

"I'll stay on the line until they've caught up," Harry said. "I'm in radio contact."

"I've got a radio, but I don't know if we're on the same frequencies."

"You're not," Harry said.

"Uh-oh, Trini just hung a right." She followed and gave Harry the street name.

"My guys are getting off the interstate now, headed east."

"Then they're probably a mile or so behind me. Tell them to step on it; they can slow down when they see me."

"Okay."

"Trini's turning left." She gave him the street name.

"One car thinks he has you in sight," Harry said.

"Tell him to pass me," Holly replied. "Hang on, Trini is stopping. Stand by." Holly drove slowly past Trini's Explorer and saw him go into a shooting range, a different one from where she had seen him before. She gave the name to Harry.

"Okay, we've got it. You get out of there," Harry said.

"Will do."

"Now, you and I have to meet; I want to see that notebook. You go back to I-95 and head south; I'll head north. There's a Burger King about twenty miles down the interstate." He gave her the exit number. "I'll meet you there in, oh hell, I don't know, half an hour, an hour?"

"I'll have a burger," Holly said. She hung up, made a couple of turns, and headed back toward I-95.

38

Holly was polishing off a double bacon cheese-burger when Harry walked in with another agent. He got something to eat and joined Holly, while the agent took another table.

"Why do you guys always have to look like FBI agents?" she asked him. "You'd think J. Edgar Hoover was still alive."

"You're not telling me he's dead, are you?" Harry asked, looking alarmed.

Holly laughed. "No kidding, the least you could do is dress like somebody who lives in Miami."

"I dress like a banker who lives in Miami," Harry said. "Let me see the notebook."

Holly put her bag on the table and fished it out.

Harry stuck his finger in the hole in her purse. "Did you forget to draw before you fired?"

"I didn't have time. I figure the FBI owes me a really good handbag."

"If I like the notebook, you can send me a bill," he replied, opening it.

"Look at the dates," she said. "He kept track of everything, along with who."

"I'll send it to our lab," Harry said, turning the pages. "They've got code people."

"Harry, a six-year-old could figure it out."

"They ought to see it anyway."

"Show it to a six-year-old!"

"Can we put Carlos with Pellegrino at any time?"

"Yes, his girlfriend was with Carlos when he stopped at the restaurant to see Pio. She stayed in the car, but they came out together after a few minutes and talked on the sidewalk."

"That's good. Will she testify?"

"I believe she will."

"Who made the silencers on Carlos's weapons?"

"I don't know," she said honestly, "but we don't need the mechanic; we've got the weapons."

"You're sure the guy who owns Miami Bullseye isn't in this?"

"He wouldn't have helped me if he were in it, and don't you go rousting him; he's a good guy."

"Okay, okay."

"Harry, do you ever have the feeling that this business is bigger than an attempt to buy a piece of real estate on the cheap?"

"No."

"Well, I do. I don't think they would have killed Carlos, otherwise. He did what he was paid to do, except that he missed my friend Ed Shine."

"If they'd wanted Shine dead, they'd have

tried again, but it got too late; he'd won the auction and bought the property. If they'd killed him, it would have gone into his estate, and not back to the General Services Administration."

"My point is, they must have killed Carlos because, alive, he could have led the law to them. I mean, down the road, he gets busted for something, and he gives them up for immunity or leniency."

"That makes sense, especially since Carlos was an outside contractor, not one of them."

"Makes you wonder how long Trini Rodriguez has to live, doesn't it?" Holly asked.

"Maybe Trini's an insider; who knows? They've had time to pop him, since he popped Carlos, but they haven't. Following him is going to have to produce something soon; I can't spare the manpower if it doesn't."

"I was going to ask you to put a team on Pedro Alvarez, too, but I guess there's not much chance of that, is there?"

"Not much. Why Pedro?"

"Because, according to the notebook, he's been in on this since the beginning. He had me thinking that Carlos was in it alone, but the notebook says different."

"Yeah, but he's an outsider, like Carlos; they're not going to let him know anything."

"I guess you're right," Holly admitted.

"I kind of like Trini, though. I think he might be worth the trouble," Harry said.

"He's going to be pissed off about his relative getting dead," Holly said.

"You think he knows you blew the guy away?"

"I don't see how he could," Holly said. "Not yet, anyway, not unless it makes the local papers."

Harry raised a finger, then produced his cellphone and a Palm Pilot and dialed a number. "This is Agent in Charge Harry Crisp," he said. "Let me speak to Captain Ames." A short wait. "Charlie? Harry Crisp. How goes it? Same here. Listen, I need your help on something. Earlier today, an out-of-town cop had a good shooting of a perp on your turf, a guy named Rodriguez. Yep, that's the one. Have you released anything to the papers yet? That's good. I'd appreciate it if, when you release it, you'd just say that a cop shot the guy and not identify her or where she's from. Because if you did that, it could put her in harm's way. She's working on something with us, and I don't want to get her killed. Can you handle that? Good, I owe you one, Charlie."

"Tell him I want my weapon back," Holly whispered.

"She says she needs her pistol back. Yeah, I'll tell her. Golf sometime? Call me." Harry hung up. "That's taken care of," he said. "You'll get your piece back if you promise not to shoot anybody else on his turf, and Trini won't know who shot his kinsman."

"Thank you, Harry."

"You're no use to me dead," he said.

"Oh, Harry, you're such a sentimentalist."

The agent at the other table answered his cellphone, then got up, walked across the room, and handed it to Harry.

"Harry Crisp."

"Yeah, when? Any other details? Thanks." He hung up and handed the phone to the agent, who returned to his table.

Harry was looking thoughtful.

"What?" Holly asked.

"Pedro Alvarez just got dead."

"How long ago?"

"An hour or so."

"Trini did it."

"That's a reasonable assumption," Harry said.

"It isn't an assumption," Holly replied. "After I left Marina's house, I wanted to talk to Pedro; I parked outside and started reading the notebook first, and while I was waiting, Trini drove up, got out, went into Pedro's shop, stayed three minutes, then left. That's when I started following him. Let me guess: one or two shots from a small-caliber pistol equipped with a silencer."

"You're right up to a point," Harry said. "We won't know all until somebody digs the slugs out of him. Sounds like Trini's cleaning house, doesn't it? You think Marina's in danger?"

"I've already sent her out of town. My guess is, one reason Trini went to the shop was to find out where she was, and Pedro didn't know."

"Where is she?"

"At her mother's sister's in Sarasota. Or at least, she's on the way. I stayed with her until she left the house. I'll bet Trini was there moments later, because he got to Pedro's shop almost as fast as I did."

Harry was looking at her funny.

"What, Harry?"

"You think maybe Pedro told Trini about you? They had to be talking about something for the three minutes they were together."

"Harry, I'm afraid you have a point."

"Holly, go home. Get out of here right now, and I think you ought to have an officer with you every hour of the day."

"I don't think that's —"

"Holly, you met Trini at Miami Bullseye."

"Yeah, but he didn't know who I was."

"He probably does now; and he knows what you look like."

"Well, you're going to have to pick up Trini now; that should be easy, since you've already got a team on him."

"We'll notify Lauderdale PD that we have a witness in the murder, and we'll give them his location. They'll pick him up, then we'll get our turn at questioning him about our matter. In the meantime, this is what I want you to do," Harry said. "My agent over there is going to follow you up I-95, toward home. You call your office and get somebody to meet you halfway and relieve him."

"Thanks, Harry, but —"

"Just do it, Holly. I've got my own car outside, I'll get back to the office okay. You're going to need protection until Trini is in the Lauderdale lockup."

"All right, Harry, and thanks. I owe you one."

"Makes a nice change, doesn't it?" Harry said.

That night, alone in bed, an officer parked outside her house, Holly allowed herself to think about what she'd been avoiding. She'd killed a human being that day. She didn't stop crying until she was asleep.

39

Howard Singleton, head of the Miami office of the federal General Services Administration, opened the file on his desk and started reading. Halfway through the document he stopped and scratched his head. This was like going to a movie he had already seen. He got up, took the file, and walked down the corridor to the office of Willard Smith, his deputy.

"Smitty, have you read this?" he asked, tossing the file onto Smith's desk.

Smith looked at it. "I wrote it," he said.

"Doesn't this sound familiar to you? Except this time, we're talking about a South Beach property instead of that thing up the coast at . . . what's the name?"

"You mean the Orchid Beach property?"

"Yeah, that's the one — Palmetto something."

"Palmetto Gardens."

"Yeah. I mean, it's the same pattern; we're getting lowball bids out of Central America, but not much local. Next thing you know, some prospective bidder is going to get himself killed, just like before."

"Jesus, Howard, we just advertise these properties, remember? We're not the FBI."

Singleton looked at his watch. "I've got to go to a meeting at my church at five, so I have to leave now. Will you call that guy at the FBI — Harry something . . ."

"Crisp."

"Yeah, call him and tell him I think we're developing a similar situation to the Palmetto Gardens property, and I thought he ought to know about it."

"Sure, Howard." Willard Smith picked up the phone and started dialing.

Singleton went to the meeting at his church, which lasted an hour and a half, then he made for home, digging out a shopping list his wife had given him at breakfast. He was the last to leave the parking lot, which was empty now, except for his car and a red Explorer parked near the exit. He had to make three stops to fill his wife's list — the grocery store for tonic water and limes, the liquor store for wine, and someplace for cocktail napkins. They were giving a dinner party that evening. As he put the car into gear, he began planning his route home.

Then, as he approached the parking lot exit, the red Explorer suddenly drove across his path and stopped. Singleton slammed on his brakes, just short of smashing into the car. "What the hell?" he said aloud. He started to reach for his door handle when he saw the darkened window on the front passenger side slide down. He stopped and looked at the figure behind the wheel, who seemed to be leaning over to the passenger window, as if to say something to him.

But the man said nothing. Instead, he held out his hand, and the windshield of Howard Singleton's car turned white, except for the two holes in front of the driver's seat.

Singleton didn't have time to think about anything else.

Trini Rodriguez exited the parking lot, driving at a normal pace. When he was a block away, he pressed a speed-dial button on his car phone.

"Yeah?" a man's voice said.

"Bingo," Trini said.

"And not a moment too soon," the man replied, then hung up.

Harry Crisp arrived at his office at eight forty-five A.M., as he did habitually. Coffee was already made in the little kitchenette off his waiting room, and he poured himself a cup. He didn't mind asking his secretary to come in early and make coffee for him, but he always poured it himself, for appearances' sake. He went back to his desk and picked up his copy of the *New York Times* national edition, scanning it quickly for stories related to federal law enforcement in general, and the Miami office of the FBI in particular. There was a knock at his open door, and he looked up. One of his agents stood there.

"Morning," Harry said. "What's up?"

"A federal official was murdered in Miami last evening," the agent said.

"Who?"

"Howard Singleton, head of the local office of the GSA."

"What were the circumstances?"

"He left work half an hour early yesterday afternoon, in order to get to a five-o'clock meeting at his church. As he left the meeting in his car, about six-thirty, somebody fired two rounds through the windshield, into his head."

"What kind of rounds?"

"Small caliber, according to the Miami PD."

"Jesus, there's a real epidemic of small-round shootings in South Florida, isn't there?"

"No more than usual, really. What do you want me to do about this?"

"Send a man over to Miami PD to get a copy of the file. We'll keep track of the PD investigation and not get any more involved than we have to. Send a memo to D.C. saying that we're on it."

"Okay. Say, did Lauderdale PD pick up Trini Rodriguez yesterday?"

"Yeah. We gave them a heads-up and his location, then I pulled the tail off him."

"It didn't exactly work out that way, Harry."

"What do you mean?"

"I mean, he made the tail and lost our guys."

"Oh, shit. Call Lauderdale and find out if they got him."

"Will do." The agent left. Harry's secretary buzzed. "There's a man named Willard Smith, from the GSA, on line one."

"Why do I want to talk to him?"

"His boss is the man who was shot last night."

"Oh, yeah." Harry picked up the phone. "Harry Crisp."

"Mr. Crisp, this is Willard Smith at the General Services Administration."

I know that, dummy, Harry thought. "What can I do for you, Mr. Smith?"

"Well, as I expect you know, my boss, Howard Singleton, was murdered after work yesterday."

"Yes, I know; we've got a full investigative team on that right now."

"I've been made acting director, pending the appointment of a new one," Willard Smith said, "and I just wanted you to know that we certainly want to cooperate in any possible way with your investigation."

"Thank you, Mr. Smith. Can you think of anything that Mr. Singleton was working on that might have involved criminal activity? Maybe something like the Palmetto Gardens thing that got those two Miami developers killed?"

"No, not a thing," Smith said. "Everything has been quite routine, lately. We're still working on getting you more office space, of course."

"Thanks, I appreciate that. Well, we'll let you

240

know if you can be of help," Harry said. "Goodbye, Mr. Smith."

"Goodbye, Mr. Crisp."

Harry hung up. "Denise," he called to his secretary, "did my copy of *Golf Digest* arrive yet?"

"Not yet, Mr. Crisp."

"Be sure you put it on my desk the minute it comes in."

"Sure, I will, just like always."

Good girl, Harry thought. He turned back to his *New York Times*. The Singleton killing hadn't made the deadline, he noted, reading the National Report. Maybe tomorrow. By that time, Miami PD would have some jealous husband in custody, and he could forget about it.

When the agent came to report back to Harry, he had left the office. The agent left a note on his desk.

40

Holly put in a full day at the station, meeting with each of the four officers Hurd Wallace had chosen to take over his duties. At the end of the day, she drove home and was looking in the fridge for something to eat when Daisy was suddenly on her feet, growling, looking at the door to the beach.

Holly grabbed her 9mm and walked to the door, the weapon held at her side. She turned the knob slowly, then kicked open the door and stepped outside.

Grant Early was lying in the sand, a bottle of wine beside him. "Hey, is this how you always greet a neighbor? I was about to knock when the door hit me."

Holly offered a hand and helped him to his feet. "I'm sorry, Grant, it's been a little tense around here."

He picked up the bottle and dusted off the sand. "I just thought you might like some dinner."

"I feel like pizza; that okay with you?"

"Sure, I'll order. Anything you don't like on your pizza?"

"I like everything but green peppers; I *hate* green peppers."

Grant picked up the phone and called in the order. "So why are things so tense?"

"Long story," Holly said.

Grant began opening the wine. "I've got all the time in the world." He poured them both a glass, and they went to the sofa and sat down.

"Okay, yesterday I shot and killed a man; he has a relative who might have taken it badly. Fortunately, Harry already had a tail on him, and he told me Lauderdale PD picked him up yesterday, but I guess I'm still a little spooked."

"Are you okay?"

"I'm fine."

"I mean, are you okay with the shooting?"

"It was a good shooting; I'm getting over it."

"I know how that feels," Grant said. "The first man I killed haunted me for a long time."

"There was more than one?"

"Two. They were both good shootings, but it was still hard to live with. You might want to talk to somebody."

"I'm talking to you," she said.

"I was thinking of somebody more professional," Grant said.

"Who's more professional than you? You understand it a lot better than any shrink would."

"Tell me about it."

"I got a call yesterday from a woman who had some evidence in my case. I drove down to Lauderdale to get it, and when I walked into her house, somebody else was already there, wanting it too. He tried to draw down on me, and I shot him once, middle of the target. Blew a hole through my handbag."

"Did you play it by the book with the local cop shop?"

"I did."

"Then you're in the clear."

"Yeah, Harry called some captain there for me, asked them not to put my name in the paper, just in case Trini read about it."

"Who?"

"Trini Rodriguez."

Grant sat up. "Holy shit."

"Huh?"

"You killed his brother?"

"Or his cousin; don't know for sure."

"He had a brother, Ernesto."

"That's the one. How do you know about Trini?"

"The Rodriguez brothers are famous, in certain circles," Grant said.

"What circles?"

"Enforcement circles."

"What kind of enforcement?"

"Loan collections, used to be. Last I heard they'd branched out into contractual work."

"Hit men?"

"Yes, but nothing too refined."

"Not like anything that required accuracy with a rifle?"

"Nothing like that, requiring any sort of finesse; more the kind, like, walking up to some-body and shooting him in the head. They're remorseless killers. Does Trini know you shot Ernesto?"

"Maybe, I'm not sure. You remember I told you about Pedro Alvarez? My floater's cousin?"

"Sure."

"I was sitting outside Pedro's shop when Trini walked inside, stayed two or three minutes, came out, and drove away. Later, I was sitting with Harry at a Burger King when we heard that Pedro had been popped, and the time was about when I was sitting outside Pedro's shop."

"You think Pedro told him about you?"

"I think if Trini asked, Pedro told him. I actu-ally met Trini, sort of, at the firing range, so he'd remember my face, though he wouldn't know my name."

"But Pedro knew your name and where you were from."

"Yes."

"Well, Trini and Pedro were talking about *something* for those two or three minutes."

"I figure Trini heard about Ernesto's getting dead, and he went to Marina's house, then, when she wasn't there, he went to Pedro's shop to find out where she was."

"Did Pedro know where Marina was?"

"No."

"He probably wanted to know who shot Ernesto, too."

"Yeah, but Pedro didn't know I was involved.

He wouldn't even have known Ernesto was dead; it was too soon."

"Where is Marina?"

"With her mother and her mother's sister, in Sarasota."

"Did Pedro know about the mother's sister?"

"Marina says not."

"Would Marina ever have told Carlos about her mother's sister?"

"I don't know, but Carlos is dead."

"What was this evidence you went to get from Marina?"

"A notebook with a lot of incriminating information in it."

"Incriminating for Trini?"

"Yes."

"Where's the notebook now?"

"Harry has it. He may have sent it to Washington."

"Let's recap: Trini may know who you are and where you're from, right?"

"Right, but it's okay; Lauderdale picked him up yesterday."

"Trini has colleagues. Are you in the phone book?"

"No. But . . ." Holly had just thought of something.

"What?"

"Carlos broke into my house and bugged my phones; he was probably reporting to Trini."

The doorbell rang, and they both jumped.

"It's gotta be the pizza," Grant said.

The doorbell rang again. "Pizza delivery!" somebody shouted from outside.

"I'll get it," Holly said.

"No, I'll get it," Grant replied, getting up.

Holly handed him her pistol. "If it has green peppers on it, shoot him."

"I don't think that will be necessary." Grant set the pistol on the coffee table, went to the door, cracked it, and peered out. "It's pizza," he said. Then Grant flew backward as somebody kicked open the door.

41

The deliveryman stepped into the room, a pizza in one hand and a small submachine gun in the other. Daisy hit him from the side, knocking him off his feet, just as he began to fire.

Grant grabbed for the weapon and diverted it from where Holly sat. She grabbed her pistol from the coffee table and fired twice at the deliveryman, aiming as much away from Daisy and Grant as she could. The pizza man stopped firing, and Grant held up a hand. "Hold your fire!"

Holly ran around the sofa, her gun still pointed at the man. As she kicked his weapon away from him, more fire erupted from outside the house. "Stay, Daisy!" she yelled. She didn't want the dog to run outside and directly into fire. She flattened herself against the door jamb and took a quick look outside, snatching her head back. As she did, she heard the spinning of tires on gravel and saw the shadow of a car heading up her driveway toward A1A.

"Pizza man's dead," Grant said. "Are you okay?"

"Fine," Holly panted, "how about you?"

"My pride is wounded, nothing else. How could I let that happen?"

"We were expecting pizza," Holly said. She looked out the door again. "Seems to be all clear."

"Where's the real pizza guy?" Grant asked.

"Oh, no," Holly said, stepping outside. She ran to the driveway and saw a car parked near the top. As she approached it, gun in hand, a figure got out of the car. "Freeze, police!" she yelled. And the figure stopped moving.

She came closer and found a young man holding his head, which was bleeding. "Who are you?" she demanded.

"Pizza delivery," he said. "What happened?"

"You come with me," she said, taking his arm and pulling him down the driveway.

Finally, the police, the ambulance, the crime-scene tech, the medical examiner, the pizza man, and the corpse had left the house.

"Jesus, what an evening," Grant said, picking up the pizza and examining it. "You know, I think the pizza is okay; shall I stick it in the oven?"

"Considering we nearly died for it, it would be a shame to waste it," Holly replied.

Grant turned on the oven and put the pizza in to warm up.

Holly was examining the row of bullet holes in the bar counter that separated the kitchen from the living room. "I think I'll leave these," she said. "They're kind of cute. I mean, who else has bullet holes as part of their decor?"

"I'm glad they're in the counter, instead of us," Grant said, retrieving his wineglass. "Or the wine bottle. I think I need this right now." He took a deep draft of the wine.

"Me too," Holly said. "That's two people I've killed. So Trini has friends, huh?"

"It would appear so."

Holly picked up the phone. "What was Harry's home number again?" Grant gave it to her, and she dialed.

"Hello?" Harry sounded terrible.

"You sick?"

"Terrible cold," Harry said. "I didn't go in today. What's up?"

"Tell me Trini Rodriguez is in the Lauderdale jail."

"I assume so. Like I said, I didn't go in today. Why?"

"Because two guys with Uzis visited me tonight."

"Are you okay, Holly?"

"Barely. One of the shooters is dead, and one is being sought."

"Anybody else hurt?"

"A pizza deliveryman got a lump on the head, that's all."

"Let me call you right back," Harry said.

Holly hung up the phone. "Harry has a cold; home in bed. He's going to call back."

Three minutes later, the phone rang. "It's

Harry. Lauderdale PD didn't get Trini; he's at large."

"I'll call my department," she said. "You call the state police and have them look for him on I-95 South. My guess is he's headed toward home. And I'd stake out that bar Tricky's, too."

"I'll take care of that. Let's talk tomorrow." Harry hung up.

Holly called her department and gave Trini's description to the duty officer, with instructions to radio it to all cars.

"Pizza's hot, I think," Grant said, pulling it from the oven and putting it on a platter.

They sat down to eat.

"Who did you tell your cops I am?"

"A neighbor," she said. "Your cover is still intact. You ready to tell me what you're working on yet?"

"No can do; nothing has changed in that regard."

"Have some more wine," Holly said, pouring him some. "Then we'll talk about it."

"Wine will not loosen my tongue."

"*In vino veritas,*" she said.

"Not yet. You're exciting to know," he said.

"Thanks; you're pretty dull."

"What do you mean, dull?"

"The most interesting thing about a person is often his work," she said. "And I don't know anything about yours."

"I've regaled you with stories from my undercover past," he said. "Isn't that enough?"

"And I've given you my body; doesn't that count for something?"

"It counts for a very great deal," Grant said. "In fact, once or twice, when you were giving it especially well, I nearly blurted out everything. You want to try again?"

"I'm eating pizza," she said. "It's hard to give your body and eat pizza at the same time."

"Later?"

"We'll see."

"Listen, when we've eaten, I want you to pack a bag and come home with me."

"Why?"

"If it was Trini out there, I wouldn't be surprised if he comes back."

"You have a point," she said, kissing him and leaving tomato sauce on his mouth.

"He's not going to stop trying, you know. He has a reputation for persistence."

"I'm sorry to hear it."

"Don't be sorry, be safe," he said, kissing her back.

"Listen, if we're going to keep exchanging tomato sauce, let's do it at your place."

"Pack a bag, and pack Daisy a bag, too. Enough for a couple of days, or until they find Trini, whichever comes first."

Soon, they were walking hand in hand up the beach toward Grant's house, with Daisy gamboling in the dunes. Holly had the gun in her other hand, all the way.

42

Holly was in her office reading about the death of Howard Singleton when Harry called.

"I want to bring you up to date," he said.

"You still sound terrible, Harry. Are you at work?"

"Yes, but soon I'm going home and to bed."

"Okay, bring me up to date."

"Nobody has found Trini Rodriguez so far, but there's a statewide APB out for him; sooner or later he'll turn up."

"I hope he doesn't turn up on my doorstep again," Holly said.

"Grant gave me an account of the evening. Sounds like you saved his neck."

"I'm always happy to pull the FBI out of it. By the way, have you seen this morning's Miami papers?"

"No."

"The head guy at the GSA, Singleton, got hit yesterday."

"I know about that."

"It's got to be related to the Palmetto Gardens thing."

"It's not. I spoke to Singleton's deputy yester-

253

day, a guy named Willard Smith. He says they weren't working on anything similar. My guess is a jealous husband."

"Yeah? Well, my guess is Trini Rodriguez."

"Why would Trini and his people want Singleton dead?"

"I think that would be a real good thing for the FBI to figure out, Harry. A federal employee is dead, and that puts it right in your lap, doesn't it?"

"I prefer to let the local cops lead on things like this, unless there's a pressing reason for it to go federal."

"Call Singleton's replacement and ask him if he wants to be next; that might get him thinking about why the man was killed."

"I told you, I've already talked to him, and they aren't working on anything remotely related to this other stuff."

"Harry, can I remind you that we don't know what the hell this other stuff is about?"

"Not yet."

"If we don't know what it's about, how do we know that Singleton's killing wasn't related? I think his death ought to be on the federal front burner."

"You'll have to let me make that judgment, Holly; it's what I do."

"You are the most exasperating man," she said.

"You sound like my wife."

"Listen to her, Harry." Holly hung up. She thought for a minute, then called information and got the number for the Miami office of the General Services Administration and dialed it. Shortly, she had Willard Smith on the line.

"My name is Holly Barker, Mr. Smith. I'm chief of police in Orchid Beach, Florida, up the coast."

"What can I do for you, Chief?" He sounded in a hurry.

"It appears that the death of Howard Singleton might be related to a case I'm working on up here."

"And what case would that be?"

"Perhaps you'll recall that there were two murders and another attempt that were related to your office's auction of the Palmetto Gardens property?"

"I know about that. Listen, I've already talked to the FBI about that."

"I know; I've just talked to Harry Crisp."

"Then your question must be the same as his?"

"Yes. Is there anything at all you're working on that sounds like the Palmetto Gardens deal?"

"Nothing."

"You mean you have no confiscated properties for sale?"

"All the time, Chief, but not like that one. In that case, we appeared to have lowball bidders who had been killing off the competition, but when they failed to kill Mr. Shine and the sale to him went through, they had no further reason to kill people."

"But what I'm asking is, is there another sale pending which might attract the same sorts of bidders?"

"You mean a criminal element?"

"Yes."

"Absolutely not. I've been through every sale on Howard's desk — and incidentally, I was the one who put those sales on his desk — and neither Howard nor I has spotted anything remotely similar to the Palmetto Gardens case. I've been reviewing the files again this morning, just to be sure, and there's nothing. Now, if you'll forgive me, I have a great deal of work to do today."

"Will you call me if something similar comes up?"

"I will certainly do that, Chief," he said, then hung up.

And he didn't even take my number, Holly thought.

Her phone rang; it was the medical examiner.

"Morning," she said. "I hope you've done the autopsy on our shooter of last evening."

"I have, and he died of two gunshot wounds to the chest, both from your weapon."

"Anything else?"

"He had amalgam dental fillings, just like the other one."

"So he's Cuban?"

"I don't think so."

"Why not, if the fillings are the same?"

"Well, he's blond and blue-eyed, for one thing."

"Aren't there any blond and blue-eyed Cubans?"

"I've never encountered one. And there's something else."

"What?"

"He had a tattoo on his left bicep that looks military to me."

"American military? Like a regimental symbol?"

"Like that, but not American. There was a legend underneath that was in letters of the Cyrillic alphabet."

"You mean, like Russian?"

"Yes."

"There were a lot of Russians in Cuba at one time, weren't there?"

"Yes, military advisors. I believe they were advising on how to assemble medium-range ballistic missiles. But that was back in the sixties, and this guy is in his early- to mid-thirties."

"Could it be a Cuban outfit?"

"Then the legend would be in Spanish, wouldn't it?"

"You have a point," she admitted.

"The tattoo is of crossed daggers, and I had the legend translated. It says, 'Blood and Loyalty.' "

"Send me a photo of the tattoo, will you?"

"It's already on the way."

"Anything else about the guy that was unusual?"

"I think he might have been a boxer — or at

least someone who has taken a beating on more than one occasion. He had a broken nose — twice, according to the X-rays — and some broken ribs that had healed, too. I've sent his prints along with the photo."

"Thanks, Doc." She hung up and tried to figure out why a Russian might be involved in this.

43

Holly drove to Grant's house after work, an unmarked car following her. She had arranged for around-the-clock cops to be parked outside.

She entered the house to wonderful smells of cooking. "Hello there," she called.

"Dinner's in half an hour," Grant called back.

"Mmmm," she said, sniffing the air and kissing him. "Did you ever do an undercover job as a chef?"

"Short-order cook once, for a week. The worst work I've ever had to do; it nearly put me off food."

She fed and walked Daisy, and came back to the house. "I'm going to grab a shower while you're finishing dinner," she said.

When she came back downstairs, dinner was on the table — a risotto with shrimp and asparagus, and a lovely chardonnay.

"So, how was your day?" Grant asked.

"Not bad. The ME called, said the dead pizza guy was Russian."

"How could they tell? Was he carrying a passport?"

"No ID at all, but he had amalgam fillings,

which you don't find in this country anymore, and he had a Russian military tattoo." She described it to him.

Grant shook his head. "Blood and loyalty. I've never heard of anything like that. Crossed daggers doesn't sound military, either; crossed swords, maybe."

"I saw a photograph; it's definitely daggers."

"Send it to Harry; he can run it against the Bureau's files."

"Good idea."

"You run the guy's prints?"

"Yes, but we came up with nothing."

"If he's an immigrant on a visa, his prints should be on file with INS. Tomorrow, run them against their files. They may not have gotten passed on to the Bureau yet."

"Thanks for the suggestion."

Grant started clearing the table, and Holly helped. Then her cellphone rang.

"Hello?"

"Miss Barker?" The voice was female and quavering.

"Yes, who's this?"

"It's Marina Santos."

"Is something wrong, Marina?"

"I went to the grocery store, and when I came back . . ." Her voice broke, and she seemed unable to go on.

"Marina, what is it? Tell me."

"My mother and my aunt are dead."

"Oh, God."

"There was blood all over the kitchen; they were shot."

"Marina, where are you now?"

"I'm on my cellphone in my car, parked on the street outside my aunt's house."

"What's the address?"

Marina gave it to her, and Holly wrote it down. "All right, Marina, here's what I want you to do. I want you to start your car and drive away — don't hang up. When you drive away, check your rearview mirror to see if anyone is following you. Now, go ahead."

"All right."

Holly heard the car start.

"I'm driving down the street, and no one is behind me."

"All right, give me your cellphone number." Holly wrote it down. "Now, I want you to go to a public place, very well lighted, like a supermarket parking lot, and park right in front of a big store. I'm going to call the police, and then I'll call you back with further instructions."

"All right," Marina said.

Holly hung up and called Ham's house.

"Yo," Ham said.

"It's me," Holly said. "Is Ginny there?"

"You don't want to talk to your old man?"

"Not right now, old man; let me talk to Ginny."

Ginny came on. "Hi, Holly, what's up?"

"Ginny, can you fly me to Sarasota?"

"Sure, when?"

"Right this minute; it's urgent."

"All right."

"Tell me the name of the closest airport; we're going to pick up a passenger."

"It's called Sarasota-Bradenton, and it's near the north-south interstate, north of Sarasota. You can tell your passenger we'll meet him at Dolphin Aviation."

Holly heard Ham speak up in the background. "Tell her I'm coming, too."

"Tell Ham to come armed," Holly said. "I'll see you at the airport, just as fast as I can get there."

"Right."

Holly hung up. "I've got to fly to Sarasota; Trini has killed my witness's mother and aunt."

"Jesus," Grant said. "I'm coming with you."

"Drive me to the airport," Holly said. "I don't know how much room there is in the airplane."

"Hang on." Grant went upstairs and came back putting on a jacket over a shoulder holster.

"Daisy, you stay here and be a good girl," Holly said.

Daisy put her head on the floor, but watched them as they left.

In the car, Holly called Marina back.

"Hello?"

"Marina, are you all right?"

"Yes, but I'm very scared."

"Do you know how to get to the Sarasota-Bradenton Airport?"

"No."

"Do you know how to get to the interstate?"

"Yes, I can see it from here."

"Get on the interstate going north and look for signs to the airport. When you get there, find a place called Dolphin Aviation and wait for me there; I'm flying in."

"Dolphin Aviation?"

"If you can't find it, ask. You'll get there before I will, so just go inside and make yourself comfortable. Tell them you're being picked up if they show any interest in you."

"All right."

"And keep your cellphone with you."

"All right."

Holly hung up, called the Sarasota Police Department, and asked for the duty commander.

"This is Lieutenant Brower," a voice said.

"Lieutenant, this is Chief of Police Holly Barker, from Orchid Beach, Florida."

"Where is that?"

"Directly across the state from you, east coast."

"Oh, yeah, I've got it on the map. What can I do for you, Chief?"

"I've just learned about a double homicide in your city." Holly gave him the address.

"How did you hear about it?"

"The person who found the body called me."

"Why didn't he call us?"

"There are very good reasons, Lieutenant," she said. "The FBI are on this, too. The person who found the bodies didn't witness anything.

263

I'll get back to you so you can talk to the witness later. In the meantime, I'm responsible for that person's safety, and I'm taking steps." Holly gave him her cellphone number. "You can reach me on that number later tonight or tomorrow morning at my office."

"All right, Chief."

"Now, listen. The shooter is very likely a man named Trini Rodriguez." She gave him a complete description. "He may be hanging out in the neighborhood, waiting for my witness to come home. He drives a red Ford Explorer sometimes."

"We'll keep an eye out for him."

"He's wanted for murder in Fort Lauderdale, and the FBI want him, too. He'll be armed and extremely dangerous."

"What is your witness's name?"

"I'll let you know about that when the witness is secure. Goodbye." She hung up. "Step on it, Grant," she said. "Don't worry about getting a ticket."

Grant stepped on it.

At the airport, Ginny was waiting beside a larger airplane than the one Holly had flown. "We'll take the Saratoga," she said, "since we've got so many people."

Holly introduced Grant to Ginny and Ham.

Ham looked Grant up and down, then turned to Holly. "Are you two . . . ?"

"Shut up, Ham, and get in the airplane."

44

Holly was in the pilot's seat, taking instruction, and she spotted the airport beacon, flashing green and white. "I have the airport," she said.

"Good," Ginny replied. "The automated weather tells us the wind is three-zero-zero at six knots, so we're landing on runway thirty-two."

"I see the runway lights," Holly said.

"And which one is thirty-two?"

Holly looked at her compass. "The one going left and right."

"Good. Now switch on your landing lights." She pointed at the switch. "Make a normal approach, just like with the Warrior. This is a heavier airplane, and it will take more of a pull on the yoke when you flare. This is a night landing, and the thing about a night landing is that it feels as if you're a little higher than you really are, so expect the gear to touch down sooner than you think."

Holly announced her intentions on the radio and was cleared to land. She reduced speed, put down the landing gear, and followed the landing check, as Ginny read it to her from the checklist.

"You're a little high and hot," Ginny said, "but you've got plenty of runway. A little less throttle."

Holly made the adjustment and landed a little harder than she'd expected to.

"That's a night landing for you," Ginny said.

Following Ginny's instructions, Holly taxied to Dolphin Aviation and went through the shutdown checklist. When the propeller had stopped, a lineman chocked the nosewheel, and everybody got out.

"You a cop?" Ham asked Grant as they walked toward the Dolphin lobby.

"Nah," Grant said.

"Then how come you're packing?"

"Seemed like a good idea," Grant said, grinning.

"Well, yeah," Ham said.

Holly led the way into the lounge and looked around. Empty. The reception desk was unmanned. Holly unholstered her gun, and Grant and Ham followed suit.

"I'm going to the ladies' room," Ginny said, "and I'm not coming out until the shooting stops." She headed off.

"Grant, will you check the pilot's lounge, down that hallway? Ham, you come with me." She led him through the front doors and out into the parking lot. "There," she said, pointing at Marina's little Ford. "That's hers."

The two approached the car with caution and

checked the inside. The driver's door was un-locked.

"Better check the trunk," Ham said.

Holly found the trunk release and heard it pop open. She walked to the rear of the car, her heart in her mouth, lifted the trunk lid, and looked inside. A spare tire, nothing else. Holly looked around the lot for a red Explorer but didn't see one.

"What do you think?" Ham asked.

"I don't know what to think," Holly said, heading back inside. She got out her cellphone and was dialing Marina's number when Ginny came out of the ladies' room with Marina fol-lowing.

Holly walked over and hugged her. "I'm so glad you're all right," she said.

"Mama and Tia Rosita are not all right," Ma-rina replied.

"I'm so sorry, Marina."

"It was Trini, wasn't it?"

"Probably. How did he know where you were? Did you tell anyone?"

"It had to be Pedro," she said. "He must have known more than I thought."

Holly didn't tell her that Pedro was dead, too. She was upset enough already. "I'm going to take you where you'll be safe," she said, "and my policemen will protect you." She led Marina outside toward the Saratoga.

"An airplane?" Marina asked. "I've never flown in an airplane."

"It's fun," Holly said. "Ginny is a great pilot. And I want you to meet my father, Ham, and my friend Grant."

Marina solemnly shook hands with everyone.

Holly and Grant sat in the rear seats with Marina, and Ham sat in the copilot's seat. Marina seemed nervous at first, but she soon relaxed and watched as the lights of the Sarasota-Bradenton area grew scarce, giving way to the lights of small towns and farms. She said nothing for the remainder of the flight.

Finally back at Grant's house, they gave Marina some soup.

"Why did Trini do it?" Marina asked.

"Because he's a mad-dog killer," Holly replied. "The police and the FBI are looking for him everywhere right now, and they'll find him soon."

"I don't have any clothes," Marina said.

"We'll get you some new ones tomorrow," Holly replied. "You look tired; would you like to go to bed now?"

Marina nodded dumbly.

Holly led her to Grant's spare bedroom and got her settled, then came back downstairs.

"What a beautiful girl," Grant said.

"She's had more than her share of heartbreak in the past week," Holly said. "I don't think she's feeling very beautiful now." She went to the phone and called the Sarasota police.

"Lieutenant Brower."

"Lieutenant, it's Holly Barker."

"Hello, Chief. We've worked our crime scene; two dead, as you reported. Looks like executions; he used a nine-millimeter."

"Any sightings of Rodriguez?"

"Not a thing. Where's my witness?"

"Asleep. You can talk to her on the phone tomorrow, unless you'd like to come to Orchid Beach."

"It's a woman?"

"The daughter of one of your victims and the niece of the other."

"You're satisfied she had nothing to do with their deaths?"

"Yes. They went to Sarasota to hide from Rodriguez. Somehow he found them, but Marina was at the grocery store when the shootings took place."

"I faxed the FBI in Miami the report, since you said they wanted Rodriguez, too."

"That was the right thing to do. I'll call you tomorrow morning, and you can talk to Marina Santos."

"Thank you. Good night."

Holly hung up and went to bed, happy to have Grant to sleep next to.

45

Holly took Marina to her office the following morning. She put her in Hurd Wallace's empty office, called Lieutenant Brower in Sarasota, and put Marina on the phone with him. She gave instructions to check the dead Russian's prints against the INS database, then faxed the photograph of his tattoo to Harry Crisp. Then she called in a policewoman, who was in civilian clothes, and gave her some money.

"I've got a witness in Hurd's old office; her name is Marina Santos. I want you to take her out to the outlet mall and buy her enough clothes for four or five days."

"Yes, ma'am," the woman said.

"I want you to go armed. Someone is trying to kill her, and although he's unlikely to look for her at the outlet mall, you should be alert." She gave the officer Trini Rodriguez's description. "It may not be him; he has friends."

Holly introduced the two women and let them get on with their shopping trip.

Hurd Wallace, slightly itchy in his new uniform, drove slowly around the Blood Orchid property, taking in everything. Two houses were in the early stages of construction, and others were being renovated, with workmen going in and out. The golf courses were beautiful, he thought; he didn't play golf, but maybe it was time to take up the game, since membership in the golf club was part of his compensation package. As he passed the ninth hole, he saw Ed Shine playing with a Hispanic man, who seemed never to have played before, and Ed waved him over.

"How's it going, Hurd?"

"Everything's fine, Mr. Shine."

"Call me Ed; everyone does."

"We seem to be in good shape, Ed."

"You meet your new employees?"

"Yes, one's on the gate, and the other is back at the station, manning the phones."

"When is your first golf lesson?"

"I haven't scheduled anything yet."

"Start soon; the pro is bored rigid."

"I'll do that, Ed. See you later." Hurd drove on past the empty tennis courts, then turned and went out to the airfield. A King Air twin turboprop, belonging to Shine, was the sole aircraft parked there. Then, as he watched, a business jet came whistling in and landed on the six-thousand-foot runway. A large van bearing the Blood Orchid logo drove up, just in time to meet the airplane as it taxied in. Hurd saw a group of four men, all accompanied by rather flashy women, disembark and be greeted by the salesman. They all piled into the van, while the airplane's crew stowed their luggage in the rear, then they drove off, just another group arriving to hear Ed Shine's sales pitch. They'd be put up in the guest cottages and would, no doubt, be on the golf course by mid-afternoon.

Hurd drove back to his office and parked the Range Rover. One of his two officers sat, his feet on the desk, obviously talking to a woman. Hurd pushed his feet off the desk to get his attention, and the officer put his hand over the phone.

"Yeah, what is it?" he asked irritably.

"Hang up the phone; you're at work."

"I'll call you back, baby," the man said, then hung up.

"Not from the office, you won't," Hurd said, "and not from a patrol car, either. Talk to her on your own time; right now, you're at work."

"There isn't any work," the man said.

"Then find a broom and sweep up," Hurd said, going into his office. The man had a point, he thought; the golf pro wasn't the only staffer who was bored rigid. He looked out his window at the shop across the street, where a truck of goods was being unloaded. This was the first of the shops to be reopened, and Hurd had not met the man who ran it.

He got up and went across the street, introduced himself to the man, whose name was Carter.

"What sort of shop are you opening?" Hurd asked.

"Jewelry," the man said, setting down a carton on a showcase and lifting out a number of trays filled with diamond earrings and bracelets.

"Looks expensive."

"You better believe it," Carter said. "That's the way Ed wants it."

"You know, we're a little underpopulated here so far; it may be a while before you have some customers."

"Hurd, my first customers are already here," Carter said, nodding at the group approaching the shop. The people who Hurd had seen get off the jet walked in and started shopping immediately, forcing Carter to open more cartons.

Hurd left them to get on with it and went back to his office. He had nothing else to do, so he started setting up a file system, one for each property on the place. It took him less than an hour, and when he was finished, he had nothing to do. He picked up the phone and called the golf club.

Holly found Harry Crisp on the other end of the phone.

"Afternoon, Harry," she said.

"Hello, Holly." His cold sounded a little worse. "Where did you get this tattoo you sent me?"

"From the guy who came to my house with pizza and tried to kill me," she said. Somebody came into the room and handed her a report on the man's fingerprints. "And his prints were on file with the INS."

"What's his name?"

"Alexei Bronsky. He emigrated to the States less than a year ago, supposedly resides in New York."

"What else do you have on him?"

"Just his prints and the tattoo. The ME said he might have been a boxer at one time; there was evidence that he'd taken one or more beatings, although he looked like the kind of guy who'd be delivering them. What did you get on the tattoo?"

"This is really weird," Harry said. "D.C. had only seen one other like it, also on a dead guy. They traced it back to a special branch of what used to be the KGB, a branch that was devoted to rough stuff. Your dead guy was probably not a very nice person."

"That was my impression when he was shooting at me," Holly replied. "You get anything yet on the background of Pio Pellegrino?"

"Nothing yet," Harry said. "I'll let you know."

Harry didn't sound very convincing.

"Harry, you're not holding out on me, are you? Remember the two-way information highway?"

Harry ignored her. "I got the report from Sarasota about the double homicide."

"Yeah. We've got to get Trini off the streets or we'll be wading in blood."

"I've got Lauderdale, Miami, and the state police all over it," Harry said. "We'll pick him up soon."

"Harry, how did your tail lose Trini after I called you in?"

"They, uh, just lost him; the guy's good."

"How does a red Explorer just vanish?"

"Holly, let it go, will you? I'll talk to you later." He hung up.

Holly had the distinct feeling that the two-way information highway was running in only one direction again.

46

Holly arrived back at Grant's house to find Grant and Marina having a drink in the living room. Marina was wearing her new clothes, but she still seemed very subdued.

"You look very nice," Holly said, pouring herself a bourbon and sitting down.

"It's a very nice mall — big discounts," Marina said. "Holly, what am I going to do about burying my mother and my aunt?"

"There are certain procedures the Sarasota police will have to go through before the bodies can be released," Holly said. "It will probably be a few days. Do you know of a funeral home in Lauderdale?"

"Yes, the one that buried Carlos," Marina replied. "They were all right."

"You might want to call them and put them in touch with the Sarasota police, so that they can bring the bodies home."

"All right, I'll call them tomorrow morning."

"Remember not to tell them where you are."

"I'll give them my cellphone number," Marina said. She set down her drink. "If you'll excuse me, I'd like to go and have a nap before dinner." She rose and went upstairs.

"So, how was your day?" Holly asked Grant.

"Okay," he replied. "And yours?"

"Less than okay. I'm getting the distinct impression that Harry is holding out on me again."

Grant looked uncomfortable but didn't say anything.

"He and I supposedly had an agreement to share information," she said, "and it's not happening. I tried to talk to him about the background check on Pio Pellegrino, and he cut me off and hung up."

Grant stared at the ceiling and sighed.

"What?"

"I'm trying to think of a way you could have found this out, other than from me."

"Find what out?"

"You're going to have to keep this to yourself, Holly; if Harry should find out . . ."

"Grant, what are you talking about?"

"Pio Pellegrino's real name is Pietro Falcone; his father kept his old name, Ignacio. He was known in New York as Iggy the Finger."

"Iggy the Finger? That's colorful. What does it mean?"

"If Iggy wanted a guy taken out, he would point his finger at him and wiggle his thumb, like the hammer on a gun. He always smiled when he did it, but the guy who got the finger got dead."

"Why did they change their names?"

"Iggy was high up in the New York mob, one of three or four top guys. He got off on a murder rap about four years ago and just faded into the wallpaper. We finally stopped tapping his phones, it got so boring. Then he just dropped off the map."

"What about Pio?"

"His daddy's boy. He had a clean sheet, but he was a main go-between for the old man. They disappeared together. A year or so later, Pietro opens the restaurant in Miami, and he has a success. Nobody made him and the old man for a while, and when we did, we figured they were retired."

"And how long has Harry known about this?"

"From the beginning."

Holly felt as if someone had kicked her in the stomach. "You mean, he knew who Pio and the old man were before I told him about them?"

"Yes."

"That miserable son of a bitch. Why wouldn't he tell me?"

"I guess it's just Harry's natural reticence," Grant said.

"Well, it's obvious from the connection with Trini Rodriguez and the hiring of Carlos Alvarez that they're both into *something*," she said.

"Well, yeah."

"Does Harry know what it is?"

"Not really."

"Do you?"

"I have my suspicions, but I can't talk about that."

"Why not?"

"Because it pertains to what I'm working on in Orchid Beach, and you know I can't tell you about that."

"Grant . . ."

"Listen, Holly, I'm trying to help you out here, but I can't tell you more than that."

"Grant . . ."

"All right, one more thing: Trini is a registered FBI informant; has been for a couple of years."

"You mean, he's working for Harry?" Holly asked, astonished.

"It's not like that; he's not an undercover agent. He's just a guy on the street who gets paid for information."

"Well, I'm relieved to hear it. Do you think that his status as a snitch has kept Harry from busting him?"

"Maybe, when all this started. Right now, Harry wants him off the street as bad as anybody."

"I don't believe this. I'm busting my ass trying to figure out stuff that Harry already knows but won't tell me?"

"It's the nature of the beast, Holly. I told you before that the Bureau likes to know more than everybody else, and it doesn't like sharing."

"You know," Holly said, "I would really like to just bow out of this whole thing, except that I can't, because Trini Rodriguez is trying to kill me and that poor girl upstairs."

"Believe me, I know how you feel, but whatever you do, don't let Harry find out that you know what you know, or I'll be an undercover seal on an ice floe in Alaska by this time next week."

"All right, Grant, but you will try and help me not to get killed because of something Harry didn't tell me?"

"I'm not going to let you get killed," he said, kissing her on the cheek.

"Okay, but you're answering the doorbell from now on, while I hide under something."

"Okay, deal."

"And try and do a better job than you did with the pizza guy."

She went and poured herself another drink. Sobriety was not in the cards for this evening.

"First time I've seen you have more than one drink before dinner," Grant said

"First time I've needed more than one," Holly replied.

47

The following day, Holly worked listlessly, hungover and depressed, a bad combination. Just before lunchtime, she got a phone call.

"Hey, Holly, it's Ed Shine," he said.

"Oh, Ed, it's good to hear from you."

"How about dinner tonight?"

"Thank you, Ed, but I'm tied up."

"Sounds like I've got competition."

"Well, maybe."

"How about lunch; you free?"

"Sure."

"Come on out to Blood Orchid; meet me at the clubhouse, and I'll show you what my new chef can do. Then we'll play some golf."

"Oh, I don't think I can take the time for golf, but I'd love lunch."

"Half an hour?"

"See you then."

"I'll leave your name at the gate."

"Bye."

Holly freshened up and put on civilian clothes, then drove out to Blood Orchid. The guard waved her through the gate, and she drove to the clubhouse. As she got out of her car, she looked over toward the practice range and saw a very peculiar sight: Hurd Wallace taking a golf lesson! She went inside.

Ed was waiting for her at a table overlooking the golf course; he was the only other person in the dining room. She gave him a kiss and sat down.

"Drink?"

"Maybe a glass of wine with lunch," she said.

"I've already ordered for us," Ed said. "Trust me?"

Holly smiled. "Anytime. How's it going with Blood Orchid?"

"I'll tell you, this is going to turn out to be a better investment than I thought. I've sold six houses and three building lots; we've already got construction started on two houses."

"How so fast?"

"The corporation already had the building permits, and the buyers liked the plans."

"That's great, Ed."

A waiter arrived with soup: lobster bisque.

"This is wonderful," Holly said, tasting it.

"This new chef is a wonder, that's why."

"Where'd you find him?"

"In New York; he was the number-two man in a big-time restaurant, but he wanted to get out of the city. I was able to offer him a very attractive package, and he jumped at it. He's got a lovely wife and two kids, one of whom is starting school this year. I've helped him get the boy into a good private school."

"Sounds like a wonderful deal for him," Holly replied. "But how about you? Is this going to be a big enough operation to afford that kind of talent?"

"I want only the best," Ed said, "and by this time next year, the place will be generating big revenues. Everybody I've hired has been the best available — except for my security chief, of course; he's second-best."

"I saw Hurd out on the practice range, having a golf lesson," Holly said. "Never thought I'd see that."

"Oh, Hurd's a natural," Ed said. "The pro thinks he's going to be quite good."

"Does he have time for golf lessons in the middle of the day?"

Ed grinned sheepishly. "Well, he's a little underworked at the moment — will be until the place really gets going. I knew that would be the case, that's why I gave him a golf club membership."

"The course looks wonderful," Holly said.

"I had the designer back to install some improvements, and we're already under way. I'm keeping one of the three courses untouched while the other two are being worked on. That way, my members won't be bothered with the construction."

They finished their soup, and the waiter brought their main course.

"What is it?" Holly asked.

"It's fresh sea bass, cooked in a potato wrapping, with an excellent sauce," Ed said.

The waiter poured them a glass of white wine.

"And that's a Batard Montrachet, 'eighty-nine," Ed said. "The bastard of Le Montrachet."

Holly tasted it. "Wow," she said softly.

"Exactly. Now tell me, what's up with you?"

"Oh, Ed, I'm up to my ears in a huge mess."

"Tell me about it," Ed said, concerned.

"Well, for a start, we found the guy who took a shot at you."

"Hooray for that!" Ed said. "Who is he?"

"Was. His name was Carlos Alvarez, and we found him floating in the Indian River with a bullet in his head."

"I never heard of him."

"He was a hired hit man, the same one who killed the two Miami developers. He was quite a shot, too; you were very lucky."

Ed gave a low whistle. "I guess I was. Who hired him?"

"I don't know," Holly admitted. "We've traced Alvarez back to some people named Pellegrino, in Miami."

"There's a restaurant by that name," Ed said. "I've had dinner there; very good."

"Pio Pellegrino and his father, Ignacio. Turns out the old man is a former mafioso from New York named Falcone. He disappeared a few years ago and turned up in Miami with his son and a new name."

"So I had dinner in a Mafia restaurant?" Ed said, sounding delighted. "That's a new experience. Are they the people who wanted me dead?"

"Yes, and whoever they work with or for. We haven't gotten past them yet, although the FBI is working on it."

"I guess they really wanted this property bad, then."

"Yes, but you're safe now, since you own it. There's nothing in it for them to try to kill you again."

"Who killed . . . what's his name? The hit man?"

"Another hit man named Trini Rodriguez."

"He doesn't sound like Mafia," Ed said.

"There's all kinds of Mafia, Ed. We've even got a Russian involved in all this."

"This is the craziest business I ever heard of," Ed said, shaking his head. "I'm glad I'm out of it."

"I wish I were out of it; these people have already tried to kill me."

Ed's eyebrows went up. "My God! Are you safe?"

"I work on it every day."

"Listen, I've got a couple of guest cottages here; why don't you move into one of them? They're very comfortable, and this has to be the most secure place in Orchid Beach."

"Thank you, Ed, that's very sweet of you. I'm staying with a friend at the moment, but if that doesn't work out, I might take you up on your invitation."

"Is your friend anybody I know?"

"Maybe; his name is Grant Early. He looked at some property out here."

"Oh, yes, I met him in our office; nice fellow. Some sort of dot.com millionaire, I believe."

"Yes, he apparently got out just in time, before the crash in those stocks."

"Some people are just lucky, I guess," Ed said.

"Yes, and you're one of them."

"Keep me posted on your case, will you? It's fascinating. I lead such a dull life compared to you."

"Believe me, Ed, you're better off with a dull life."

48

Holly felt better after lunch, the wine having helped her hangover, but when she got back to Grant's house after work, she was tired.

Marina was sitting in the living room alone, a drink in her hand.

"Hi," Holly said.

"Hello," Marina said disconsolately.

"Where's Grant?"

"He went to the grocery store," she replied. "I wanted to go with him, but he wouldn't let me."

"It's best you stay in the house, until we know you're safe," Holly said.

Marina nodded listlessly. "I spoke to the undertaker this morning, and he called back this afternoon. They're releasing my mother's and my aunt's bodies tomorrow, and the undertaker is taking them back to Fort Lauderdale. I want to go back tomorrow to make the funeral arrangements, but my car is still at the airport in Sarasota."

Holly sat down next to her. "Marina, you can't go back to Lauderdale while Trini is still on the loose. He's looking for you."

"I don't care," Marina said. "I have to bury

my mother and my aunt; there's nobody else to do it."

"I understand, but you're going to have to postpone the funeral until it's safe."

"While their bodies rot in a funeral home?"

"The undertaker will take care of them; they'll be embalmed and kept in cold storage."

"Yes, at a hundred and fifty dollars a day," Marina said. "I've already missed a lot of work because of Carlos's funeral, and now this. They're not paying me for the time off, either, and I only have a little in savings. I'll have to put all this on a credit card, and I just got them paid off."

"Marina, I know it's expensive, but isn't protecting your life worth a few hundred dollars?"

"Oh, I suppose so, but I feel so helpless."

"Tell you what, I'll send someone over to Sarasota to bring back your car. Do you have the keys?"

Marina opened her purse and handed them to Holly.

"I'll send two officers over there tomorrow, and one can drive your car back."

"Thank you."

"But you can't leave here, Marina. I hope you understand that."

Marina nodded. "I understand."

Grant came in from the garage, his arms filled with groceries. "There's more in the car," he said. "Give me a hand?"

Holly went out to the garage and got the remaining bags from Grant's trunk. The top was down on the Mercedes convertible, and as she walked back into the house, something in the car caught her attention. It was a matchbook, lying on the console between the front seats, but she could read the name on it. TRICKY'S, it said. BAR AND GRILL.

They finished dinner and watched TV for a while, then Marina excused herself and went to bed.

"She's getting pretty antsy," Grant said.

"I know. She wants to go back to Lauderdale to bury her mother and aunt."

"You're not going to let her, are you?"

"Of course not." They were both quiet for a moment. "Grant, what else do you know about the Pellegrinos?"

"Nothing I can tell you," he replied.

"Oh, come on, there must be something else that you can tell me without compromising your investigation."

"They're very well connected," Grant said.

"With whom?"

"You name it — if it's a criminal organization, they're plugged into it."

"What sort of activities?"

"Whatever turns a million bucks — prostitution, gambling."

"Prostitution? I thought that was a free-lancer's market these days."

"There are some very fancy whorehouses in

Miami," Grant said. "You wouldn't believe how fancy, and how beautiful the girls are. Or boys."

"And the Pellegrinos are into that?"

"The Pellegrinos *own* that."

"Jesus. And what sort of gambling? Bookie operations?"

"They've gone way beyond a bookie operation," Grant said. "They're on the Internet."

"The Internet?"

"Come on, I'll show you." He led the way into the study and switched on his computer. He hit the Internet connection, then typed in an address. A title page came up, and there were buttons for football, baseball, golf, basketball, soccer, European soccer, South American soccer, dog racing, and horse racing. Grant clicked on one and got a display of odds on various games.

"Wow," Holly said. "But that's got to be illegal."

"It is, in this country, but Pio and his pop are too sophisticated to get caught at it. The operation is based on an island in the Caribbean called Saint Marks. It's a former British colony with very loose rules about gambling and banking."

"How does it work?"

"Well, let's say you want to place a fifty-dollar bet on a Yankees game. You hit the appropriate button, place a bet, give them a credit card number, and you get an on-screen receipt, which you can print out. If you win, the amount is credited to your card, and you can use it to pay down your bill, or you can take a credit refund."

"Even if you're in the United States?"

"Yep. You'd never be caught because there are too many people playing it, and the government doesn't know who."

"Can't the Feds hack into their computer and find out who their customers are?"

"They've got their own computer experts working to prevent just that, but suppose we could? We couldn't arrest everybody. What if we picked a hundred players and arrested and tried them to make an example of them? They've still got hundreds of thousands more playing. We couldn't make a dent. We've made overtures to the government of Saint Marks, but the politicians there are well paid by the Pellegrinos, and they're not going to cooperate."

"What happens to the money they make? They can't get it back into this country, can they?"

"That would be tough to do in any volume, but they own their own bank in Saint Marks, and they can wire money to any bank in the world, including ones in places with banking secrecy laws, like the Cayman Islands and Switzerland. They can launder it through dozens or hundreds of legitimate businesses. They own a resort in Saint Marks, for instance. But one of the puzzles is, exactly where is the money going?

We're working on that, but it's a hard puzzle to break."

"I don't get it," Holly said. "These guys are making all this money . . ."

"Hundreds of millions a year."

". . . and they're sitting in Miami, running a restaurant?"

"That's just cover; somebody else runs the restaurant. They live well, but not like the very rich people they are. I'd love to know where the money is going and who's getting it."

"And this is connected with your work in Orchid Beach?"

"No comment," Grant said.

After they had gone to bed, Holly thought about the Pellegrinos. And she thought about Tricky's, too, and what Grant might have been doing there. He wasn't going to tell her, she knew, and she wasn't going to ask. Not yet, anyway.

49

The following morning, Holly sent two officers to Sarasota in an unmarked car to bring back Marina's car. "Just put it in the garage," she said, giving them the address of Grant's house, "but bring the keys back to me."

Harry Crisp called just before lunch. "Good morning."

"Good morning, Harry," Holly said warily.

"I've got some more stuff on your Russian, Bronsky, from the organized crime division of the Justice Department."

"Oh?" Harry was going to supply information?

"He was part of the New York Russian mob, centered in Brighton Beach, in Brooklyn; nothing big, just an enforcer, and our information is, a particularly cold and cruel one, in an organization noted for its cruelty."

Holly was immediately suspicious. "Wait a minute, Harry: He was ex-KGB, and he's just an enforcer? That doesn't sound right to me."

"It's what my people found out, Holly. I'm sorry if it doesn't mesh with your preconceived notions about the guy."

"Does he have any connection to the Pellegrinos, apart from his association with Trini Rodriguez?"

"Nothing we can nail down."

"Then he's a dead end."

"A nice turn of phrase, in his present circumstances, but yes, his identity leads us nowhere."

"How about some information that leads us *somewhere*, Harry?"

"That's all I've got, I'm afraid. I thought you'd like to know."

"Forgive me if I seem ungrateful, Harry, but it seems like a bone for the dog. What have you found out on the Pellegrinos?"

"We're still working on that, Holly, don't worry."

Yeah, sure, Holly thought. "Any news on the search for Trini?"

"He's gone to ground, not visiting any of his usual hangouts."

"Including the bar Tricky's?"

"We're looking everywhere, Holly, don't worry."

"Somehow, I have the idea that if Trini wanted to kill you, instead of me, you'd be looking a lot harder."

"We have to leave that sort of pursuit to the locals and the state boys; we don't have enough personnel to run dragnets. It's always been that way; our people are investigators; they don't set up roadblocks or search for hideouts."

"Yeah, and in the meantime, Trini's going to

keep trying to kill me and Marina because he thinks one of us has the notebook. Can you get something in the papers saying that *you've* got the notebook? Maybe that would take the heat off Marina and me."

"I'll see what I can do."

"Well, thanks for the information on the Russian, Harry. Goodbye." She hung up, pissed off.

Her officers showed up around three with Marina's car keys, and Holly worked until six, then went home. The guard outside the house showed himself when she arrived.

"Hi," she said. "Everything okay?"

"Very quiet," the young man replied. "Two of your officers showed up around mid-afternoon with a car; they put it in the garage."

"Right. I've got the keys in my pocket." She went inside. "Hello?" she called. "Anybody home?" No answer. She checked the garage to see if Grant's car was there, and it wasn't. Neither was Marina's.

She ran upstairs to check the guest room, but it was empty; Marina's things were gone. She ran back to the front of the house and grabbed her officer. "The car that was brought here this afternoon is gone. When did it leave?"

"I didn't know it had," the officer said.

"Did you leave the front of the house at any time?"

"Sure, I check the perimeter every twenty

minutes or so. It could have left when I was on the beach side of the house."

Holly looked up to see Grant turning into the driveway, and she ran over to his car.

"Hi," he said getting out and handing her a box of wine bottles. "I picked up a few things to drink."

"Marina's gone," she said.

"How?"

"I had her car brought back from Sarasota. I kept the keys, but she must have had another set."

"She's obviously headed for home," Grant said. "Call the state police and have them pick her up on the interstate. Tell them she's a material witness."

Holly shook her head. "Problem is, she's not a witness to anything; she didn't see Trini shoot anybody."

"In that case you couldn't have stopped her anyway."

Grant parked, and they went into the house. Holly picked up the phone and dialed Marina's cellphone.

"Hello?"

"Marina, it's Holly."

"I'm sorry, Holly; I know you're angry with me."

"I'm not angry, I'm worried about you."

"I don't feel in any danger," Marina said. "They're looking for Trini everywhere; he won't come near me."

"That may not be true. Don't go home, Marina. Can you stay with a friend?"

"I'm going to my house," Marina said. "I'll be there in fifteen minutes. I'm going to cook myself some dinner and watch TV, and tomorrow I'm going to work."

"I'm going to call the Lauderdale police and ask them to put a guard on your house."

"I think it's a waste of time," Marina said, "but I can't stop you. I have to hang up now, Holly; I'm at the grocery."

"Listen, Marina, the FBI is going to get something in the papers stating that they now have the notebook. Once Trini knows that, he won't be interested in you anymore. Wait until that happens before going home."

"No, I'm going home. I'm tired of this."

Holly had a thought. "Marina, have you scheduled the funeral yet?"

"The day after tomorrow at ten A.M., at Santa Maria."

"Be careful," Holly said.

"I will. I stopped and bought a gun."

"Marina, you're more likely to get shot with your own gun than protect yourself."

"It makes me feel better. Goodbye, Holly." She hung up.

Holly called the Lauderdale police and got the duty captain on the line.

"What can I do for you, Chief Barker?" the man asked.

"I've been protecting a woman that Trini Rodriguez has been trying to kill; he shot her mother and aunt in Sarasota."

"I'm aware of that crime; every car we've got is looking for Rodriguez."

"The woman's name is Marina Santos." Holly gave him Marina's address. "Do you think you could put a man on her for a few days, until Rodriguez is picked up?"

"I think I can do that," the captain said.

"She's burying her mother and aunt at Santa Maria, the day after tomorrow."

"I'll put somebody on her at least until after the funeral."

"Thank you very much, Captain. If I can ever do anything for your department, please let me know." She hung up.

"Feel better?" Grant asked.

"Not yet. Give me Harry's home number again." She dialed it.

"Hello?"

"Harry, I think I know how we might catch Trini Rodriguez."

"How."

She told him.

50

Holly sat on a folding chair in the steeple of the church of Santa Maria, next to an FBI marksman with a sniper's rifle. It was a quarter to ten, and they had an excellent view of the churchyard and part of the square.

"I hope to God they don't ring the bells," the marksman said.

Holly handed him a pair of earplugs; she had already inserted hers.

"How many more people have we got, besides you and me?" the agent asked.

"Close to thirty," she said. "Between the Bureau and the Lauderdale department, we've got a dozen guns in the square, and all the approach streets are being watched."

"Shit," the man said, "I hope somebody else doesn't get the shot."

Holly reflected on how she had felt when she had shot Trini Rodriguez's brother, and compared it to this agent's eagerness to get a kill. No comparison. This guy wanted another notch on his rifle stock. She looked at the weapon, but there were no notches.

"How many people have you taken out?"

she asked.

"Over twelve years, nine," he replied. "FBI and police snipers don't get shots as often as you would think. More often than not, it's a hostage situation, and the suspect surrenders or shoots himself." He took aim at something in the churchyard and made a minute adjustment to his gunsight. His weapon was mounted on a tripod, so that the barrel would not protrude from the steeple, making it visible to an opponent.

"What do you shoot for?"

"The head," he replied. "In most of these situations, you've got a suspect who's trying to kill cops or threatening to kill a hostage. You don't want to gut-shoot him, because he might still be able to empty his weapon, and a chest shot won't incapacitate him every time, either. What you want to see through your scope is an exploding head."

Holly gave a little shudder.

"Position one, this is position three."

Holly picked up her handheld radio. She was position one, and position three was a soft-drink delivery truck on a corner of the square. "Three, this is one."

"We've got a couple of funeral-home limos approaching from the northwest."

"Those will contain family and friends," Holly said. "Don't bother watching them; look for any threat to them."

"Roger," the cop said.

Holly saw the two limos now, driving slowly. The hearse had already delivered the two coffins to the church, and now the two long, black cars parked next to the hearse near the front entrance. This was the first real opportunity for a shooter to get a shot at Marina.

"Condition red," a commander said over the radio. That meant maximum readiness.

The sniper next to Holly swung his weapon slowly back and forth through his assigned target area, looking for a gun barrel or a vehicle that seemed suspect.

Seven or eight people, Marina among them, got out of the two cars and walked slowly up the front walk and into the church. Forty or fifty other people were already inside, having arrived earlier.

"Condition blue," the commander said. That meant that the snipers could relax; the onus was now on the officers inside the church. Organ music wafted up into the steeple: Bach, Holly thought. The choir joined in.

"That's nice," the sniper said, leaning back in his chair and taking out his earplugs. "I don't often get a job that has musical accompaniment."

Holly removed her earplugs, too, to better hear the music. It was comforting, somehow, fulfilling the composer's intention. The piece ended, and the priest began to chant something; the words were unintelligible up in the steeple, but Holly thought it sounded like Latin. Then he seemed to change to English, but she could still pick up only a word or two, here and there.

"You're up the coast at Orchid Beach?" the sniper asked.

"That's right."

"The wife and I have driven through there; seems like a nice spot."

"It is; it's the way Florida should have turned out, but didn't," Holly said. "No high-rises on the beach, very green."

"Might be a good place to retire," the agent said. "Fairly crime-free?"

"I recommend it," Holly replied. "It's normally free of major crime, except lately; we've had a couple of killings."

"I heard."

The two chatted sporadically as they waited, then the music got louder, meaning the front doors of the church had opened.

"Condition red," the commander said over the radio.

Soon a procession, led by the priest and two coffins, made its way from the church into the churchyard, toward two open graves, side by side.

"I want a maximum effort now," the commander said. "These people are at their most vulnerable."

Holly's companion had shifted his position and brought his sights to bear on his assigned portion of the churchyard perimeter. Traffic had been stopped on all the streets leading into the square for the duration of the brief graveside service, and, somewhere in the distance, an occasional driver made his impatience known with his horn. Apart from that sound, the square had become extremely quiet, unusual for an urban area.

Holly, having no assigned quadrant, swept as much of the area as she could see with her binoculars, looking for any kind of suspicious activity.

The priest spoke for a minute or two in English, then reverted to Latin.

"Position one, this is position five." Harry.

"Five, this is one."

"Nobody has seen a damned thing," Harry said, "not a whit of threatening activity."

"He wants her, and this is his best chance," Holly replied.

"I hope to God he makes an attempt," Harry said. "I want this to be over."

"Nobody more than I," Holly replied. She was glad she was not standing, exposed, in the churchyard by the two coffins and the two open graves. Maybe five minutes to go, and they'd be clear; Marina would be back in the limo, headed home.

The priest concluded his ceremony, and one or two people came forward and picked up handfuls of dirt to sprinkle as the coffins descended into their graves. But first, there was another small ceremony.

Marina Santos, dressed in funereal black,

stepped forward to the heads of the coffins, bearing two red roses. She kissed one coffin and placed a rose upon it.

Holly watched with sadness through her binoculars.

Then, as Marina kissed the second coffin, both caskets exploded.

The shock wave set the bells in the steeple to ringing. Holly and the FBI sniper, knocked off their seats, writhed on the wooden floor, clutching their ears.

51

Then Holly was on her feet, running down the stairs, her radio pressed to one ear, but with her ears still ringing, she could hear nothing. "He's in the square," she said into the radio. "Trini's in the square. Find him."

She reached the ground and ran into the churchyard, which looked like a war zone. Headstones for yards around had been toppled and thrown about; a good-sized tree had been knocked down. And there were bodies and parts of bodies everywhere. She saw a smoking torso that was what was left of Marina. Holly let her anger replace her revulsion.

A car screeched to a halt at the curb, and Harry Crisp and a uniformed police captain came running toward her.

"He's in the square, Harry!" she said. "We've got to find him!" She was barely in control of her fury.

"Take it easy, Holly," Harry said.

"It was a radio-controlled detonation," the captain said. "He could be anywhere."

"He was watching," Holly said. "He waited until she kissed her mother's coffin, then he blew it. I'm telling you, we can still get him."

The captain began barking orders into his radio.

Holly looked around: She counted at least eight dead bodies, and there were another dozen or fifteen badly injured people.

Sirens were screaming in all directions now; ambulances arrived, so did police cars, marked and unmarked.

Holly began running; all she wanted was a shot at Trini. She ran down one side of the square, looking into shop windows, some of them blown out, and at second-story windows and into parked cars. A commercial van was parked just ahead of her. She yanked open the driver's door and stuck her gun out. "Freeze, police!"

A startled uniformed cop stared back at her.

"Sorry," she said, and slammed the door. She continued down the street, turned a corner, and kept going. She didn't stop until she had covered the whole square.

Harry was waiting for her. "He's gone," he said. "We won't get him today."

"Shit, Harry, we blew it," Holly said, "and I got a lot of people killed."

"It isn't your fault, Holly, it's Trini's fault."

"Bust the Pellegrinos, Harry, do it now."

"That would not be a good move, Holly. There's more going on than you know about."

"Oh, I believe that," Holly said. "I don't know a goddamned thing!" She was fuming.

"Holly, I think you ought to move out of Grant's house," Harry said. "You've been there too long, and I'm afraid Trini or one of his people will find you. Is there somewhere else you can go? To Ham's, maybe?"

Holly shook her head. "No, Ham has a girlfriend living there, and there's only one bedroom." Then she remembered something. "There is someplace else, though."

"Where?"

"I'll let you know," Holly said.

Holly drove back to Orchid Beach, the scene in the churchyard playing back in her head, over and over. She kept seeing Marina's image through the high-powered binoculars, and then Marina didn't exist anymore.

She drove into the driveway and was met by her own officer.

"Everything all right, Chief?" he asked.

"No," Holly said. "Nothing's all right." She left him standing there and went into the house. Grant was on the phone, but he ended his conversation and hung up.

"I heard," he said. "It's been all over the TV. I'm sorry, Holly."

"Me too," she said, starting upstairs.

"Do you want a drink?"

"I have to get out of here, Grant."

He followed her up the stairs and came into the bedroom, where she was stuffing her things into her bag. "You shouldn't go home, Holly."

"I'm not going home."

"Are you going to Ham's?"

She started back down the stairs. "No."

He followed her across the living room. "Then where are you going?"

"I'm not going to tell you," she said.

"Why not?"

"Because I want to stay alive. I'm not going to tell anybody. Come on, Daisy," she said to the dog. They both got into her car, and she started the engine. "You can reach me on my cellphone." She reversed out of the driveway and drove down the street, leaving Grant standing there.

She made sure she wasn't followed, turning down small streets and watching her mirror, then she got back onto A1A and headed for safety.

Ed Shine was waiting for her in his car at the entrance to Blood Orchid, and when he spotted her car, he waved for her to follow him. They drove around the golf course to a small road near the airport, where Ed turned in. Finally, he stopped before a cottage under some trees and got out.

"Here we are," he said. "I'm glad you called; I've been worried about you since our talk."

"Thank you for taking such good care of me, Ed," she said, giving him a kiss on the cheek.

"I'm glad to help," he said, leading her into the house. "Here we are — living room, dining room, kitchen, and the bedrooms are back here — two of them, take your pick."

Holly chose one and dumped her bag on the bed. "It's lovely, Ed."

"I had them redone first thing. You can stay as long as you want. You'll hear airplanes taking off and landing now and then — the airfield is right behind the house — but there isn't much traffic, just prospective buyers coming and going, so it shouldn't bother you too much. Would you like a drink?"

"Yes, I would," Holly said, following him into the living room.

He opened a cabinet to reveal a well-stocked bar with sink and ice machine. "Bourbon?"

"That would be lovely; I need it."

He poured her a drink and himself a scotch, and they sat down.

"Now tell me," he said, "what's happened?"

Holly took a sip of her drink and poured out everything, describing the scene in the churchyard as vividly as she dared without beginning to cry.

"Nine dead, twenty-six wounded, five of them in critical condition," she said.

"Good God!" Ed said, holding her hand.

"And it's all my fault; it was my big idea to trap Trini Rodriguez, using Marina for bait, since she refused to be protected anyway."

"Then it would have happened anyway, whether you'd had your idea or not, Holly. Stop blaming yourself; you did everything you could."

★ ★ ★

That night, she went to bed trying to think of what else she might have done. She fell into a troubled sleep, having thought of nothing.

52

Holly holed up for two days in the guest cottage, watching TV and listening to the airplanes come and go two or three times a day, and talking with Grant, Ham, and her office on the phone. Daisy was her only company. She felt so paranoid by now that she would give no one her location, not even Ham, just her cellphone number.

The cellphone rang.

"Hello?"

"Holly, it's Ginny. How are you?"

"Alive," Holly said.

"I don't know where you are, but it's not good for you to be alone right now, not after all that's happened."

"I'm staying here until they catch Rodriguez," she said.

"Why don't you come flying with me? Nobody who's looking for you would ever suspect that."

"I don't know . . ."

"Come on, Holly. Who'd be looking for you at the airport?"

Holly had a thought. "Ginny, you know that

311

long strip at the Palmetto Gardens property?"

"You mean Blood Orchid?"

"Yes. I'm not too far from there. Could you land and pick me up? Then I wouldn't feel too exposed."

"Sure, glad to. When?"

"Are you at the airport now?"

"Yes."

"In an hour, say?"

"Sure. Do you know if they have a CTAF?"

"What's that?"

"A Common Traffic Advisory Frequency. Haven't you been reading your flight instruction manual?"

"I'm afraid not, and I don't know about the CTAF. I do know there's no tower, though. But there's not much traffic — two or three flights a day."

"Okay, I can deal with that."

"See you in an hour. Can Daisy come?" Holly asked.

"Sure."

Holly made herself a sandwich from the fully stocked refrigerator, put on some jeans, and drove around to the airstrip. She could have walked, it was so close. She parked in the ramp area and got out of the car, scanning the skies for Ginny's little airplane. As she looked around, a business jet entered the traffic pattern and was soon on final approach. Holly moved her car to allow the aircraft plenty of parking room, and watched as it taxied to the ramp and killed its engines. The rear door opened, and two men got out. They were casually dressed, not in the uniforms that corporate pilots wore, and they stood, looking around, waiting for something. They saw Holly, and one of them called out to her in Spanish.

She shook her head. *"No hablo español,"* she yelled back. They were maybe fifty yards away. Then a large van arrived, bearing the Blood Orchid logo, and backed up to the airplane. The two pilots began unloading boxes, quite heavy boxes, judging from their body language. The boxes kept coming, until Holly realized that there could not be any seats in the airplane, that it was being used for cargo.

The men finished their work, and the van drove away. The two pilots began arguing about something, and one of them gestured toward Holly. Then one of them got back into the airplane, while another made a cellphone call, occasionally glancing at her.

That was all right, she thought; he was calling the Blood Orchid office, reporting someone loitering on the airstrip. Then he finished the call, got aboard, closing the door behind him, and shortly, the airplane's engines started and it taxied to the runway. The jet took off, headed north, and was soon out of sight.

Then Holly heard the sound of a small airplane and spotted Ginny's Piper Warrior at about a thousand feet, seemingly on a base leg for landing. The airplane turned final, landed, and taxied to the ramp. Ginny shut down the engine and got out.

"You take the left seat," she said.

Holly put Daisy in the rear seat and climbed aboard and ran through the startup checklist with Ginny. Soon they were rolling down the runway for takeoff.

"Let's do some touch-and-goes," Ginny said over her headset. "Just enter a left crosswind, then turn downwind and make a normal approach. The procedure is touch down, then apply full power and retract flaps, then take off again without stopping."

"Okay," Holly replied, turning crosswind and climbing. She climbed to a thousand feet, turned downwind, and began running through the landing checklist. She turned base leg, then final, put in full flaps, and set the throttle for landing. When she touched down she applied full throttle, retracted the flaps, and watched the airspeed indicator climb toward sixty knots, her takeoff speed. As she pulled back on the yoke there was a loud noise, and the windshield exploded.

"I've got the airplane," Ginny shouted. She grabbed the controls and continued climbing

"What happened?" Holly shouted over the newly increased noise.

"I don't know," Ginny said. "Maybe we hit a bird. I'll come back around and land."

Then, as they turned crosswind, Holly felt something jar the airplane, and a hole appeared in the Plexiglas window next to her head. "Get out of here!" she shouted at Ginny. "Somebody's shooting at us!"

53

Ginny leveled off at a thousand feet and reduced power to cruise, then she moved her headset microphone close to her lips. "I'm going back to the Orchid Beach airport," she said. The airplane was vibrating heavily.

"No," Holly replied. "We can't go there; it's not safe. That's what whoever was shooting at us will think we'll do. Is there someplace else nearby?"

"There are half a dozen airports within a few minutes' flight, but with all the vibration, I think the propeller must have been hit, and if that's true, it could come off the airplane any time, and we'd be done for. Without the prop up front, the airplane balance would be so affected that we couldn't fly; we'd be too tail-heavy."

"Then let's put it down on a road or something."

Ginny was looking around now, and she swung the airplane onto a northerly heading. "There's a disused World War Two training field a few miles north. I'm going for that."

Holly sat in her seat and stared forward, searching for the airfield. Only her big sunglasses made it possible for her to keep her eyes open, with so much wind in her face. She glanced at the airspeed indicator: Ginny had slowed the airplane down to eighty knots, but that was still a lot of wind.

"There!" Ginny said, pointing just to the right of the airplane's nose.

Holly spotted the three runways, set in a triangle, and a large hangar. "I've got the field."

"You want to land it?" Ginny asked.

"No! You do it."

Ginny laughed. "We'll land in the same direction as at Blood Orchid; the wind direction and speed will be about the same." Then the airplane began to vibrate even more. Ginny reached over, yanked out the mixture knob, and the engine stopped.

"What the hell are you doing?" Holly demanded.

"I think we were about to lose the prop," Ginny replied, starting a turn toward a runway. "It's still windmilling, but with no power, there'll be less stress on it. Turn off the master switch."

Holly switched it off. "Do we have enough altitude to make it?" Holly shouted, her headset no longer of any use with the power off. The airplane seemed awfully low to her.

"We're about to find out," Ginny yelled back. "Never mind the wind direction, we're going for the runway straight ahead. Tighten your seat belt and brace yourself."

Holly yanked on her seat belt until it hurt, then turned and held onto Daisy's collar, then she braced against the instrument panel, elbow slightly bent, so the impact wouldn't break her arm. It was becoming clear that they weren't going to make the runway.

Ginny flew the airplane lower and lower. "Hang on!" she yelled as she flared.

The airplane was headed straight toward a drainage ditch about fifty yards short of the runway. Ginny began pulling back slowly on the yoke, and the stall warning horn began to shriek.

The airplane stalled and fell the last ten feet to the ground, landing with a noisy slam, then bouncing a couple of times. They came to a stop on the very end of the runway.

"Well," Ginny said, "we made the runway."

"A little late, though," Holly replied. "I'm glad you were able to miss the ditch."

Ginny pointed straight ahead: the propeller had stopped straight up and down, and the tip of the blade they could see was missing. "That accounts for the vibration," Ginny said.

They got out and walked around the airplane. Daisy seemed remarkably unconcerned. Apart from the shattered windshield and the punctured window, there was a line of bullet holes running from just aft of the pilot's seat upward and aft. Holly counted seven holes.

Ginny stood back and looked at her wounded bird. "What this airplane needs is a new windshield, new prop, new pilot's window, and a lot of patching — plus a very thorough annual inspection. I think the engine is going to have to be torn down to see if there was any damage from that awful vibration."

"All that sounds expensive," Holly said.

Ginny nodded. "That's what insurance is for, although I'm not sure how I'm going to explain this to the insurance company." She climbed into the pilot's seat. "Come on, let's see if this thing will start."

"Start?" Holly asked, alarmed. "You're not going to try to fly it again, are you?"

"No, I'm going to try and taxi it over to that old hangar," Ginny replied, pointing. "It beats pushing it."

Holly got into the passenger seat. "Right. And anyway, somebody might be looking for us from the air."

"The thought crossed my mind," Ginny said, "although we're both probably completely paranoid." She flipped on the master switch, pushed in the mixture, cracked the throttle, and turned the key. The engine fired as if nothing had happened, and they began to move down the runway.

Shortly, they were in the shade of the big hangar, which had been built to hold many airplanes. Ginny shut down the engine, and they got out and looked around. The roof was full of holes and the floor was covered with light debris, but it sheltered the airplane from prying eyes.

Ginny took out her cellphone and tapped in a number. "Ham," she said, "come get us, we're on the ground. We're okay, just a little problem with the prop. You drive north on highway one . . ." She continued with the directions. "That's only approximate, since I've never been here on the ground. Just keep hunting until you find us." She punched off. "Ham's not too concerned," she said.

"It takes a lot to concern Ham."

"You know," Ginny said, "I think it might have been the tip of the prop that broke the windshield. I mean, when a bullet came through your window, it made a hole but didn't shatter."

"You could be right," Holly said, looking at the prop. "Looks like there's about six inches missing, and that's a pretty good-sized piece of metal."

"Holly, who was shooting at us?"

Holly thought about that for a minute. "I'm not sure I know," she said. "You think I could sleep on the sofa tonight?"

"Of course you can. Better yet, we'll make Ham sleep on the sofa, and you and I will share the bed."

Holly laughed. "I'll let you break the news to him."

Ginny walked around the airplane, inspecting it. "I think the shooting was coming from ahead of us when we were doing the touch-and-go. Then, when we made our left crosswind turn, it was coming from the side of the airplane; that's how your window got hit. Looks like the shooter was somewhere around the end of the runway, to the north."

"It's good that you chose to keep flying, instead of setting her back down."

"You know, I don't know why I did that," Ginny said.

"I'm real glad you did."

54

Holly insisted on sleeping on the living room sofa. They had had dinner and talked, and Ham and Ginny respected her reluctance to talk about what had happened in the past few days. Holly's response to any conversation was desultory, and they finally gave up and went to bed.

Holly made up her bed on the sofa and got into it, and Daisy lay down beside her. Holly was tired from the stress of the day's events, but she did not sleep for a long time. Then, in the middle of the night, she came wide awake and sat up. Had she been dreaming, or just thinking? Somehow, she had answered a question in her sleep, then another. Pieces slid toward one another, and if they did not seamlessly interlock, at least there was a logic present. She found her cellphone in the dark and called Grant's number.

"Hello?" He sounded sleepy.

"It's Holly," she said.

"What's wrong?"

"I won't know that until I talk to you," she replied. "I'm at Ham's. Do you know where that is?"

"No."

She gave him directions. "I want you to come and get me."

"*Now?*"

"Now. I think I can put this thing together, with your help."

"What thing?"

"Come get me." She hung up.

Holly dressed and waited for Grant at the gate, so as not to wake Ham and Ginny. When he came, she waited for him to turn around, then put Daisy in the backseat and got into the car. It was a warm Florida night, and the top was down.

Grant found his way back to the bridge before he said anything. "What's going on?"

"Listen to me carefully," she said, "and don't interrupt me until I'm finished."

"All right."

"I've been staying in a guest cottage at Blood Orchid, courtesy of my friend Ed Shine. I've been kind of stunned, I guess, since the bomb went off in the cemetery. Mostly I've been watching TV — old movies, sitcoms, anything I could find. I tried not to think, but I believe a part of my mind was working, because I began to think of things.

"Yesterday, Ginny called me on my cellphone and invited me to go flying, said it would be good for me. I asked her to pick me up at the Blood Orchid airfield, and while I was waiting for her, a business jet landed and offloaded a bunch of heavy boxes into a Blood Orchid van. The guys flying the airplane noticed me, and before they took off, one of them made a cellphone call. I think it was about me.

"Ginny came, and we took off; I was flying left seat. We went around the pattern once and did a touch-and-go, and as we started to lift off, somebody opened fire on the airplane. The windshield exploded, and we took some rounds in other parts of the airplane. Ginny flew us to a disused field not far from there, and we landed safely, and Ham came to get us. Got all that?"

"Yes."

"Does any of that tell you anything?"

Grant hesitated. "I'm not sure."

"Did I mention the boxes the jet unloaded were heavy?"

"Yes."

"What weighs a lot?"

"Metal . . . liquid . . . paper."

"Yes, paper."

"You know about what was going on at Blood Orchid when it was Palmetto Gardens, before the Feds went in and broke it up?"

"Yes, they were shipping money out of the country, money from drug sales in the U.S. They were flying it out of their own airstrip to wherever they wanted, in South or Central America."

"Do you think they're doing that again? Is that your idea?"

"No."

"Then what?"

"The Pellegrinos are taking in huge amounts of money from their offshore banking operations and putting it into their own offshore bank, right?"

"Right. But you didn't hear that from me."

"Yeah, sure. So they can send as much money as they like to any bank in the world, right?"

"Right."

"Now, say you're running a drug ring in the U.S. Say you're associated with other people who're in the same business. It's a cash business; you don't take checks or credit cards, and you don't put the money in the bank, right?"

"Right; it would be noticed by the bank examiners if huge amounts of cash were being deposited, and they'd notify Treasury or the Bureau."

"Right. So they've got to get the money out of the country."

"Right."

"You know about this network of informal banks that people from the Middle East use to send money to relatives? They don't actually wire-transfer it; somebody deposits it with a bank in the sending country, then a phone call is made and the relatives go and collect it from a so-called bank in the receiving country. There's no paper trail, as with a wire transfer."

"Yes, it's thought that some terrorism operations may have been funded that way. It's very difficult to stop."

"Right. Now, the Pellegrinos are sitting on large sums of cash in Saint Marks that they can't send back to the U.S., right?"

"Right."

"And the drug dealers in the States are sitting on large sums that they can't get out of the country, right?"

"Sort of. There are other ways to get money in and out of the country; it's called money laundering."

"Yes, but you leave a paper trail that someday might be discovered."

"Maybe."

"So, suppose the drug dealers in this country ship their money to a predetermined spot in the United States, where it's counted and stored in a safe place. Then somebody makes a call to Saint Marks, and an identical amount of money, less a healthy handling fee, of course, is then transferred to someplace else in the world, an account of the drug dealers' choice."

"I believe I get the picture."

"It's what you've been working on, isn't it?"

"I will neither confirm nor deny that."

"I think what I saw today was boxes of cash being unloaded and very probably taken to a facility that was built for the purpose back when Blood Orchid was Palmetto Gardens. It's a building with underground vaults, just like a bank."

"Possibly."

"You know that's what's happening, don't

you, Grant? It's what you've been working on all this time."

Grant said nothing.

"Then why haven't you rolled up the operation? Not enough evidence yet?"

Grant still did not speak.

"All right, then, just answer me one question, just one. Will you do that?"

"If I can," Grant replied.

"Who is Ed Shine?"

55

Grant looked at her. "Ed Shine is Ed Shine," he said. "He has no criminal record; he has a history in New York as a property developer; he's even in *Who's Who*, for God's sake. The Bureau checked him out thoroughly; he is who he says he is. What is it that worries you about Shine?"

"Everything I've just told you," Holly replied. "If my theory is correct, he has to be a part of it. And it bothers me that our airplane was shot at by someone on the Blood Orchid property."

"How do you know that? The fire might have come from the river, or the beach, or a road somewhere around Blood Orchid."

"The angles were right," Holly said.

"Angles of fire can be deceiving," Grant said, "especially when you're the one being shot at. Anyway, you've been staying at Blood Orchid for two days, haven't you?"

"Yes."

"Well, if Shine wanted you dead, why didn't he just drop by and pump a few bullets into you?"

"Good point," Holly admitted. "He certainly had ample opportunity. But that guy from the airplane that unloaded the boxes was staring at me, and he made a call. Shortly after that, we were fired on."

"I stare at you all the time," Grant said. "Any red-blooded male would. And people make cellphone calls all the time, too. You're making a connection where there isn't one."

Holly sighed. "Maybe you're right."

"From what you've told me about Ed Shine, he's been nothing but nice to you. There are things that don't add up in this case, but Shine isn't one of them."

"All right, but let's go back to my theory about the exchange of money between criminal elements."

"Run your theory by me again."

"The Pellegrinos collect drug profits from various criminals in the States, then reimburse them with profits from their off-shore gambling operation."

"Oh, that theory."

"My question is, what do the Pellegrinos do with the money they collect inside the United States? It doesn't make any sense to just warehouse it in a vault at Blood Orchid; they have to do something with it."

"Like what?"

"Like buy up large chunks of real estate in Florida and, maybe, in other places. I mean, where did Ed Shine get the sixty million bucks to buy the place from the GSA?"

"He's a rich guy."

"Did the Bureau run financial checks as well as background checks on Ed?"

"I don't know."

"Grant, when you checked out Ed, how did you go about it?"

"I called the Bureau, and they did the legwork."

"Who did you call?"

"Harry Crisp."

"Why?"

"He's my boss; I'm assigned to the Miami field office, and he's the agent in charge. Harry also runs me, personally."

"Do you have any other way of running a check on somebody, without going through Harry?"

"Sure, I could call somebody I know in D.C. and get a check done, but why would I want to do that?"

"Did you ever ask Harry to run a check on the Pellegrinos?"

"Yes, I did."

"And what answer did you get?"

"The first time, no criminal record."

"And the second time you found out who they really were?"

"Yes."

"And what period of time passed between your first request and when you found out who they really were?"

Grant thought about it. "Two, three weeks, I guess."

"Did it ever occur to you that Harry might have known who they were all along?"

"Why are you asking me this?"

"Because quite a lot of time passed between when *I* asked Harry to check out the Pellegrinos and when I learned who they were. And I didn't learn it from Harry, I learned it from you. Harry has *never* told me that the Pellegrinos were the Falcones."

"Yeah, but you're not Bureau; I am."

"But what did Harry have to gain by keeping me in the dark about the Pellegrinos?"

"Nothing, probably. I've told you that the Bureau likes to keep information to itself."

"In that case, why did Harry keep *you* in the dark about the Pellegrinos? After all, you're Bureau; why should he hide anything from you?"

"Are you suggesting that Harry is somehow involved with the Pellegrinos?"

"Well, I was going to suggest that Harry Crisp is a self-aggrandizing son of a bitch who likes to take credit for other people's work, even his own agents', but I'm willing to entertain the thought that he might be dirty."

Grant shook his head. "Harry hasn't got it in him," he said.

"That's my take on Harry, too, but we could both be wrong. Look, Grant, I know that an agent doesn't get ahead in the Bureau by questioning his boss's honesty, but I think that, for our current purposes, you at least have to consider the possibility."

"All right, so Harry sometimes withholds information he shouldn't. Tell me something else that might suggest that he's dirty."

"Well, how about the murder of the guy at the General Services Administration?"

"What about it?"

"Why was he murdered?"

"I don't know."

"If you remember, it was that guy who first tipped Harry to the connection between Blood Orchid and the murders of the two Miami developers and the attempt on Ed Shine."

"It was?"

"Harry didn't tell you that?"

"Not that I recall."

"He probably told you that he turned up that information, but he actually got a call from the guy at the GSA, Howard Singleton, who alerted him to the connection."

"Okay, let's say that's true. What of it?"

"Wouldn't it make sense that Singleton was murdered by the Pellegrinos for that very reason? Because he noticed something funny and tipped off the FBI? And because they don't want it to happen again?"

"Maybe, but how does popping Singleton solve their problem? Harry told me he was already working with Singleton's successor, a guy named Willard Smith. He called Smith and asked if there were any other sales pending by the GSA that might be like the Blood Orchid sale, and Smith said no, nothing."

"So, what if Smith is the Pellegrinos' inside guy at the GSA? What if he was all along? He knows the GSA has another deal brewing, and he tips off the Pellegrinos that Singleton is about to queer it by going to the FBI."

Grant nodded. "That makes sense. And when Harry calls Smith about any other pending sales, Smith tells him there's nothing, just waves him off."

"You're starting to look interested in my theory, Grant."

"I have to admit that it makes a kind of sense, but it still doesn't mean that Shine tried to kill you."

They had reached Grant's house and pulled into the driveway.

"Turn around," Holly said.

"And go where?"

"Back to Blood Orchid."

"Are you nuts? You think somebody there is trying to kill you, and you want to go back?"

"I have an opportunity to be on the inside at Blood Orchid, and I think I can do more good there than on the outside. I've got you on the outside."

Grant turned around. "Well, if you go back, then maybe Shine won't think you suspect him."

"Let's hope not, but in the meantime, you've got to call your friend at Bureau headquarters and run a check on Ed that doesn't get filtered through Harry Crisp. And you've got to do more than just an ordinary background check."

"What else do you want?"

"Everything possible — credit history, education, every piece of information that might connect him to any other person or organization."

"That's going to take manpower, and they'd want Harry's approval for that."

"You've already been through Harry; can't you get it done without his knowing?"

Grant sighed. "I'll have to call in every marker."

"Isn't it worth it?"

"I hope so."

They reached the Blood Orchid gate and were passed through. As they drove in, Holly looked back at the gate and saw the guard making a phone call. They drove to the airfield, picked up Holly's car, and returned to the guest house.

When they arrived at the house, Holly and Daisy jumped out. "Come on in for a minute," she said. "I just thought of something."

He took her arm and stopped her. "Has it occurred to you that the house might be bugged?"

"No," she said.

"Behave as if it is."

In the house, she went to the wet bar and opened the shutters that concealed it. The two glasses she and Ed had used for their drinks on her first day there sat on the marble counter, still unwashed. She sniffed the glasses. "That one was the scotch." She got a Ziploc plastic bag from the kitchen, dropped the glass into it, and handed it to Grant. He held it up to the light, looked at it, and nodded.

Outside, she said, "Don't you want to look for bugs?"

"Why bother?" he replied. "If we found one, we wouldn't want to disable it; that would tip them off. Just don't say anything in the house or on the phone that you wouldn't want the bad guys to hear."

"Okay. Run the prints against every available database."

"Will do," he said. He put an arm around her. "I don't like leaving you here."

"I've got my cellphone," she said, patting her pocket. "I can use it outside the house to call you if I need you. If you call me, it may take a few rings for me to get outside, so don't hang up."

Grant gave Daisy a pat. "You take care of her, girl."

56

Holly got a little sleep, and was awakened by the doorbell. She opened the door to find Ed Shine standing there.

"Hi," Ed said. "I tried to call you for dinner last night and didn't get an answer. You been off the reservation?"

"Come in, Ed," Holly said, kissing him on the cheek. "I have a lot to tell you. I've got some coffee on; would you like some?"

"Don't mind if I do," Ed said, settling on the living room sofa.

Holly poured the coffee and brought milk and sugar.

"The gate guard said somebody brought you back here."

"Yes, that was Grant Early, my neighbor. I've been seeing him."

"Is it okay for him to know where you are? I've been worried."

"It's okay."

"So, what's up?"

Holly told him about her experience of the day before, and she watched his reaction closely. He appeared to be shocked.

"That's the most awful thing I've ever heard," Ed said. "You think it was this Rodriguez fellow?"

"Him or a friend of his."

"But how could he know that you were here? Have you told anybody?"

"No, no one, until yesterday. I spent the night at Ham's place. Grant picked me up and brought me back here. I still think this is the safest place I could be."

Ed picked up the phone and dialed a number. "Hurd? This is Ed. I'm over at guest house number two. Can you come over here right now? I need to talk to you. Good." He hung up. "I want to get Hurd on this right away."

"That's a good idea," Holly said. "I haven't told any of my people, but Hurd is like family."

"What happened to the airplane?" Ed asked.

"They'll remove the wings, load it onto a truck, and take it back to the Orchid Beach airport, where it will be repaired."

"God, you were lucky to get down in one piece." He scratched Daisy behind the ears, and she reacted with pleasure.

"I know we were lucky. Ginny's a fine pilot, and she got us down safely; it could have turned out differently."

There was a knock on the door and Hurd Wallace entered. "Morning," he said.

"Hurd, sit down," Ed said. "Holly's got something to tell you."

Hurd listened calmly as Holly related the

events of the day before. "I was on the practice tee, hitting some balls," he said, "and I heard something that sounded like a string of fire-crackers going off."

"It wasn't firecrackers," Holly said.

Hurd stood up. "I want to go and take a look at the area around the airfield right now," he said. "I'll report back to you as soon as I can, Ed."

Ed nodded, and Hurd left the house.

"What do you think all this means, Holly?"

"Well, Trini Rodriguez has got to be behind it," she replied. "And he knows that I'm the one who put the law on him."

"But how could he find you here?"

"I don't know. Have there been any people on the property the last couple of days that you don't know?"

"Just the construction crews," Ed replied. He looked at his watch. "I have to be going in a minute; someone's picking me up; I'm showing a house this morning."

"Ed, when I was waiting for Ginny to land, a business jet came in and dropped off some packages that were taken away by one of your vans. What would that have been?"

"Let's see," Ed said, scratching his head. "Plumbing supplies, I expect; special-order stuff. We needed them in a hurry, and a friend sent them down from Atlanta in his airplane."

"And who were the pilot and copilot?"

"They work for my friend; they're his regular

crew. Why? Do you think they had something to do with this?"

"I don't know. One of them made a cellphone call just before it happened, and he had been looking at me."

"Oh, Holly, I don't think he would have been involved. He was probably reporting to his base about having arrived here."

"I guess you're right, Ed. Maybe I'm getting paranoid."

There was a knock on the door, and a man stepped inside — fiftyish, tall, slender, dressed in an expensive-looking suit. "Hi, Ed, you ready?"

Ed Shine put down his coffee cup. "Yep. Holly, I'll tell Hurd to come tell you if he found anything out there."

"Thanks, Ed."

"You want to come look at a house with us?"

"Thanks, but I'm a little tired; think I'll try to get in a nap."

"We'll be going, then. Oh, Holly, this is Willard Smith. He's thinking of retiring to Blood Orchid."

Smith held out his hand and gave her a little smile. "Everybody calls me Smitty," he said.

57

Holly slept for an hour, then was wakened again by the doorbell. Hurd Wallace came in and tossed her a plastic bag with a shell casing inside. "I found that," he said, "behind some bushes at the north end of the runway."

"Thirty-caliber," Holly said, looking at the casing. "Military weapon, I guess."

"There's a lot of surplus stuff on the weapons market," Hurd said. "It could have come from anywhere. If somebody was firing on auto out there, he cleaned up after himself; I found just the one casing. What's going on, Holly?"

She tapped her ear with a finger and moved her hand in a circle.

Hurd frowned, but he seemed to get her point.

"It's this guy Rodriguez," she said. "There's a statewide APB out for him."

"We got a fax from the state police," Hurd said. "Nobody like that has been seen around Blood Orchid. There are so few people about that any visitor would be noticed."

"I guess so," Holly said, handing him back the cartridge case. She took his arm and walked him outside.

"You think the house is bugged?" Hurd asked.

"I don't know, maybe."

"Who do you think would be listening?"

"I don't know, but somebody here tried to kill me, and that's been happening way too often. I think I'm entitled to be a little paranoid."

"You suspect Ed Shine of being involved in something?"

Holly didn't hesitate. "No, Ed is the sweetest guy in the world, and he's been great to me." She wanted to trust Hurd, but she didn't know how deeply Ed had his hooks into his security chief.

"Me too," Hurd said.

"It may be that Rodriguez has just tracked me down. Will you keep an eye out for any strangers?"

"Sure I will, and I'll alert my whole force to do the same, all two of them."

Holly laughed.

"Do you have a weapon?"

"I've got my Beretta," she replied.

"Take an extra magazine," he said, handing her one.

"Thanks, Hurd."

"I'll talk to you later, if I find out anything."

"Use my cellphone number," she said. "You still have it?"

"I know it by heart."

"Hurd, you remember that building over on the north side of the property that has the vaults?"

"Yeah, I got a look at it once, after the Feds busted everybody."

"Do you know if there's been any activity around that building?"

Hurd blinked. "It's back in the trees, and the driveway has a sawhorse across it and a No Trespassing sign."

"If you get a chance to do it discreetly, could you have a look at the place, see if there's any sign that people have been in and out of it recently?"

"Sure."

"Don't let anybody see you."

"Okay, I'll be careful. You want me to mention this to Ed?"

"No, keep it to yourself."

"All right." He got into his Range Rover and drove away.

Her cellphone vibrated in her pocket, and she answered it.

"Hi, it's Grant. You okay?"

"Yep."

"I pulled some prints off your glass —"

"You mean you have a Junior-G-Man fingerprint kit with you at all times?"

"Sort of. Now listen."

"I'm listening."

"They're already working on it. We should have some answers tomorrow."

"Have you talked to Harry today?"

"Yes, and there's nothing new down there."

"Well, there's something new here," Holly

said. "Ed came by this morning and introduced me to a man who's thinking of buying a retirement home here. His name is Willard Smith."

"The guy from the GSA?"

"How many Willard Smiths can there be?"

"I'd better get back to Harry with that."

"Are you sure you should, Grant? I mean, in light of our conversation last night?"

"It's something Harry ought to know," Grant said.

"It's something Harry may already know," Holly replied. "If he's dirty."

"I'm going to have to think about that. The guy you met may not be the GSA Willard Smith, you know."

"Call the GSA and ask for Smith," Holly said. "I'm betting that he's not at work today."

"All right, I'll do that."

"Get back to me?"

"Sure."

"Bye."

"Bye." Holly punched off and went back into the house. Daisy was waiting, her leash in her mouth.

"Okay, baby," Holly said. "Let's take a walk."

They started out from the house, and Holly had an idea. The golf course outside her door was empty, so she cut across it, letting Daisy off her leash. The happy dog ran in big circles, enjoying the open space, just as she did on the beach. Holly looked around and still saw nobody, except a man in the distance mowing a green.

She reached the other side of the golf course and clipped the leash onto Daisy's collar again, as they walked along the road, heading north. Her recollection was that the driveway to the vault building was around a curve ahead of her, about a quarter of a mile along. Then she heard an airplane overhead.

She looked up to see a twin-engine turboprop circling to land at the Blood Orchid airfield. It wasn't Ed Shine's King Air; it looked more like a Piper Cheyenne. Holly crossed the road and walked into the woods far enough that she couldn't readily be seen from the road. Then she sat down with her back against a tree and waited, with Daisy lying beside her.

Nearly half an hour passed, and Holly saw a Blood Orchid van drive past. She and Daisy ran back to the road and just far enough to see around the big curve in the road.

The van had stopped, and a man got out of the passenger seat and moved aside the sawhorse blocking the drive. The van drove in, the sawhorse was replaced, and the van disappeared down the driveway.

Holly went back into the woods. "Come on, Daisy," she said, "we're going to do a little spying."

58

Holly walked through the woods with Daisy, keeping roughly parallel to the road, toward where she remembered the building to be. There had been two floors of administrative offices, she recalled, then the basement with vaults.

She saw the building through the trees and brush sooner than she had expected, and she realized that she was approaching it from the rear. She began to work her way to her left, in order to circle the building and see what was happening on the front side. Noise became a factor now, and she made her way slowly through the woods, keeping Daisy on a short leash and being as quiet as possible. Soon, she could hear voices.

There wasn't much in the way of conversation, just grunts and a word or two here and there about work. Holly turned more to her left, lest she come upon them too quickly and be spotted.

Finally, she moved past a corner of the building and could see what was taking place out front. Two men were unloading the van and moving the contents inside the building. This time there were no boxes, but an odd collection of old briefcases, suitcases, and trunks, all strapped shut with duct tape. Some could be carried by one man, others required a hand truck.

The unloading was going slowly, and this was what was causing what little conversation there was, mostly complaining. Holly wanted to see inside the front doors of the building, so she continued to work her way to the north, giving the parking area a wide berth. Once she had covered some ground, she could see three cars parked in the lot, all of which had been screened from her view by the van. She could see through the open doors of the building, too.

Not that there was much to see. The two men were loading the cases and trunks into an elevator. Then one of the men got on with them and pressed a button. The doors closed, and the lights above indicated the car was going to the basement. That left one man dealing with the remaining cargo.

Then Holly saw something that interested her. Half a dozen cases had been unloaded from the van and were waiting to be carried inside. The one man left was struggling with a foot-locker-sized trunk that seemed to be very heavy, and next to the rear of the van sat a good-sized plastic briefcase — like the others, taped shut.

Holly turned to Daisy. "Down, Daisy," she said, and the dog lay down. She dropped the leash on the ground and, holding up a hand, said firmly, "Stay. Stay, Daisy."

The dog looked at her and waited for a further signal.

Holly turned back toward the van; five yards of woods and twenty yards of parking lot separated her from it. The man was still struggling with the footlocker — the hand truck must be in the elevator, she reckoned, and the other man would be unloading the elevator in the basement. She worked her way left, until the van was between her and the second man, then she moved as silently as she could through the brush and ran for the van.

Reaching it, she stood beside the left rear wheel of the vehicle so her feet would be hidden from anyone on the other side who happened to look under it. She could hear the man dragging the trunk into the building. She darted her head out a foot, then back again. Through the window of the rear door, she caught a glimpse of the building's doorway, and the man could no longer be seen.

She got down on her knees and peeked again; he was still inside the building. Quickly, she crawled under the open van door and grabbed the briefcase. As she did, she could hear footsteps from inside the building, and they were coming toward her. The man had taken his burden inside and was returning for more. Holly flung herself and the briefcase back under the door and behind the van.

She sat by the rear wheel, hugging the briefcase and pulling her knees up as far as they
would go. She felt the van move as the man
went inside for more cases. Now was her best
chance. She got to her feet and ran for the
woods, lugging the briefcase, which was surprisingly heavy.

"Hey!" a man's voice yelled.

Holly dropped to the ground, holding out her
hand, signaling Daisy to stay.

"Hey, give me a hand with this trunk, will
you?" the man called again.

"Just a minute," came the reply.

"What's the holdup?"

"I thought I had another piece here, but I
can't find it."

"What do you mean, you can't find it?" The
first man's voice was louder now; he was coming
out of the building.

"It was right here at the rear of the van, a
briefcase. I know it was here."

Holly inched her way toward Daisy, who
waited four or five yards from her. Then she
heard a very unwelcome noise — an electronic
chime. Her cellphone was letting her know that
its battery was low. She dug into her pocket and
got it free just in time for it to chime again before she could hit the off switch.

"What was that?" one of the men said.

"What?"

"I heard something, like a little bell."

"What are you talking about?"

348

"Shut up and listen." Both men were quiet for a minute.

Holly had stopped moving, afraid of making even a tiny noise. Her left hand had fallen across a trail of ants, and now they began to bite. She rubbed her arm as much as she dared to get them off.

"I swear to God I heard a little bell-like thing," the first man said.

"Do you hear it now?" his companion asked.

"No."

"Do you hear angels singing?"

"What?"

"If you do, it's because I'm about to kill you if you don't start unloading again."

"Oh, all right, here — take this one." The normal noises of moving the luggage resumed.

Holly began to crawl toward Daisy again, rubbing her arm against her clothes to kill the ants, who were stinging like crazy now. "Stay, Daisy," she whispered as she crawled past the dog, putting yardage between herself and the van, moving the heavy briefcase before her.

She moved another five yards before she chanced a look over her shoulder. The van was no longer visible. She got to her knees and signaled Daisy to come. The dog trotted to her, dragging her leash, which made noise.

Holly hugged the dog, catching her breath, then took her leash in one hand, the briefcase in the other, and, in a crouch, put some more distance between herself and the van.

Finally, when she reckoned she was sixty or seventy yards away, in deep woods, she stopped. She lay the briefcase on its side and reached into her pocket for a miniature Swiss army knife she always carried.

She opened the large blade and slit the duct tape, then holding a hand over each, opened the latches. She raised the lid and looked inside.

"Good God," she said.

59

Holly stared at the money. There were rows of it, bound with rubber bands, twelve across and eight down — she lifted several stacks and counted — stacked six deep, all hundred-dollar bills. She quickly counted one stack. One hundred hundred-dollar bills — ten thousand dollars. She did the math: the case held five million, seven hundred and sixty thousand dollars.

Holly sat down and took a deep breath. She had never had her hands on so much money. For a moment she entertained the thought that she was a thief, stealing from bad people who deserved it, but she shook that off. She got up and, lugging the case, began to make her way back toward the golf course, following a slightly different route, so as not to beat down a trail that might be noticed later.

When she caught sight of the golf course through the trees, she stopped and looked around. She didn't want all that money in the house with her; she needed to hide it. She was standing in a grove of live oaks, dripping Spanish moss, none of them more than about twenty-five feet high.

She looked closely at a number of them, then chose one, hoisting the case onto a low limb and climbing up to it. She repeated the process until she was a good fifteen feet off the ground, where she found an ideal cradle for the case — two stout limbs, one growing out of the other, making a fork — at just the right angle from the trunk. She hoisted the case up and wedged it tightly between the two limbs. A hurricane wouldn't move it, she reckoned. And nobody ever looked up.

She climbed back down the tree, brushed the woods off her clothes, collected Daisy, and started toward the guest house. She waited before crossing the road to be sure no one could see her leaving the woods, then she and Daisy ran onto the golf course again. The man mowing the green was gone; they had the expanse of green grass to themselves. Holly found a stick and spent a few minutes tossing it for Daisy, who loved to retrieve, then she started back toward the house, thinking about what to do next.

When she arrived at the house there was a car parked out front. She walked into the living room to find Ed Shine and Willard Smith waiting for her. Daisy ran over to Ed and greeted him with a nuzzle.

"Hi," Ed said. "We just dropped by to see if you'd have dinner at the club with a bunch of us tonight."

"Sure," Holly said, thinking fast. "Do you

mind if I invite my friend Grant to join us? I sort of had a date with him tonight."

Ed hesitated for only a moment. "We'd be delighted to have him. Shall I pick you up at eight?"

"I'll call Grant and get him to pick me up."

"Go ahead," Ed said. He didn't move from his seat.

Holly picked up the phone, dialed nine for an outside line, then Grant's number.

"Hello," he said.

"Hi, it's Holly," she said brightly. "Listen, instead of our going out tonight, how about we have dinner at Blood Orchid? Ed Shine has invited us to join him and a friend, Willard Smith." She hoped he'd pick up on the name.

"Yeah, that sounds great."

"Good. Pick me up at the guest cottage at seven-thirty?"

"Okay, see you then."

Holly hung up. "All set," she said to Ed. "Can I get you guys a drink?"

Ed stood up. "No, thanks. We'll see you at eight, then?"

"You bet."

"I'll let the gate know Grant is coming." The two men left. Holly went out to the back patio and called Grant on her cellphone, which was still chiming its low-battery news.

"Hi, it's Grant," the recording said. "Leave a message, and I'll get back to you."

"It's Holly. Will you bring the battery charger

for my cellphone with you tonight? It's on the bedside table. I have a lot to tell you; I couldn't talk freely before." She punched off and went back inside, suddenly tired. She fed Daisy and stretched out on the sofa for a nap.

Holly was awakened by a knock on the door, then Grant's voice: "Hello? Anybody home?"

"Grant?" she said, sitting up. "Come in. My God, I've been asleep all this time. I've got to get dressed. Fix yourself a drink." She went into the bedroom and quickly changed her clothes and freshened up, then returned to the living room.

Grant handed her a drink, but she refused it. "I don't think we have time," she said. "Let's get going."

As soon as they were in the car, Holly began talking, rapid-fire. "It's money," she said. "They're bringing in money, just like I thought. I even stole some of it."

"Holly . . ."

"Don't talk, listen," she said.

"Holly . . ."

"Grant, will you shut up? I have things to tell you."

"No, *you* shut up. You're going to want to hear what I have to say."

"Oh, all right, say it."

"My people in Washington have been working like beavers. They got a make on the prints on the glass."

"Whose are they?"

"They belong to two people; one is Ed Shine."

"Yes, go on."

"The other is Gaetano Costello," Grant said.

"Who the hell is Gaetano Costello?"

"He was in the files — he's a second cousin to Frank Costello."

"Who?"

"Frank Costello was the number-one man in the mob after Charlie Luciano got deported in the late thirties. You may remember that he starred in some congressional hearings many years ago."

"So, tell me about Gaetano."

"He emigrated from Italy in July of 1938, at the age of thirteen, quite legally; that's when he got printed. Pretty soon, he had acquired the mob sobriquet of Eddie Numbers, because of his facility with math and money."

"Go on."

"Then, two years later, we have the appearance of Edward G. Shine on the scene. Little Eddie Shine entered a New York City public high school in September of 1940, giving his age as thirteen. His parents were listed in the school records as Mr. and Mrs. Alvin Shine, and here's the good part. Mr. and Mrs. Shine lived in the same apartment building as Mr. and Mrs. Meyer Lansky."

"Holy shit!"

"My very words when I heard about it. It appears that the mob recognized talent when they saw it, and they went to some trouble to hide little Gaetano's light under a bushel. He graduates as Edward Shine, with honors, in June of 'forty-five, just in time to get drafted. Not surprisingly, little Eddie turns up at his physical with a perforated eardrum, making him ineligible. He applied for and was issued a passport the following year."

"He was already a citizen?"

"Somehow, a birth certificate in his name appeared in the public records, stating that he was born in 1927 to Mr. and Mrs. Shine. I think we can attribute that to the fine Italian hand of Frank Costello, who owned many politicians. Little Eddie studies in Italy for a year, it's not certain where, then returns to the U.S. and enters NYU, graduating in 1951 with a degree in accounting and business management. The following year, he builds his first office building."

"What a precocious boy," Holly said.

"From then on, he's in the New York commercial real estate business big time, and he never seems to have any trouble getting financing."

"Because his mob friends are laundering their cash through his projects?"

"Exactly." Grant pulled into the parking lot of the Blood Orchid Club and parked. "And guess who he's doing most of his business with."

"Who?"

Then somebody opened the car door.

60

Ed Shine stood at the car door. "There you are," he said, beaming. "Come inside, there are people I want you to meet."

Holly and Grant got out of the car and followed Ed into the club. "Are you armed?" she whispered to him.

Grant shook his head.

There was one large, round table set for eight by the windows overlooking the golf course.

"I believe we're all here," Ed said, waving at some people at the bar. "Let's be seated," he called to them.

From the shadows of the bar, two men and two women approached. Holly knew two of them.

"Holly, I believe you've met Pio Pellegrino at his restaurant in Miami."

"Of course," Holly said.

"I believe you had a different name that evening," Pio said smoothly.

"Forgive me; a single woman alone in Miami, I was being careful."

"Of course."

"And this is Pio's father," Ed said, "Ignacio. We call him Iggy."

The old man bowed his head slightly, un-smiling.

"And this is Iggy's daughter, Allegra, and Pio's wife, Barbara; we call her Babs." Babs was thin and elaborately coiffed, with big eyes and a wide mouth. Allegra Pellegrino was a tall, solidly built woman with black hair and blacker eyes. "Everybody, this is Holly's friend, Mr. Grant Early, who may yet be a resident at Blood Orchid. Grant, I don't believe you've met Willard Smith."

Grant shook hands all around.

"Please be seated," Ed said, waving a hand at the table. "There are place cards for everyone."

Holly found herself seated between Ed and Pio. "What a beautiful table, Ed," she said. "The flowers are lovely." She glanced over at Grant, who was seated between Barbara and Allegra Pellegrino. He was chatting amiably, as if this were the most normal of dinner parties.

Holly couldn't figure out why she was here, and she didn't like it. Nearly everybody in the world she wanted to arrest was in this room.

"We're starting with beluga caviar and a Veuve Clicquot Grande Dame champagne," Ed announced to the group, as plates were set before them.

Holly figured there were at least four ounces of the black roe on her plate. Blinis, sour cream, and chopped onion were passed around. Holly ignored them, picked up a small spoon, and began to eat the caviar unaccompanied. The champagne was a perfect accompaniment.

Grant seemed to be enjoying it, too.

Holly found the atmosphere more and more oppressive. "Will you excuse me, Ed?" she said. "And could you point me to the ladies' room?"

"Of course, Holly," Ed replied. "Allegra, why don't you show Holly where the ladies' room is?"

Holly rose and walked toward the bar area. Allegra silently fell into step with her. Holly felt as if she were under armed guard, and maybe she was: Allegra was carrying a very large handbag.

Holly went into the farthest stall, while Allegra washed her hands. Holly was grateful for the noise of running water, since it covered the sound of her dialing Harry Crisp's home number on her cellphone.

"Hi, we're out," Harry's voice said. "Leave a number at the beep, and we'll call you back." As Holly started to speak, her phone bleeped and went dead. The battery was flat. She left the stall and washed her hands. Allegra was messing with her makeup.

"I didn't know Pio had a sister," Holly said, trying to find out if the girl could speak.

"Yeah," Allegra replied, snapping shut her compact.

They went back to the table, where waiters were removing the plates from the first course. Holly sat down.

"You know," Pio said conspiratorially, "you're

a good-looking girl. Maybe we could get together sometime?"

"Why, Pio," Holly said, "whatever would your
wife say?"

"She'd enjoy it," Pio replied with a smile.
"She likes to watch."

Holly gulped at the thought.

"Now, our main course," Ed announced.
"*Boeuf* Wellington."

A waiter appeared carrying a large platter and
presented the mound of pastry to the diners.
Everyone clapped lightly.

The waiter sliced the beef into thick slabs and
served it.

Holly felt as though this were a last supper of
sorts, but at least it was a good supper. She
began trying to think of a way to get out of here.
Grant was annoying her now, blithely chatting
up Barbara Pellegrino, who looked as though
she would like Grant for her main course, instead of the beef. He knew who these people
were; he could at least have the grace to look
worried, she thought.

Holly directed her attention to Ed, pointedly
ignoring Pio. "So, Ed, is this a business dinner,
or just pleasure?"

"A bit of both, sweetheart," Ed said in his af-
fable way. "I hope you're enjoying yourself."

"The food is wonderful," Holly replied.
"What sort of business are you in together?"

"Real estate, of course. This is really sort of a
celebration of a new property we've just bought

in South Beach, Miami. In less than a year, we're going to have the hottest hotel on the beach."

"Another deal like Blood Orchid?" Holly asked.

"Very much the same," Ed replied. "Smitty, over there, is the new head of the Miami office of the General Services Administration, and this is the second property we've bought from them. There will be more, you may be sure."

"Sounds wonderful," Holly said.

"Oh, it is, believe me. Within five years we're going to be the second largest holder of resort property in Florida, right after Disney. And by that time, gambling will be legal in Florida, and we'll be the largest operators of casinos."

"Gambling legal in Florida?" Holly asked. "I haven't heard anything about that."

"You will," Ed replied.

Holly glanced at Grant to see if he was hearing any of this.

"We're out shopping for state legislators right now," Ed said.

"Ed," Holly said, "I thought Blood Orchid was your swan song in real estate; I thought you were going to retire here."

"I hope you'll forgive that little fib, Holly. I didn't want anyone to know what my plans were. Did I mention that we bought a bank in the next county?"

"No, you didn't."

"You can't imagine what a convenience it is to own a bank," Ed said, grinning.

Dessert was served — baked Alaska — and Holly declined, instead continuing to toy with her beef. Her head was spinning with the scale of what Ed Shine and the Pellegrinos were planning. Certainly, funding it all was no problem, not with all the cash piling up in the vaults across the golf course from where they sat.

"Well, Holly," Ed said, "have you digested all that?" He wasn't referring to dinner.

"Not quite, Ed, I'm still working on it." It worried her that he was telling her all this, as if he didn't expect her to be able to pass it on.

"Well, while you do, let me tell you a little story about myself." He put down his napkin and turned toward Holly. "I've been coming to Florida for more than forty years, you know."

"No, I didn't."

"No reason why you should. You may recall that I told you I didn't have any children?"

"Yes."

"Well, none to speak of, as they say. A little over thirty years ago, I spent a few weeks in Miami, and I had a rather passionate liaison with a young lady of Latino extraction. That union produced a child, and while I wasn't on hand for all the usual occasions — birthdays, Christmas, and so on, I certainly kept a fatherly eye on his rearing, and the boy has turned out to be very useful to me in my business."

A figure had appeared in the shadows of the bar, and Ed waved him over. "Enrico, come over here; there's someone I want you to meet." Ed turned to Holly. "He's been dying to meet you."

Holly turned and watched the man approach.

"Holly," Ed said, "this is my son, Enrico."

Trini Rodriguez, dressed in a severely cut black suit, smiled a broad smile.

61

This was bad. Holly saw Grant getting to his feet and offering Trini his hand. "How do you do?" he asked.

Trini ignored him and continued to stare at Holly.

"Grant!" Holly said. "Have you got a weapon on you?" It was a stupid thing to say, but it caused everyone to look at Grant, while Holly dropped her napkin onto her steak knife and gathered it into her lap.

"What?" Grant replied, incredulously. "A weapon, did you say?"

"Only joking," Holly replied.

"Why would I have a weapon?" Grant asked, as if he thought she were insane.

"Yes, Holly," Ed said, "why would he? You seem to be very nervous, sweetheart."

Holly turned to Ed. "I take it you're fully informed of your son's activities over recent days?"

"Why, of course," Ed replied. "Enrico does only what I ask him to." He turned to Trini. "And, Enrico, right now I'd like you to take Miss Barker back to her cottage."

"Why?" Holly asked. She slipped the steak knife into her waistband under her jacket.

"Yes, why?" Grant echoed.

"Because my son has expressed an interest in having some time alone with Miss Barker," Ed said.

Holly felt a wave of nausea.

"Enrico," Ed said, "you may as well deal with Mr. Early, too," Ed said.

Grant was on his feet, looking wary. He turned to face Trini.

Trini raised a hand containing a semiautomatic pistol and shot Grant in the chest. Grant flew backward onto the floor, knocking over his chair.

Barbara Pellegrino began screaming, and Holly got up and rushed around the table to Grant and bent over him. "Grant, Grant," she was yelling.

Grant opened his eyes and winked at her, then closed them again. Then she realized there was no blood, just a neat hole in his shirt. She put her hand on his chest and felt the vest underneath his shirt.

Holly stood up and faced Trini, who was walking toward her, holding the weapon at his side. "You miserable son of a bitch!" she yelled at him. "You've killed him!"

Trini smiled and drew back his empty hand to hit her. Holly ducked, and Trini's knees suddenly buckled as Grant reached up, grabbed his coattails, and pulled him off balance. She got ahold of his gun hand with both hands and held on for dear life. Then Grant got ahold of Trini's belt and pulled him over on top of himself. Holly followed, falling on Trini. His gun went off.

There was a scream from behind her; the bullet had found its way to somebody, but Holly couldn't see who. Grant was twisting Trini's arm now, and Holly could let go with one hand. She felt for the heavy steak knife at her waist, got ahold of it and plunged it into Trini's neck, twisting it and yanking it out the way she had been trained in the army. Blood began to spurt rhythmically from Trini's jugular.

Grant got the gun free from him and was getting to his feet when a man with a shotgun stepped up and hit him across the back of his head with the butt of the weapon.

Where the hell had he come from? Holly wondered. He was pointing the shotgun at her now, motioning for her to drop the knife. She dropped it.

Willard Smith was sitting back in his chair, blood all over his chest, so Holly knew where the stray round had gone.

Ed Shine had run around the table and was kneeling at his son's side. "What have you done?" he shouted at Holly.

"What he's been doing to everybody else," Holly said.

"Enrico," Ed was saying, trying to stanch the flow of blood with his dinner napkin.

Trini's eyes were fluttering, and he looked panicked, but it was clear to Holly that he was bleeding out very quickly. A moment later, he stopped moving.

Ed stood up, his hands covered with Trini's blood. "I was fond of you," he said to Holly. "I was going to make you a rich woman."

"When, after Trini had finished with me? He's been trying to kill me for some time, you know, and you've already said he does only what you want him to."

Other men with shotguns were in the room now. Shine turned to one of them. "Take these two over to the admin building and put them into vault number two, the empty one, then set the security system to the emergency mode."

Someone drew Holly's hands behind her and she felt herself being handcuffed. Grant had begun to stir, and he was handcuffed as well. They were frog-marched out of the building and tossed into the rear of a Blood Orchid van. While one man sat in the rear seat, covering them with a shotgun, another drove rapidly toward the administration building, where a vault awaited them.

62

Grant shifted his body until he was lying close behind Holly, and he put his lips close to her ear. "Can you roll over and reach my cellphone?" he whispered. "It's in my inside jacket pocket, down low. Your hands are near it now."

Holly groped behind her and felt his belt buckle.

"To your left six inches," Grant said.

Holly found the phone.

"Now, pry it open — it's already turned on."

Holly got the phone open.

"Press one and hold it down for a few seconds."

Holly felt the keypad of the phone, located the number one, and held it down.

Grant waited a moment, then began shouting. "Now!" he yelled. "Do it now!"

"What?" Holly asked, as if he were talking to her.

"You two shut up," the man with the shotgun said.

"Why now?" Holly asked, hoping to confuse the man.

"Now! Do it now!" Grant yelled again.

The man with the shotgun rapped him sharply on the top of the head with the barrel. "I told you to shut up."

"Why do you want to lock us in a vault?" Grant asked the man loudly. "Why can't you just shoot us?"

"Believe me, I'd just as soon shoot you, but the boss says to put you in the vault!" the man yelled back. "He didn't say I couldn't crack your skull first, though, and that's what I'm going to do if you open your mouth again!"

The van stopped, and the driver got out and opened the rear doors. He dragged Holly and Grant to their feet, and the two men unlocked the front door and shoved them roughly into the building, then into the elevator.

Holly and Grant each stood in a corner of the elevator, looking at each other as they descended one floor.

"Don't open your mouths," one of the men said.

They were dragged off the elevator in the basement and taken down a hallway to a vault, the door of which stood open. The two men kicked them into the vault and then swung the foot-thick door slowly shut.

Holly heard the mechanical sound of the bolts closing. "Well, shit," she said.

"My sentiments exactly," Grant replied.

"Back in the van, who was on the other end of the cellphone?"

"I hope to God it was Harry," he said. "He's out there somewhere with forty or fifty men."

"Out where?"

"Outside Blood Orchid, ready to storm the place at my signal. At least I hope he is; that was the plan. I didn't have time to tell you everything in the car. As soon as we figured out who Shine was, Harry went into action, getting warrants and marshaling resources."

"You think he got your signal?"

"I was yelling loud enough, wasn't I?"

Then came the sound of running water.

"What's that?" Grant asked.

"The sound of running water," Holly replied. "Do you think that was what Ed meant by 'emergency mode'?"

"Oh, shit," Grant said, and as he spoke a sheet of water made its way across the floor of the vault. They heard the sound of another valve opening, and more water began to pour in.

"Why the hell would anybody want to put water into a vault?" Holly asked. "Apart from drowning us, I mean?"

"I think the vaults at Fort Knox can be flooded. Maybe that's where they got the notion. Any ideas?" Grant asked.

Holly stepped around him and nuzzled close. "Put your hand in my pocket," she said.

"Is sex all you can think about at a time like this?"

"The left-hand pocket," she said. "Get ahold of my car keys."

"You want to drive somewhere? That's okay with me."

The water was up to their shins now, and rising fast.

"There's a handcuff key on my key ring," Holly said.

"Oh," Grant replied, groping in her pocket. "Got them."

Holly turned around and backed up to him. "Now, unlock my cuffs and don't drop the keys."

Grant dropped the keys.

"I told you not to drop them!" Holly moaned.

"I'm sorry, they were slippery."

She put her back against the wall and slid down into a sitting position, then began groping around the floor for the keys. Sitting down, the water was up to her chin. "Don't just stand there, help me!"

Grant sat down beside her and joined the effort.

"Got them!" Holly said, and her mouth filled with water. Leaning against Grant, she struggled to her feet. "Can you stand up?"

"I'm trying," he said.

"Lean against me."

He managed to get to his feet.

"This time, I'll do the unlocking," she said, feeling for Grant's wrists. After a moment she got one of his cuffs off.

He took the key and unlocked her cuffs and his other wrist. "There," he said, "that's better."

"Not much," Holly said. "What do we do now, the backstroke?" The water was waist deep and rising.

"Brackish," Grant said, tasting a finger. "River water."

"What is this, a tasting? Or do you want to get us out of here?"

"My cellphone's in the van; how about yours?"

"Dead battery; I tried it in the ladies'. I doubt if we could get a signal inside a steel basement room, anyway."

"You have a point," Grant said, then he ducked under the water and started feeling the vault door.

Holly watched him, wondering what the hell he was doing.

Grant came up for air. "There's got to be some sort of safety feature in this thing. Surely they can't let people get locked into vaults these days without having a way out."

"Let's both look," Holly said "At least the lights are on."

The lights went off.

"We'll just have to feel," Grant said.

Holly took a couple of deep breaths and began running her hands over the inside of the vault door. Her air gave out, and she came up. The water was up to her neck.

Grant surfaced. "I don't think this is going to work," he said. "Anything you want to say to me before we drown?"

"Yes," Holly replied, "what are you working

on in Orchid Beach? What's your assignment?"

"I can't tell you that," Grant replied. "It's a secret."

Holly burst out laughing. The water was up to her nose now, and she was forced to tread water.

"Come on, let's keep trying," Grant said, and went under again.

Holly dove after him, wondering if there would be any air left in the vault when she came up.

63

Holly came up for air again, and her head bumped against the ceiling before her nose cleared the water. She leaned back and sucked in air, trying to pack it into her lungs. She heard Grant doing the same thing. Then she dove under again.

She swam to the bottom of the door, running her hands desperately over the smooth surface. Then she came to a handle, like that on a cupboard. She turned it and a door opened. Inside was another handle, like a lever. She pulled hard on the lever. Grant was above her, doing something.

Then, in the darkness, three green lights began to flash in sequence. She watched them, her lungs bursting, and then she heard a mechanical noise.

She didn't even have to push the door; the pressure of eight feet of water did that. Light streamed in from the hallway as Holly and Grant poured out of the vault along with the water.

Holly landed on top of Grant as they both sucked in lungfuls of air.

"What happened?" Grant asked.

"I found a door and a lever, and I pulled it."

"I knew something had to be there."

"I'll remember that if I'm ever locked in a flooded vault again."

They sat on the floor, leaning against the wall.

"I don't know if I can stand up," Holly said.

"If you can do that, help me."

Together they struggled to their feet. "Let's get out of here before somebody comes," Grant said.

"Not the elevator," Holly said. "The electrics may have gotten wet." They were splashing around in a couple of feet of water. She pointed at a lighted exit sign. "There, the stairs."

A moment later, they emerged one floor up into the upstairs lobby. The front doors were locked.

There was a small steel table and a chair in the lobby, as if for a guard to use. Grant picked up the table and hurled it at one of the glass doors, which shattered. A siren went off, and lights began to flash.

"Follow me," Holly said. "I know how to get out of here." She ran around the building and into the woods. There was a moon, and after her eyes had become accustomed to the dim light, she could see her way. "You with me?"

"Right behind you. Where are we going?"

Holly stopped. "What was the plan?"

"What plan?"

"The plan for Harry and his people to take

this place? Where were they going to come from?"

"From all sides," Grant said.

"Let's head for the airfield. When the balloon goes up, Ed might try to get out that way."

"Whatever you say," Grant replied.

Holly set off at a trot, with Grant close behind. After two or three minutes, she stopped.

"What is it?" he asked.

Holly looked above her. "I'm looking for something."

"What?"

"Just something. Hang on for a minute." She knew she was somewhere close by.

"Holly, we're in the middle of the woods. What are you looking for?"

"There; this is the tree. I don't have a knife. Have you got one?"

Grant fished in his pockets and came up with a pocketknife.

Holly took it and began carving something in the tree trunk.

"That's sweet of you, Holly, but I don't think this is the time for you to carve our initials into a tree."

"Not yours, just mine," she said, pointing at an *H*. "Okay, we can go now. I want to go back to the guest cottage."

"Why?"

"It's on the way to the airfield, and I want Daisy with me. Come to think of it, my gun is there, too."

"You take Daisy, I'll take the gun."

"We'll see." She stopped him at the road's edge and looked around. "Come on!" She sprinted across the road and onto the golf course. It took her less than a minute to cross the course to the trees on the other side, and she stopped to get her breath.

Grant pulled up beside her. "Jesus, I haven't run that fast in years."

"It's not much farther. Come on." She jogged off in the direction of the cottage. There was still a light on in the living room, and she looked through a window before opening the door. Daisy was on her feet, alert.

Holly rushed into the room and hugged the dog.

"Hi, Daisy," Grant said. "Holly, where's the gun?"

Holly went into the bedroom and came back with her Beretta and two clips. "You think we can risk using the phone to call Harry?"

"We can't," Grant said.

"Why not?"

"Because I can't remember his cellphone number. I had it programmed into mine, and that's in the back of the van now. Where's yours?"

"In my purse, back at the clubhouse."

Holly picked up the phone, dialed nine, and got a dial tone. She dialed a number she knew by heart.

"Hi, this is Hurd," the machine said, "leave a

message." Holly hung up and dialed another number.

"Wallace," he said.

"Thank God you've got your cellphone."

"What's up, Holly?"

"Everything." Then she stopped herself. If someone was listening, she couldn't blow the imminent arrival of the FBI. "Call your former workplace," she said. "And order a six-six-six."

"Where?"

"You know where. I'm heading for where you found the shell casing."

"Got it."

Holly hung up.

"What's a six-six-six?" Grant asked.

"Doesn't the FBI have a six-six-six?"

"No. What is it?"

"It means everybody converge with everything they've got. Devil's drill."

"I hope they don't think it's a drill."

"I hope they don't start shooting at the FBI," Holly said, "but we've got to get *somebody* here."

A car's lights flashed across the windows, and there was the crunch of gravel in the driveway.

"Let's get out the back way," Holly said, crouching and running. "Come on, Daisy."

64

Holly ran out the back door, through the bushes, across a road, and into more bushes. Two minutes later, they could see the landing lights of the runway, ending almost at their feet. Ed Shine's King Air was sitting on the ramp, near the middle of the runway, and two pilots in white shirts were walking around the airplane, as if to preflight it.

"I don't suppose you're a good enough shot to hit the tires of that airplane from this distance," Holly said.

"How far is it?"

"The runway is six thousand feet, so three thousand, give or take."

"More than half a mile, with a handgun? Yeah, sure."

"Me neither," she said. "We need to get closer to the airplane."

"It's all open ground between here and there," Grant said. "And there's a moon up there, remember?"

"They're not expecting us," Holly said. "And they're looking at the airplane. Come on." She got up, crossed the runway, and began running down the opposite side, Daisy keeping pace with her. As she ran, she saw the headlights of a vehicle approaching the ramp, down the road on the other side of the runway. From the direction of the main gate she heard four or five gunshots. She began to run faster. How long did it take to run half a mile?

She could see the van stopping at the airplane and people getting out. Their movements were not leisurely; they were in a hurry. Half a dozen people boarded the airplane.

"We're not going to make it," Grant said.

Holly stopped running. They were still at least five hundred feet from the airplane. "We don't have to," she said.

"What?"

"I can get a shot from here."

"Holly, you might hit something with a rifle and a scope, but not with the Beretta."

The airplane's engines started, and it began to move.

"They've got to use the runway to take off; let's let them come to us." The airplane was taxiing down the runway in the opposite direction.

"Where's he going to go?" Grant asked.

"The Bahamas? The Dominican Republic? Haiti? Wherever he can get fuel, and then he's off."

Grant lay down on the ground and pulled his knees up. "Brace on my knees," he said. "Keep your arm straight and fire one round at a time

— no rapid fire. Try for the nosewheel."

The airplane had turned and was starting down the runway, the two turboprop engines screaming as they achieved full power.

"Don't pan with the airplane," Grant said. "Let it come to you, then fire, re-aim, and fire again."

"Daisy, down," Holly said. She braced herself against Grant's knees and took aim about a third of the way down the runway. She reckoned she could get off three shots that had any hope of connecting — one early, one abeam of her, and one late.

"Lead it a little," Grant said.

The airplane was picking up speed now, and in a second, Holly would fire her first shot. She squeezed off the round and saw sparks as the bullet ricocheted off the runway, a yard ahead of the airplane's nosewheel.

"Next one is the toughest," Grant said. "Lead a lot."

As the airplane drew abeam of her, Holly fired her second round and saw nothing, no effect.

"Now don't lead," Grant said.

Holly swung the gun around, aimed carefully, and fired. The airplane's nose dropped a little, and sparks flew as the tire disintegrated and the metal wheel ran along the runway. The pilot lifted the nosewheel off the ground.

"Shit, he's going to take off!" Holly yelled.

The airplane rose at a nose-high angle, and the main gear came a couple of feet off the ground. But it wasn't gaining any altitude. She saw the landing gear come up.

"He doesn't have enough airspeed," Grant said. "He's going to stall it."

As if on cue, the King Air fell onto the runway from a height of about six feet. The airplane skidded down the runway, turning sideways, then swapping ends.

Holly was on her feet, running, amazed by how far the airplane could slide. Finally, the airplane slowed, then stopped. It was a thousand feet away, and Holly knew the pilot would want to get his passengers off in a hurry. The door fell open, banging on the runway, and people began to pour out.

Grant yelled, "FBI! Freeze! FBI! Stop or we'll fire."

From somewhere in the distance, Holly heard the siren of a police car. "That's my people," she said.

Then the firing started. Someone in the group from the airplane began automatic fire, but he didn't know exactly where to shoot, so the shots went wide.

Holly hit the runway on her belly, her gun out in front of her, and took aim at the man with the assault weapon. She squeezed off two shots and heard somebody yell in pain.

"You're shooting well tonight," Grant said. "Let's just stay right here until the cavalry arrives."

But Holly was already up and running.

"Come on, Daisy, stay with me." She was looking for Ed Shine, and she wanted him badly. She could smell jet fuel now. A tank had ruptured.

Somebody fired a shotgun in her direction, only a yard wide. Holly stopped running and aimed at the runway under the airplane's wing. She fired two more rounds, sparks flew, and the fuel caught fire. The airplane had been spilling fuel as it slid, and the blaze raced up the runway toward Holly; she sidestepped it and kept running, Daisy alongside her.

Then the flames under the airplane spread upward and both wings exploded, a fraction of a second apart. A man with a shotgun threw it aside and ran in circles, covered in flames. Other figures could be seen running away from the airplane, one with snowy white hair.

"Daisy," Holly said, pointing at him. "Get Ed! Get Ed! Guard!" Daisy took off after him, while Holly skirted the burning airplane, looking for other people with weapons.

Two cars, a white Range Rover and an Orchid Beach PD patrol car sped down the runway toward the airplane, lights flashing and sirens on. Both cars screeched to a halt beside Holly. "Holly?" Hurd's voice said from the Range Rover.

"Right," Holly replied. "Half a dozen people left that airplane before it caught fire, and they've scattered out there somewhere," she said, swinging her arm across the area beside the runway. "Hurd, you stick with me. You go round up those people and cuff them," Holly yelled at the other car. "Some of them may be armed, so be careful." The car sped off. "You follow me, Hurd. Stay behind me, I need your headlights."

Then Holly heard a man yelling from out in the darkness. "Get off me, get off me!"

"Ed, is that you?" Holly asked, running toward the voice, the Range Rover following.

"Get the dog off me!" he yelled back.

Holly saw him now, lying on his back, with Daisy standing beside him in the guard position, fangs bared, growling. "Daisy, sit; stay," she said.

Ed Shine sat up, then struggled to his feet. "You! How did . . ."

"Vault doors have safety releases on the inside, Ed," she said. "Sorry about your airplane."

"Why don't you just shoot me?" Shine said disconsolately.

"No, Ed," Holly said. "I couldn't stand it; that would be too much fun." Hurd cuffed him and put him into the back of the car.

"I don't know what's going on here, Holly," Hurd said, "but it looks like I'm out of a job."

"Hurd," Holly said, "as far as I'm concerned, you never left the department; the job is still yours."

Then a black van with a flashing red light on top drove up, and Harry Crisp got out, wearing full FBI battle regalia — body armor, helmet, the works. "Okay, Holly, I'll take it from here," he said.

"The hell you will, Harry," Holly said. "This is my collar. You can have whatever stragglers you can pick up."

"This is a federal matter, Holly," Harry said.

"Tell it to a judge," Holly replied. "You're on *my* turf, Harry."

Grant walked up. "Harry, where the hell have you been? Didn't you get my call?"

"Yeah, but I didn't know exactly what it meant," Harry replied.

"You didn't know what NOW, do it NOW! meant?"

"I think you fellows need to have a little chat," Holly said, getting into the Range Rover. "Have a nice evening." She drove away.

65

Holly and Grant lay on a double chaise beside the swimming pool at The Marquesa, a small but luxurious Key West inn, sipping rum and tonics. Daisy slept in a puddle of shade under a nearby tree.

"This isn't bad, is it?" Grant asked.

"I've been in worse places," Holly agreed. "You know, this is the first vacation I've had since I took the job in Orchid Beach? I was supposed to have a honeymoon, but . . ."

"Yeah, I know. I'm glad you could take the time now. Harry's still pissed off at you, you know."

"Why? I told him he could have Ed Shine as soon as he's done his time. If Harry had been straight with me about a few things, he'd be a lot happier now."

"I haven't mentioned that to him, but you're right," Grant said. "You've committed the cardinal sin with Harry, you know; you prevented him from taking all the credit."

"Yeah, and I'm really crushed about that."

"There are rumors that he may get transferred to a less desirable post."

"Oh?" Holly asked. "What will I do for entertainment?"

"In the meantime, he's got another assignment for me. Undercover again."

Holly sat up on one elbow. "Where?"

"I can't tell you; it's a secret."

Holly poured her icy drink on his chest. "Just for that, I'm not going to tell you where the five million seven hundred and sixty thousand dollars is."

"What?" Grant asked, flicking ice off his chest and mopping with a towel.

"I took five million seven hundred and sixty thousand dollars from Ed's stash at Blood Orchid," Holly said.

"How the hell did you do that?"

"I was watching them unload a van at the admin building, and I filched it when they weren't looking. I wanted to know what was inside. Then I hid it."

Grant sat up and looked at her. "The tree," he said. "The one where you carved the *H*. You buried it near there."

"I'm not talking," Holly said smugly.

"You can't keep it, you know."

"I was thinking of giving it to you," she said playfully. "But not if you're going to disappear on me."

"It belongs to the government."

"Why should it? I stole it, fair and square."

"No, you stole if from the government."

"At the time, the government had not even

expressed an interest in it, let alone possessed it."

Grant lay back on the chaise. "This is an interesting situation," he said. "You stole it from Ed Shine, which means drug dealers. He probably doesn't even know it."

"I shouldn't think so."

"You're not a federal employee."

"No, I'm not."

"But it's still grand theft."

"Who is the complainant?"

"There isn't one, I suppose," he admitted.

"It was my intention to give the money to the FBI and have them use it as a basis for a search warrant, but, of course, I was overtaken by events."

"I should probably arrest you," Grant said.

"For what?"

"For stealing that money."

"What money?"

"The money buried under the tree."

"What tree?"

"The one with your initial on it."

"I think if you could actually find the spot where we were that night — not that we were ever there — you wouldn't find my initial on any tree in the woods."

"You moved the money?"

"What money?"

"I give up," Grant said, lying down.

"Smart move."

"Probably not."

"So, when are you leaving for your new assignment?"

"First of the week."

"And when will I see you again?"

"I don't know how long this will take."

"I'd rather you didn't go," she said.

"Holly, it's what I do."

"No, it isn't."

"Yes, it is."

"I'm telling you, it's not what you do. Not anymore."

Grant sat up again. "Do you know something I don't?"

"I know a lot of things you don't," she replied smugly.

"What? Come on, tell me."

"I know a lot of stuff."

"I'm going to go get my gun."

Holly raised her hands in surrender. "Well, let's see: The rumor about Harry's reassignment is true, but as I understand it, they haven't yet found a place awful enough to transfer him to."

"Who have you been talking to?"

"A gentleman named William Barron, who, I believe, is a deputy director of the FBI."

"Barron? How the hell do you know him?"

"I don't know him, exactly; he came to see me after we shut down Blood Orchid."

"Why?"

"He had a lot of questions about how the whole thing came off. He wanted to know everything, right from the beginning."

"And what did you tell him?"

Holly shrugged. "Everything."

"Holly, are you telling me that you blew Harry Crisp out of the water?"

"Nope, all I did was to tell that nice Mr. Barron everything I knew. I didn't cast any aspersions; he drew his own conclusions."

"When does Harry go?"

"I believe he's already gone."

"And what was that you said about my work not being my work?"

"Come Monday, you're going to have a new job," she said.

Grant sat up straighter. "How do you know this?"

"Because I have a little handwritten note from Mr. Barron in my bag; it was delivered this morning."

Grant grabbed at her bag, but she snatched it away and put it where he couldn't reach it.

"Holly, you're killing me."

"Well, I certainly don't want to kill you. Not now, anyway; maybe later."

"Do you know what my new assignment is?"

"Yes. That was the purpose of Mr. Barron's little note. He thought you might like to hear it from me, while the Bureau is doing whatever they have to do to produce an official letter."

"What? Where?"

"Agent in charge. Miami office."

He grabbed her and pulled her up to his face. "This is not some sadistic joke on your part?"

Holly reached in her bag and produced the note. Grant read it and handed it back, then he waved at a waiter. "Two more rum and tonics," he said.

"So, how do you feel?"

Grant lay back on the chaise. "Lighter than air," he said. "There's only one problem."

"What's that?"

"Now I *have* to arrest you for stealing that money."

"What money?" she asked.

Acknowledgments

I want to express my thanks to all the people at Putnam who have worked so hard to achieve success for this and past books, particularly my editor, David Highfill, who has been wonderful.

I am always grateful to my literary agents, Morton Janklow and Anne Sibbald, and their superb support group at Janklow & Nesbit, for their continuing management of my career over the past twenty-two years. It is important for a writer to know he is in good hands, and I have always appreciated the hands in which I rest.

Author's Note

I am happy to hear from readers, but you should know that if you write to me in care of my publisher, three to six months will pass before I receive your letter, and when it finally arrives it will be one among many, and I will not be able to reply.

However, if you have access to the Internet, you may visit my website at www.stuartwoods.com, where there is a button for sending me e-mail. So far, I have been able to reply to all of my e-mail, and I will continue to try to do so.

If you send me an e-mail and do not receive a reply, it is because you are among an alarming number of people who have entered their e-mail address incorrectly in their mail software. I have many of my replies returned as undeliverable.

Remember: e-mail, reply; snail mail, no reply.

When you e-mail, please do not send attachments, as I *never* open these. They can take twenty minutes to download, and they often contain viruses.

Please do not place me on your mailing lists for funny stories, prayers, political causes, charitable fund-raising, petitions, or sentimental claptrap. I get enough of that from people I already know. Generally speaking, when I get e-mail addressed to a large number of people, I immediately delete it without reading it.

Please do not send me your ideas for a book, as I have a policy of writing only what I myself invent. If you send me story ideas, I will immediately delete them without reading them. If you have a good idea for a book, write it yourself, but I will not be able to advise you on how to get it published. Buy a copy of *Writer's Market* at any bookstore; that will tell you how.

Anyone with a request concerning events or appearance may e-mail it to me or send it to: Publicity Department, G. P. Putnam's Sons, 375 Hudson Street, New York, NY 10014.

Those ambitious folk who wish to buy film, dramatic, or television rights to my books should contact Matthew Snyder, Creative Artists Agency, 9830 Wilshire Boulevard, Beverly Hills, CA 90212-1825.

Those who wish to conduct business of a more literary nature should contact Anne Sibbald, Janklow & Nesbit, 445 Park Avenue, New York, NY 10022.

If you want to know if I will be signing books in your city, please visit my website, www.stuartwoods.com, where the tour schedule will be published a month or so in advance. If you wish me to do a book signing in your locality, ask your favorite bookseller to contact his

Putnam representative or the G. P. Putnam's Sons Publicity Department with the request.

If you find typographical or editorial errors in my book and feel an irresistible urge to tell someone, please write to David Highfill at Putnam, address above. Do not e-mail your discoveries to me, as I will already have learned about them from others.

3|3